A DIAMOND'S ALLURE

Hawk touched Sienna's face. "When you look at me like that, what are you thinking?"

"I'm thinking you are the most beautiful man in the world. Your eyes never fail to show how deeply you feel. They change, you know. As they've changed now."

A sad smile touched his lips. "My eyes have been a blessing and a curse. There's no way for me to hide. But what about you?" Hawk's eyes darkened. "I don't always understand you, Sienna. There's nothing so obvious about you that let's me know how I make you feel."

"Then let me tell you, Hennessy, you move me beyond words."

In response, Hawk lowered his firm lips to hers. Languidly, he rubbed them against hers before the tip of his tongue made itself known and invited Sienna into a mingling kiss. All the while they clung to each other, making sacred all their memories, and the ones they would create.

"There was a moment today when I realized there'll come a time when I won't be able to hold you like this." Hawk whispered, then paused. "Death is something that comes to all of us."

"But it hasn't come yet, Hawk." Sienna interrupted him. "And I don't want to talk about that now. Not now." Her eyes implored him. "I want you to make love to me, Hawk." She placed his hand on her firm breast. "I want to feel you inside of me."

A DIAMOND'S ALLURE

Eboni Snoe

BET Publications, LLC
http://www.bet.com
http://www.arabesquebooks.com

ARABESQUE BOOKS are published by

BET Publications, LLC
c/o BET BOOKS
One BET Plaza
1900 W Place NE
Washington, DC 20018-1211

All Kensington Titles, Imprints, and Distributed Lines are available at special quantity discounts for bulk purchases for sales promotions, premiums, fund-raising, and educational or institutional use. Special book excerpts or customized printings can also be created to fit specific needs. For details, write or phone the office of the Kensington special sales manager: Kensington Publishing Corp., 850 Third Avenue, New York, NY 10022, attn: Special Sales Department, Phone: 1-800-221-2647.

BET Books is a trademark of Black Entertainment Television, Inc. ARABESQUE, the ARABESQUE logo, and the BET BOOKS logo are trademarks and registered trademarks.

First Printing: May 2003
10 9 8 7 6 5 4 3 2 1

Printed in the United States of America

To my steadfast readers,
because you believe in the dream.

One

Sienna Russell looked through the window blinds one last time before she turned out the light. It was one o'clock in the morning and Hawk had not come. It took everything she had not to dress, jump into her car and just ride aimlessly through the streets of Atlanta, emerged in a frenzied effort to nullify the hurt . . . and possibly strike back if Hawk should come later. Then he would wonder where she was at that time of morning, and Sienna hoped that Hawk would be plagued with the same kind of thoughts that were going through her mind, right now, about him. But instead of going out into the night, Sienna held on to her senses and returned to her bedroom.

This was the second time in a month that Hawk had reneged on his promise. In all the years she had known him his word had been his bond. Sienna would have staked her life on Hawk's word . . . until now. Lately, it seemed as if he was less and less accountable, and that he was gradually pulling away.

Sienna lay on her bed with her back to the bedroom door. A barrage of questions filled her mind. *Why is Hawk doing this? Is he tired of me? Us?* A hot tear worked its way out of the corner of her eye. With a brisk motion she swiped it away. "How could he do this? How *dare* he, with all we've been through?" She stopped her tirade when she thought she heard the warning tinkle of the chime hanging inside her front door. Sienna lay very still, straining to hear. Was it the chime announcing Hawk's arrival? Or was it wishful thinking?

"I thought I heard you talking to someone." Hawk announced his presence as he entered her bedroom.

Sienna's heart lurched as she sat up and faced him. Her eyes took in his familiar features. Over the years Hawk's light brown locks had grown down his back. It was only of late that he had cut them back to shoulder length. Now Hawk looked almost exactly like he did when Sienna met him eight years ago. Almost. His hair had lightened at his temples, and time had thickened his body, yet the musculature had become even more defined. Hawk's hazel eyes were as alluring as the first day she'd looked into them. But tonight Sienna searched those eyes for the answer to why he was changing, and she saw a quiet torment there.

Sienna was forced to admit, recently, she had frequently seen wisps of anguish in Hawk's gaze, although she had tried to ignore them. They reminded her of a time, years ago, when the anguish in the depths of Hawk's eyes had been all-consuming. Sienna and Hawk had been in Costa Rica. She had found the Pirate's Emerald, and as the Stonekeeper, had returned the gem to Mother Earth, hurling it into the mouth of a volcano. Afterwards, when they were all alone, for the first time, Sienna saw the proof of the secret Hawk had guarded for two years. It was a hideous growth that distorted his handsome features. A kind of punishment because he had chosen to ignore his gift as a visionary. Gift was the word

Sienna had given his abilities. Hawk considered them and himself an abomination.

To see Hawk in physical and emotional pain had been one of the most difficult moments of Sienna's life. It was so disturbing Sienna prayed she would never have to see it again, that Hawk would never be forced to experience it again.

Now all those things seemed like a waking dream. One Sienna had hoped time had put to rest. But now, staring into Hawk's glistening eyes, it was difficult to bury the past. Sienna admitted, it was also difficult to accept the things they had been through. If someone had told her of the adventures the two of them had shared and claimed the encounters to be true, Sienna might have called them a liar. But the experiences were *her* truth. They were *Hawk's* truth too. And there was no way to deny their own lives.

She looked away from the man she had come to love so deeply. *After my parents were killed in the accident and I was orphaned, all I ever wanted were the simple things in life. A family. A home. I never wanted to be . . . special. I never wanted to be born a . . . Stonekeeper.*

The last cycle of the Stonekeeper had been over six years ago, and time made the unnatural occurrences that much more dream-like. Yet there were three things in Sienna's life that made the Legend of the Stonekeeper very real. One . . . the mark of the crystal, a crystal-shaped birthmark, between her breasts. Two, the silver bangle she wore that Aunt Jessi gave her, inscribed with the Legend of the Stonekeeper and the gemstones she was destined to return to Mother Earth. And the third and most important of all was Hennessy "Hawk" Jackson.

Over the years Sienna had managed to close the

door on those other worldly things, made them a part of another life, not the ordinary life that she had desperately tried to create and protect. "I've been waiting for you since eight o'clock."

"I'm here now," Hawk replied, quietly.

His reply left her empty. "Is that all you have to say?"

Hawk remained by the door. There was heaviness in the air before he replied in a tired manner. "What would you have me say, Sienna?"

Sienna's eyes instantly blazed. "Don't do this to me, Hawk. Don't make me out to be some nagging female. I've never played that role with you. You've never given me cause to until—"

"Until now." He finished the sentence for her.

Silence filled the room again.

"You have to admit you have been . . . different lately." Sienna searched around as if looking for a way to continue. "For years it never occurred to me to question the things you said or did because I knew I could count on you no matter what. But now . . . you show up late . . . or you don't show up at all. You—"

"I was *different* the day you met me," Hawk interrupted her. "It took a long time for me to let you know how different. It was my secret. My burden. And I didn't want to put it on anyone else. You of all people should know I'm a very private man. I don't share myself or my life easily."

"*I* of all people should know that," Sienna mimicked him. "Yes, *I* should." She closed her eyes. "Somehow your words make me feel like I'm part of this huge nondescript crowd. Not someone important. Not someone who has shared your life for eight years." Sienna looked at him. "Eight years, Hawk. That's a long time. But tonight, from the way you're talking, I might as well have met you two months ago."

Hawk looked down at the floor before he looked at Sienna again. "You and I agreed, because of the legend that we would take life as it came. That it was too dangerous for us to make any commitments until the Legend of the Stonekeeper had been fulfilled."

This time Sienna's eyes filled with torment. "Yes, I agreed. But I never wanted it that way. That was what you wanted." She poked the air. "You made that decision while we were still in Costa Rica and everything that happened there was so fresh," she said, exasperated. "But what does that have to do with how you've been treating me lately?"

Hawk sat on the bed. "You know how special you are to me, Sienna." He caressed her face. "No matter what . . . you always will be."

Sienna looked into his eyes that held tired surrender. *No matter what? What does that mean?* She didn't like the fatalistic sound of the phrase. It frightened her. *Does Hawk know something he isn't telling me? And what happened to the word love? Now, after all this time, it's back to my being special, that's all?*

But beneath those thoughts, Hawk's quick mention of the promise they made concerning the Stonekeeper's cycle stirred Sienna's anger. "You know we thought the Legend of the Stonekeeper would be over and done with by now. It was supposed to be over in the year two thousand. The legend said all the stones," she forcefully counted them on her fingers, "the ruby, the emerald and the diamond would be returned by the millenium. Two thousand has come and gone, Hawk. *This* year we planned to start a real future together. We talked of marriage. But I can feel . . . it seems like," she struggled with what she was about to say, "you are pulling away from me."

"Some people believe this year, 2001, *is* the new millennium," was Hawk's reply.

"That's not important to me. I am talking about you and me, Hawk. Not about other people. Not about the millenium." Sienna didn't want to focus on the Legend of the Stonekeeper or the things that had made them different from any other couple. All she ever wanted was a normal life with Hawk, and maybe a family of her own, something that she had an intense longing for, having been an orphan. But Hawk looked at her now with this look in his eyes that said, "You know we are not like other people." It was the same thought that quietly lurked in Sienna's mind over the years. Perhaps the Legend of the Stonekeeper had held dominion over Hawk's mind too. Still, Sienna felt compelled to fight against it.

"I don't care what some people say, Hawk. It's over. Maybe all the prayers for world peace changed the outcome of things. I don't know." She threw up her hands. "I don't care. All I care about is that we're free to do what we want to do. And that we deser—"

"No," Hawk said with finality. "We're not."

"Why do you say that?" Sienna's eyes grew large. "Is there something you're not telling me?"

Hawk looked away.

"Or are you trying to make things difficult for us?" She turned his face toward her. "Are you tired of me, Hawk?"

"No," he quickly replied. "Never." Hawk kissed her softly before he pulled her into his arms.

Their bodies were a perfect fit and from the beginning their lovemaking was something they had only dreamed about. The intensity . . . the intensity was indescribable. The affect Sienna and Hawk had on one another eight years ago was overwhelming, and nothing had changed.

Sienna could feel the heat rise within her body as easily as if Hawk was a sensuous flame. Knowing his woman, he wasted no time. Hawk laid Sienna back on the bed, and when he kissed her again, there was tenderness, but it was laced with a budding desire. "You know what you mean to me, Sienna." His raspy words touched her ear.

"Tell me again, Hawk. What do I mean to you?" she asked, confused by her body's longing and her mind's need for clarity.

"You are most precious to me. The most important of all. You are a place of love, solace," then Hawk added, softly, "and justice."

A wave of nausea swept through Sienna, and she thought she would burst with it. *Justice! Justice!* She had heard him say the word justice as he held her in his arms. *But justice could only be found with the Stonekeeper! Not with me!* "Let me up, Hawk. I feel sick." She could barely speak as the nausea rose again. "Get up." Sienna pushed against him. "I feel like I can't breathe."

"What is it?" Hawk moved away. "What's wrong?"

Sienna draped one arm across her abdomen, then leaned forward with her forehead pressed into her other palm. She could feel Hawk's arm curve over her back as he attempted to comfort her. Sienna stiffened. "I have always wondered if it was me, the woman that you wanted, or was it me, the Stonekeeper that you needed. Now, after eight years I think I have finally accepted the truth, and it sickens me to my stomach." Without looking at him Sienna continued. "I want you to leave, Hawk. I want you to leave me, the woman . . . this ordinary . . . ordinary woman, alone."

TWO

Hawk looked down at Sienna as she huddled on the bed. *What had she said? That she was sick to her stomach? That he sickened her?* Hawk was stunned by the simple phrase. He waited for Sienna to raise her head. To look at him. To tell him she didn't mean it. But her body remained in the closed position. "Sienna," he called, but Sienna heaved as if she might regurgitate.

Shocked, Hawk felt a wooden numbness invade every cell of his body. He turned his face away before he rose from Sienna's bed, walked out of her room, then exited her house. When Hawk reached the end of Sienna's walkway, instead of crossing the grass and getting into his car, he continued down the public sidewalk. Tears stung his eyes. Tears! A man who had lived as a hermit; traveled the world to desolate, primitive places with no regrets, and weathered the acid-like growth on his face over and over again with barely a whimper. Even as a boy it was difficult to remember the last time he had cried. But Sienna was the love of his heart, the light of his life. The only person who knew the truth, but said she loved him anyway.

He clenched his eyes shut but continued to walk. Now Hawk wondered if Sienna had really accepted the truth. Or had she somehow convinced herself, after all they had been through, that the Legend of the Stonekeeper was not real? That what she experienced in Costa Rica and saw with her own eyes wasn't true? Hawk opened his eyes and looked up at the sky. Was that the only way Sienna could deal with seeing his distorted face? If that was the case, Hawk reluctantly admitted, Sienna had never really accepted it. Never really accepted him.

Hawk turned onto a main street where green and red neon lights glared enticingly from a store, a local bar, and a chicken shack. All of a sudden the words that started him down his unworldly path surfaced in his mind. The incantation that Hawk joyfully deciphered, then unknowingly, invoked when he had held the hieroglyph marked crystals to his chest. *Take not these crystals into your hands lightly, for they hold the power of sight. Cast them away from you if you cannot bear this worldly burden. Hold them near to your heart if you claim them as your own. But remember, in the end, justice can only be found with the Stonekeeper.*

A couple of men were standing outside the bar talking and smoking. Hawk watched a car pull up to a corner nearby and a woman climbed out. She was thin . . . almost too thin, but shapely. As she approached the men turned and looked at her. One of them whistled. The woman walked toward them with her breasts thrust forward, and an exaggerated swagger to her hips. "Either one of you want to party?" Hawk heard her ask as she got nearer.

"Maybe," the shorter man replied. "How much it gonna cost me?"

"Fifty dollars for thirty minutes," she said, her body in constant motion.

"What? Where in the hell you think you are? New York or someplace? I'll give you thirty dollars."

"Do I look like thirty dollars to you?" She placed one hand on her hip before her heavily eye-lined eyes focused on Hawk, and a smooth smile spread her red lips. "I bet tall and handsome here wouldn't offer me thirty dollars."

The would-be john turned his back. "You better hope so, because now you're not getting mine."

Still smiling, the woman fell in step with Hawk. "Want to party?"

Hawk looked into her pretty but glassy eyes. She was much younger than he first thought, and Hawk felt a sadness. Perhaps it was for her and for himself. He was on the verge of turning down her offer when a barrage of voices that started as a whisper inside his head grew to a deafening volume. This had been happening more and more lately. This was the reason Hawk was "changing," as Sienna termed it. Why he spent more and more time away. Why he was late tonight. When the voices came, sometimes they would stay for hours, and it was impossible to do anything else. Hawk felt that if he could make sense out of them, if he could get just some understanding, perhaps the experience would not be so debilitating, but as it stood, each time the voices came, Hawk felt as if he were balancing on the edge of insanity.

The woman looked at him strangely. "Did you hear me?"

The streetwalker's face was a blur, then images of the first time the woman indulged in drugs flooded Hawk's mind. She was naïve and had come from a small town. She wanted to impress a man who had taken her to a lavish party. She wanted to impress the "beautiful" people who were there. Later, Hawk could see the same man filling her with more drugs, convincing her that he had modeling and television plans for her, but she was too green for the jobs. He told her she needed more life experience, and that she needed money for a portfolio to get started. After some resistance the man was able to convince the young woman the easiest way to get both was to do a little street work. It would only be for a week or two, he'd promised. Hawk knew that was several months ago. "You need to get away from him," he finally said.

"What are you talking about?" The woman's penciled eyebrows nearly met.

"Mason. He's no good for you. He started you on drugs just so you can do what you're doing now."

Shock, then suspicion descended on her pretty, strained features. "How do you know about Mas—? I don't know you."

"I know because we're alike," Hawk said. "People who have to hide in darkness to be what we have become. But unlike me you can change. I see it." Hawk's hazel eyes became intense. "But you must stop the drugs. Then you'll see your life for what it really is. See Mason for the bloodsucker that he really is."

Abruptly, the woman stopped walking. "You're crazy," she said, turning away.

"Before you got high this morning, you looked at a picture in your wallet. It was a picture you and your sister took with your mother before you left your hometown and came to Atlanta. You prayed that they were okay and that they didn't miss you too badly." Hawk paused to let his reading sink in, before he pressed her. "You can go back. You've got your high school diploma. Stay at home until you're stronger," he advised. "Go to the junior college there. Your mother will be glad to have you back."

"Who are you?" Her words were angry at first, then tears filled her eyes. "Did God send you?"

"God . . . ?" *Once Sienna told me my abilities were from God,* Hawk thought. *I wanted to believe her. Until then I had seen myself as nothing but an abomination. I wonder if Sienna believes what she said to me then, now.*

"You know I prayed," she said softly. A tear cut a trail through her cake makeup.

Hawk took a hundred dollars out of his wallet and stuffed it in her hand. "If you don't go back for yourself, do it for me." *I want one of us to break free.*

"You must be from God. There is no other answer." Her face appeared younger. "I can't believe it. After all the things I've done I have not been forgotten." The woman looked at the folded twenty-dollar bills Hawk had placed in her hand.

"Go back to your family," Hawk said as he walked away.

"But if I go back to get my clothes Mason will stop me from leaving."

Hawk looked her straight in the eye. "Don't go back. I'll pay for a cab. It will take you to the bus station. You'll be on your way before he even misses you."

Her eyes were full of fear but she nodded her agreement.

Hawk pulled out his cell phone and dialed. "Send a cab to Black Jack's Lounge. Yes, that's it." He listened for a moment before he hung up. "A cab will be here in five minutes." He put the phone back in his pocket. "What's your name?"

"Don't you know?" Her drugged eyes held an in-appropriate innocence.

Hawk almost laughed. "No. I don't know every-thing. Just the things that come through."

"Oh. My name is Brea." She paused. "You're a psychic."

Hawk shook his head. "I hate that term."

"What do you want to be called then?" The glassy innocent look continued.

"Just Hawk." He looked up the street.

"Hawk." She repeated the name with reverence. "Ha ha!" She laughed lightly. "That's funny. Just like an angel, a hawk has wings. Maybe you are my guardian angel," Brea said softly.

Hawk was glad to see the taxi coming up the street. He had acted on a whim. He had been on an emo-tional roller coaster that started earlier that evening. It took a plunge at Sienna's place and was now tak-ing him up another hill through Brea's gentle words.

The cab stopped. Hawk opened the door. "Take her to the bus station at the airport."

"Sure," the cab driver replied.

"This should cover it." Hawk handed the man some money.

"It definitely will," the driver piped up.

"You're on your way, Brea."

"I will never forget you, Hawk." She moved further inside the vehicle. "I know you were sent by God. I know you were."

Hawk nodded and closed the door. "Goodbye."

"Goodbye," Brea said before the cab pulled away.

Hawk could see her face in the back window as she waved until the distance and darkness made it im-possible to see.

There are no coincidences, Hawk. Everything has a pur-

pose. There are messages in everything. The words of an old, wise shaman floated into his mind. Were Brea's parting words a message? Would God use someone like Brea to speak to him? *If so, would God also use a misfit like me to do the same thing?* Hawk thought as he turned back toward Sienna's street. Somehow the encounter with the young streetwalker had grounded him, perhaps even given him a glimpse of hope.

Three

Dawn entered the back room of Sienna's shop. "Boy, it sure is quiet around here."

"Hey there," Sienna said as she wrestled with the plastic covering on a box of smudging kits. Finally, she gave the wrap a mighty yank. "Actually, it's been pretty slow all morning."

"Really?" Dawn placed her purse in their secret spot. "It's normally busy by now."

"Normally," Sienna mumbled.

"Well I guess I should count my blessings while I can." Dawn chattered. "Over the last year The Stonekeeper has taken off like gangbusters." She crossed her arms and looked at Sienna. "Did you ever imagine?"

"Yes, I imagined and I hoped." Sienna attempted to sound as upbeat as her longtime employee and friend. "But I must admit business recently has been beyond even my expectations."

"You know, I was thinking about it while I drove here this morning." Dawn looked into space. "When you started The Stonekeeper there weren't many shops selling the kind of things we sell in here . . . stones, beads, ethnic artifacts, aromatherapy oils." She gave a satisfied nod. "Now you can find some of this stuff in mainstream department stores. You're a pioneer, girl."

Sienna smiled, slightly.

"And to think you named it 'The Stonekeeper' *before* you knew everything. Before you met Hawk." Dawn gave her a pointed look. "Now that is something to think about."

Sienna looked down.

Dawn reached for a box of price tags. "Speaking of Hawk, I thought he was going to change those mile high light bulbs in the showroom. I mean we could drag out that big ladder and do it"—she untangled a few tags—"but all he would have to do is use that little stepladder." Dawn motioned toward the stool before grabbing more tags.

Sienna lifted her shoulders in a minor shrug.

Dawn looked at her. "How you doing this morning?" She put the box of price tags on a shelf. "Is everything okay?"

Sienna looked at Dawn then looked away. "I'm okay."

Dawn walked over to her. "What is it, Sienna? Are you worried about your doctor's visit? I thought you said it was just your annual check up."

"Oh no. I'm not worried about the check up," Sienna reassured her, then paused. "It's Hawk."

"Hawk?" Dawn repeated with incredulity. "What is it? He sick or something? Because I know you two didn't have a fight. You never fight. At least not to the point where the situation lasts through the night." She grinned slyly.

"No, we didn't fight. I just put him out of my house last night." Sienna had difficulty saying it.

"Now I know I didn't hear you say that."

The bell at the front of the store rang.

"Aww shoot." Dawn hurried for the showroom, pointing her finger. "But you hold it right there. I want to hear the rest of this. I don't believe it."

I don't believe it either. Sienna stood for a moment before she went over to the desk and placed the receipts from the morning's activity in a yellow envelope. She could hear Dawn's cheerful greeting from the other room. "Good afternoon. Welcome to The Stonekeeper." Just hearing the name of the shop again made her think of what had happened with Hawk the night before.

Minutes after Sienna told him to leave, she went to the front window. She was relieved to see Hawk's car still parked out front. Sienna guessed he had decided to take a walk around the block to give her a few minutes to calm down. That he knew she didn't mean it, but for whatever reason, lately, her emotions had been running high. Sienna went back to the bedroom and laid on the bed, then before she knew it, she had fallen asleep. When Sienna woke up again it was a quarter to three. She went back to the front window. Hawk's car was gone. But when Sienna called his house, there was no answer.

This morning it had taken a lot for Sienna to perform her normal tasks. Her thoughts wanted to center on Hawk, but she knew business came first and she had to open The Stonekeeper. Normally, Dawn opened, but Sienna had scheduled Dawn to come in later because of her doctor's appointment.

Once she arrived at the shop keeping busy was a blessing. But she knew Hawk could walk in at any moment like he usually did whenever she was manning the store, and that kept Sienna's nerves on edge. But when Hawk didn't come, Sienna's emotional state declined even further.

The front bell tinkled again. Sienna knew it was either another customer coming in or their current customer departing. When Dawn appeared in the backroom in record time, Sienna knew it was the latter. Although Dawn knew about the Legend of the Stonekeeper, and had even gotten mixed up in the first whirlwind cycle, Dawn didn't know about Hawk's plight. Hawk had vowed Sienna to secrecy, and as difficult as it was, because Dawn was not only Sienna's first employee but a good friend, Sienna had kept the secret.

"What in the world made you put Hawk out?"

"There are some things from the past that we never really dealt with." Sienna replied vaguely. "And—"

"What kind of things?" Dawn's voice changed. "If you two can deal with, you know what, I can't imagine anything that you can't deal with."

Sienna simply looked at her.

"Well, spit it out." Dawn insisted.

"I don't have time right now." Sienna looked gratefully at her watch. "I've got to go."

The front bell rang again as another customer entered the shop.

"Literally, saved by the bell," Dawn said under her breath as they emerged from the back room together. "But don't be surprised if I give you a call tonight to see if you and Hawk have reconnected." She shook Sienna's arm playfully. "Girl, you can't be messin' up now. We need that man. And I do mean *we*. We've got three tickets for the big gem show in Hawaii, and Hawk is supposed to do all the heavy lifting for us."

"We can do it ourselves," Sienna said, stubbornly. "We did it before Hawk was in the picture."

Dawn gave Sienna a look that only a friend would be allowed to give before she greeted the customer. "Good afternoon. Welcome to The Stonekeeper," she said cheerfully.

Sienna left the shop, walked down the street and climbed into her car. Her thoughts were all over the place as she drove to the doctor's office on automatic pilot. Dawn was right. They had made big plans for the gem show on Kaua'i. Sienna had made her own private plans as well. She had dreamed she and Hawk would be married there, that they would stay an extra week on the island and turn the trip into their honeymoon. Her forehead crinkled. *How can we have a honeymoon after I threw him out?*

Sienna climbed out of her car and hit the lock button on the remote. When she reached the doctor's building an elderly woman was struggling with the heavy door. Sienna opened it for her. Afterwards she waited patiently behind the woman as she checked in with the receptionist. Sienna wondered if they shared the same doctor. She had hoped by the time a woman reached eighty she wouldn't have to put up with the intrusive examinations, but it appeared that was only wishful thinking.

"I'm Sienna Russell," she said when she reached the counter. "I have an appointment with Dr. Nelson."

"We've got you down right here," the receptionist replied. "Just have a seat please. We'll take you back in a moment."

Sienna had just started looking through a *Heart and Soul* magazine when she was taken to a room. Things moved just as quickly from there. Before she knew it all her vital signs had been taken and she was on and off the examination table. Once again she thumbed through the magazine as she waited to talk to her doctor.

"Well, Sienna . . ." Dr. Nelson opened the door with her regular opening statement.

"How am I?" She looked up from the magazine.

Dr. Nelson closed the door. "You're great. Absolutely great."

"Good. That was pretty simple." Sienna breathed a sigh of relief. "And I'll get the results of my pap smear in the mail as usual?"

"Yes, you will. You should get it in about a week, and we'll need to schedule you for another appointment two weeks from then," Dr. Nelson said.

"But why? I thought you said everything was fine." Sienna's brows knitted.

"It is." Dr. Nelson continued to smile. "But you're also pregnant."

Four

Sienna's mouth dropped open. "I am?"

"Most definitely," the doctor replied.

"But I haven't missed my period," Sienna battled with the notion.

Dr. Nelson interlaced her fingers. "It's early. You may be less than six weeks pregnant." She gazed calmly into Sienna's stunned eyes. "Are you okay?"

"Actually, I'm shocked." Sienna could feel her heart palpitating. "My cycle was shorter than usual last time but I really didn't think anything about it." She spoke for the doctor's benefit as well as her own.

"Look Sienna, it's obvious you are very surprised." Dr. Nelson paused. "I know you're not married. And I don't know what kind of relationship you share with the baby's father. So I guess you're going to have to determine how you really feel about this pregnancy. But I would like to share this with you." She paused again. "You are a well established, very capable woman. And I can't help but believe you would be just as good as a mother."

"Hawk." Sienna placed her hand over her heart.

"Beg your pardon?" Dr. Nelson leaned forward.

"Hawk. That's the father's name."

Dr. Nelson slapped Sienna's medical file gently

against her side. "Will he be happy to hear the news?"

"Yes." Sienna quickly smiled, then her expression changed. "That is . . . until recently I felt he would have." Her forehead crinkled. "Now I'm not so sure."

"Well, the smile I saw on your face let's me know where you stand. Now I guess you'll want to find out how the baby's father feels."

Dumbstruck by the idea, Sienna simply stared at Dr. Nelson. The physician walked over and patted Sienna's hand.

"I'm sure everything's going to work out just fine. But I do have one suggestion."

"And what is that?" Sienna asked, softly.

"Based on your reaction, I suggest you give yourself a little time to adjust to the idea of being pregnant. Meaning . . . really get in touch with your own feelings about the changes that will take place in your body and your life as a result of being a mother. Once you are rock solid within yourself, talk to the father about it. That way you will be clear about what you want, regardless of how he reacts. Hopefully, he will be as pleased as you initially felt he would."

Sienna nodded as she stood up. "Thanks, Dr. Nelson."

The doctor handed Sienna her medical file as she opened the examination room door. "Don't forget to make your next appointment."

"I won't," Sienna said as she turned toward the front counter. She felt as if she were walking in fog.

The trip from the doctor's office to The Stonekeeper was a blur. Finally, the warning tinkle of the front bell broke through it. Sienna hadn't intended to come to the shop. Not really. Her plan had been

to leave the doctor's office and go shopping for
clothes to take to Hawaii. But Dr. Nelson's diagnosis
changed all of that.

Sienna drew a deep breath as she glanced at the
people milling around the store. She made eye contact with Dawn who was helping a woman examine
a handcrafted water fountain.

"Sienna," Dawn remarked. "Didn't expect you
back today."

Sienna didn't know if her lips turned a smile or
not, although that was her intention. She was dimly
aware of a questioning look on Dawn's face before
she headed for the back office.

Sienna passed a display of herbal eye pillows and
other bedding products. For the first time the scent of
lavender and peppermint that she loved so much was
overpowering. Sienna fought the urge to slump down
in the middle of them, and she held herself together
and prayed she'd make it to her desk. When she did,
Sienna sat down and covered her eyes. To say she felt
overwhelmed would be an understatement, and it
wasn't simply the scent of lavender and peppermint.

"Sienna? What's wrong?"

The concern in Dawn's voice filtered through Sienna's emotional haze, but she didn't know if she
was ready to tell Dawn the truth. So Sienna's first reaction was to respond with some fancy verbal
footwork, to buy herself more time to digest it all.
But no fancy lie came. Her mind wasn't up to the
task. "I'm pregnant."

"You're pregnant," Dawn repeated in a hushed,
awed tone as she got closer.

Sienna placed an index finger up to her lips.
"Sh-sh."

"Sorry." Dawn covered her mouth. She looked out

onto the floor, then back at Sienna. "I don't know what to say. I— How do you feel?"

"All in one?"

Dawn nodded.

"It's one of the happiest moments of my life," Sienna's eyes filled with emotion, "and one of the most frightening."

"Why?" Dawn whined. "If it was me, if I was pregnant, then I could see me saying that, but you . . . I don't get it."

Sienna looked troubled. "I don't know how Hawk is going to feel about this."

"What do you mean you don't know?" Dawn ignored the tinkle of the doorbell. "I know. He's going to be ecstatic. So how is it you don't know?"

Sienna looked at the desk.

That didn't stop Dawn. "I tell you he's going to love it. He loves you. And I know he's going to love this baby."

Sienna searched her friend's eyes. She wished she could feel the conviction she saw there. "A month ago I would have said the same thing. But you don't know how things have been between us lately."

"I don't care what's been happening lately." Dawn placed her hand on Sienna's arm. "Hawk will be thrilled to know—"

Sienna's eyes widened. "Hawk." She looked past Dawn to the office door.

"Hello," he said.

For a second, Sienna searched for the love she had seen within the hazel depths of Hawk's eyes over the last eight years. Her heart felt cold when it wasn't there.

Hawk looked at Dawn. "Did I hear you mention my name?"

There was a split second of silence before Dawn looked at him and replied, "Yes, you did. You promised to put some new lightbulbs in those mile-high light sockets. And I was just beginning to wonder where you were."

"I had a somewhat . . . unusual night last night." Hawk focused on Dawn. "So I'm running a little late. But I didn't forget."

"I knew we could depend on you." Dawn's eyes were excessively bright when she looked down at Sienna. "We'll finish up later. I better get back out front and see if anybody needs help." She quickly passed Hawk on her way out.

Dawn practically ran out of here, Sienna thought as she and Hawk looked at each other. *I'd run too if I could.*

"Are you expecting a lot of business today?"

Sienna saw Hawk's lips move but her mind was going a million miles a minute. "What?"

"Both you and Dawn are manning the store today."

"Oh-h. Oh." Sienna touched her forehead. "I just stopped back by. I had some very important . . . personal things to take care of." She dropped the bait. "Dawn is actually filling in for me."

Hawk nodded. For a moment he stood quietly. Finally he said, "Where are the lightbulbs?"

Sienna swallowed. He had ignored her hint. Or perhaps he simply didn't care. She started to tell him where the light bulbs were, but Sienna didn't trust herself to speak. Not after how she'd blurted out the truth to Dawn. *Hawk didn't take the bait. He didn't take it. Why? Because he isn't interested in the things that are important in my life. That's what's been so clear this past month. He's withdrawn into his own world. Not* our *world. Not* us. *And if he isn't interested in those kinds of things, then he surely is not ready to hear that I am pregnant with his child.* Sienna got up and retrieved the box of bulbs. She handed the package to Hawk.

"There's only one in here. Will this be enough?"

"Oh. No, it won't. I—" She grabbed another box of bulbs. "How are you today?" Sienna turned intense eyes on Hawk's face. She couldn't let go. She had to find out how Hawk felt . . . if he was as miserable as she was. And if he was . . . perhaps . . . a space would open for her to tell him about the baby. But his expression was almost blank.

"I've been better."

Sienna inhaled. "Look, Hawk. There's so much going on in my life . . . in our lives that—"

"I'm not fighting you on this one, Sienna. There is a lot going on." Hawk paused and Sienna's heart seem to pause too. "And this . . . break is probably a good thing."

They stared at each other.

To Sienna silence had never been so loud. *Break? Who had said anything about a break?* Her eyes flared with emotion before she glanced down. Yes, she had put Hawk out of her house last night, but she had never thought of it as breaking up. Is that how Hawk had taken it? Is that what he wanted?

"Things haven't been quite right for a while. And until they change"—the muscle in Hawk's jaw tightened—"I guess it's better this way."

Hawk paused again and Sienna felt he was waiting for her to speak. But her throat was so constricted it was impossible. All she could do was nod her head. Hawk continued to stand there as if he was waiting for her to do something that would change the path his words had put them on. But Sienna couldn't think, couldn't feel, and most certainly could not look into Hawk's face.

"I guess I'll put these bulbs in, and . . . you can still count on me for the gem show on Kaua'i," he said before he took the bulbs, picked up the step ladder and walked away.

Five

Hawk saw Dawn look his way as he emerged from the back room. She appeared anxious. But then she turned back to the display near the entrance and went on with her work. Through clenched teeth Hawk released a ragged breath as he started across the showroom floor. Perhaps it was his imagination that created the concern in Dawn's eyes. Just like it was probably his imagination that Sienna was holding something back during their exchange in the back room, almost against her will . . . that she wanted to say she didn't want the break, but something stopped her.

Hawk looked up at the dingy light bulb and placed the step ladder beneath it. *I gave her all the opportunity I could to disagree with me. To say we didn't need a break, that we didn't need to break up not even for a moment. But she didn't say it.* Hawk moved to the top of the ladder. *And Sienna always says what's on her mind.* He nearly dropped the bulb. Before he held it so tight Hawk feared it might break. *Maybe we are better off being apart. It will give me some time to really look at things. We've been together for eight years, and I know Sienna wants more. She wants to make things permanent. Get married.* He screwed the bulb in. *Maybe that's why she didn't protest the break up because she's simply run out of patience.* Hawk stepped off the ladder and picked it up. *I understand that. I do. I want to marry Sienna, but with what I've been experiencing lately. . . .* He set the ladder down again. *I can't commit myself to anything, let alone to marriage. It wouldn't be fair to her. It just wouldn't be fair.*

Hawk changed more lights, and as he reached for the last bulb Sienna walked onto the floor. Their eyes met briefly before he looked back at the light fixture. Immediately, Hawk noticed a familiar, muffled roaring deep within his head. By the time he completed his task the sound had turned into a multitude of voices, but not a word was discernible. A daunting chaos filled his mind. Hawk stepped off the ladder, picked it up, and quickly headed toward the back room to put it away. By the time he emerged onto the floor again the sound was unbearable. *This is why I can not commit myself to Sienna. I don't know what's going to happen to me from day to day . . . from moment to moment.* He could barely hear his own thoughts now. *I can not commit anyone else to this hellhole of a life. Especially the woman that I love.*

Hawk resisted grabbing his head with both hands. As he fought the inclination, it seemed as if the force behind the voices took it as an opportunity to challenge his obstinacy, and the volume increased. It took all Hawk had not to cry out. Not to let the world know the madness that raged inside of him.

He looked at the exit door. It blurred. Now, all Hawk wanted was to get out of The Stonekeeper before he was totally incapacitated. He couldn't let Sienna see him that way. It was one thing for him to know what kind of man he really was, an inept human being under the control of evil, but it was another thing for Sienna to really know the extent of his misery.

"So you're done, huh?" Dawn's voice came out of a kind of tunnel as Hawk made his way to the door. He could see her and Sienna standing side by side near the exit, but they appeared as if they were surrounded by smoke. Dawn was smiling, but Sienna's expression was somber. "Took you all that time to get in here and didn't take but a few minutes to finish," Dawn teased.

All Hawk could do was keep his focus on the door. He was vaguely aware of a perplexed look on Sienna's face, and Dawn's look of surprise when he did not respond as he passed them, quickly. Hawk grabbed the door handle with such force, he thought, with the slightest bit more pressure he could crush it in his hand. But instead the door opened, and Hawk stepped outside and proceeded quickly up the street.

Sienna and Dawn looked at each other, then back at Hawk as he disappeared beyond the store's front window.

"What in the world . . ." Dawn's mouth hung open.

"I guess he just didn't have anything more to say to us." Sienna shrugged.

Dawn crossed her arms. She looked at Sienna and blinked several times. "Sienna, I don't think that had anything to do with us. Something was going on with him."

"Yeah. Right." Sienna could feel a lump forming in her throat. "He just couldn't stand being in here with me another moment."

"I don't think that was it," Dawn insisted.

"I do." Sienna's eyes began to sting.

"So things didn't go too well back there after I left?" Dawn asked softly.

Sienna sighed. "Not at all."

"Did you tell him?"

"No." Sienna looked at Dawn with eyes that were too bright.

"Well it doesn't make any sense," Dawn replied. "Why would he leave like that?"

Unable to speak, Sienna shrugged again.

"Look." Dawn held her shoulders. "Hawk was acting really strange, and I don't think it had anything to do with you." She shook her head. "If I were you, I'd give him a call and find out if he's okay. And then perhaps you two will have a chance to talk some more."

"I can't call him, Dawn."

"Why not?"

"He broke up with me."

"Oh no." Dawn's eyes filled with sympathy.

"Oh yes. And if anybody is going to do any calling, it won't be me. You can believe that." Sienna rushed out of the store.

Hawk bumped into another person as he rushed toward his car. This time it was a white male.

"Hey! What's wrong with you buddy?"

Hawk never turned around. He continued down the street with his head bowed.

"What's wrong with that character?" he heard the man say. "Next time you need to watch where you're going." The voice trailed behind him.

When Hawk reached his car, he could barely see how to place the key inside the lock. He fumbled, and accidentally scratched the metal before he found it. Relieved, Hawk climbed inside, slammed the door, then grabbed the steering wheel. "How can I drive if I can't see the damn keyhole?" He gritted his teeth as the voices in his head drowned out his own thought processes. It was an agonizing sound of elongated words that turned into wails. Hawk clenched his eyes shut, willing the voices to stop, but they only increased in speed. Now there could have easily been a thousand cats fighting in his head. "Who cares if I can't see?" he shouted, turning on the car. "Maybe this will be a way to end it all. Sienna will be free of me, and I will be free of myself."

Hawk pulled into the traffic without looking. A surprised horn honked behind him. He applied relentless pressure to the gas pedal, hoping there would be only one victim of his madness. Himself.

Hawk drove with abandon and surrender, placing his future in the hands of the powers that be. Beneath it all Hawk wondered if they would finally win. They had succeeded in turning his life into a living hell, by taking control of his mind and turning his face into a hideous blob that burned whenever the strange prophecies raged. What more could they do but take his life?

As he dotted in and out of traffic, Hawk railed against the powers that be and at the moment he placed the cursed crystal against his heart and read the words inscribed on it. From that time on he had been no good for himself or anyone else. With a kind of detachment, Hawk glanced into the rearview mirror. "What good is life if I am no good for those I love?" He heard several horns scream before his mind went dark.

* * *

Hawk came to in his bed. Slowly, he watched the light and shadows move across the wall. Evening was almost night. He closed his eyes as he thought, *I made it. I made it. Once again I cheated death.*

"This time," the voice said clearly. "This time."

An image began to form in his mind's eye. Hawk saw himself walking down a street. Blossom Street. He could see The Stonekeeper not too far ahead. Hawk noticed how, as he walked by, people would turn, whisper or even stare. Then he realized why. It was because of how he looked. His clothes were filthy. His pants were torn, and some of the buttons were missing from his shirt. His neatly manicured locks were long and matted in clumps. Leaves and other debris clung to them, but as startling as all of that was, it was Hawk's face, his eyes that alarmed him most. They were the eyes of a madman. Bright. So bright. Like a beaten dog that hadn't turned cowardly, but had found refuge in viciousness instead.

Hawk saw himself stop in front of The Stonekeeper's window, and place his grubby hands like parentheses against it to see inside. Sienna was in there alone, arranging candles. Slowly, she turned as if she could feel his eyes on her, and when she saw him panic blanketed her face. Sienna rushed toward the door, and Hawk saw himself move in the same direction. When Sienna realized he would reach the door before she did, she turned and ran for the telephone. In an explosion, Hawk saw himself enter the shop and run behind her. He caught Sienna's arm as she screamed for help into the receiver. They struggled, knocking items off of the shelf behind the counter.

Because of the large windows, people passing by could see them, and several good Samaritans came to Sienna's aid. They grabbed Hawk and held him down as Sienna backed away in terror. Still, even in his restrained position, Hawk's eyes never left Sienna's face. There was no love in them. There was no compassion. Only madness.

The scene changed and Hawk saw himself alone in a jail cell. He clawed at a stained mattress until he removed a makeshift knife composed of a tin can lid and a hard object wrapped in coarse string. Hawk held his breath as he watched himself take the jagged blade and slowly move it across his throat. He died in a pool of his own blood, slumped in the corner of the cold cell.

"Gifts are to be honored," the voice said. "Not judged."

In the semidarkness Hawk continued to lie in his bed. The voice in his head had stilled. The images were gone. Even the message that the voice carried quickly faded as Hawk realized, if the rare vision for himself was true, his relationship with Sienna would take an awful turn. But perhaps more sadly, before the horrible event occurred, her love for him would completely die. Murdered by his insanity.

Hawk's hand shook as it rose to the side of his face, but to his surprise there was no rash. The vision had come without it, and Hawk knew things were changing. Never before had he had a vision for himself. It was ironic, with all his visionary abilities, in his own life, Hawk stumbled in the darkness of uncertainty. Perhaps it was a sign of a chink in the armor of the powers that be. The ones that punished him for his ambition. For his desire to shine among his peers.

At last, compassion from those who had tortured him for the last eight years? Hawk thought not. Perhaps they were simply trying to warn him that he wasn't long for this earth.

Hawk almost smiled. That in and of itself did not frighten or sadden him. What did affect him, and affect him deeply, was the thought that he would completely lose Sienna. Not to death, something very natural that comes to everyone, but as a result of his mind being taken away. Yes . . . taken. Because Hawk did not feel he had lost his mind, but that his mind had been stolen. Stolen by the voices and the visions. Stolen by something he had never wanted or understood. Stolen by something he had never accepted.

Hawk turned onto his stomach. He balled his pillow beneath him and crushed it to his chest. "How can I let you go, Sienna? How can I?" He buried his face in the downed softness as his light brown locks spilled all around. Hawk's body lay still as his mind filled with Sienna's face. He could hear his heart beating. Beating. "When it is time to let her go, I will," he said, his eyelids heavy as if he had been drugged. "But that time is not now. And I will use every second that I have left showing my love for her." Hawk's eyes closed slowly. "So when that time comes, I will have no regrets, and perhaps Sienna won't either."

Six

The telephone rang. Startled, Sienna grabbed it.

"Hello." Her voice was groggy. She had finally fallen asleep. Finally, found refuge from her thoughts and worries.

"Sienna." Hawk paused. "Sorry to wake you."

Immediately, her heart surged. "I haven't been asleep long," she replied as her head began to clear. Sienna looked at the illuminated numbers of her digital clock radio. It was one thirty in the morning.

"I had to talk to you." Hawk's whispery voice reached out to her. " Hear your voice. I want to see you, Sienna."

She closed her eyes and tried to get a grasp of the situation. "I don't know what to say." Sienna watched the time change on her clock.

"Tell me you want to see me too," Hawk replied.

Sienna held her braids away from her face. *Hawk didn't say goodbye when he left The Stonekeeper. Didn't look my way. Now, he claims he can't do without me.* With all her heart Sienna wished she could believe him. She looked at the clock again. It was one thirty-three. It was late. Very late. Just as Hawk's visits had been so many times recently. *The truth is there's a name for this kind of call. And it surely isn't love,* Sienna thought. "I don't think it would be wise, Hawk." She heard him sigh.

"Don't do this, Sienna. Don't do this. I know I've been acting strange lately, but don't pretend you don't know how I feel about you."

Sienna shivered although the room was very warm. "Perhaps that's what I've been doing lately. Pretending, or maybe hoping is a better word. Hoping that things would get better between us."

"They will. I promise you. They must," Hawk added softly.

There was something different in his voice. Sienna didn't know if she had ever heard it before. It was a quiet desperation.

"I need to see you, Sienna."

The minute number changed again and Sienna closed her eyes. She wanted to tell him yes. To forget how things had been lately. But she couldn't. Not only would her mind not let her, Sienna thought as she draped her forearm across her abdomen, the baby growing inside of her deserved more. She listened to the last bars of the song playing on the radio before she spoke, softly. "I can't, Hawk."

The line went quiet.

"Why not?"

His question tugged at Sienna's heart, but she held fast. "Hawk, you can't just come and go emotionally whenever it suits you."

"But I have never left you emotionally. Never," he repeated.

"That's not how it feels," Sienna replied. "And telling you to come over tonight is not going to dissolve the emotional void I feel between us."

"Then what will fill it?" Hawk asked.

Sienna tried to think beyond the sound in her

ears. The sound of her pounding heart. "I don't know."

"My being there . . . with you," Hawk reasoned. "That's what would fill it."

Sienna's lips began to form the word, come, but she shook her head instead. "No. That would only cloud my judgment. And more than at any other time of my life, I need to be able to think clearly."

"Why? Why are you doing this? Is there something I don't know? Is there someone else?"

Sienna wanted to say, yes. A baby. Our baby. But she held back. She wasn't ready. Dr. Nelson advised her to take her time. Sienna knew the doctor was right. She needed to be mentally and emotionally strong when she told Hawk about the child. So no matter how he reacted, she would move forward with having the baby without hesitation. "We're at a crossroad, Hawk. But I guess you know that."

"Yes, I know." He paused. "But what it will ultimately mean, you don't know. So why can't we spend whatever time we have . . . together."

"It's not that simple anymore," Sienna replied. "We have too many years behind us to treat this lightly. We need to be clear about what we want when it comes to this relationship. And I don't believe we're going to get that clarity through your coming over here tonight."

They waited with dead air between them.

Finally Hawk said, "All right. Perhaps I'll see you tomorrow."

Perhaps? Sienna thought, *why aren't you sure that you will make it happen?* She squeezed the phone. "Goodbye."

"Bye."

Sienna hung up the telephone then sat up. She

stared into the darkness before she turned and looked at the place where Hawk usually slept. She ran her hand across the cool sheet. The fabric joined with her desires and played tricks on her. It felt like Hawk's body. Hard. Muscular. Smooth.

Sienna drew back and placed both hands in her lap. "Playtime is over. I have someone else to consider now." She pulled the sheet up to her neck and held it there. Tears fell from the corners of her eyes as the radio played.

"I know we don't usually take dedications at this time of morning," she heard the radio jock say, his voice far away. "But the man sounded so sincere. I've been on the air twenty years now, and I've got to say there was a kind of aloneness, not loneliness, aloneness, in this man's voice that I don't think I've ever heard before. So Sienna . . ." She looked at the radio. "I had to take his dedication. And if you're out there listening like the Birdman hopes you are, know this song is for you."

Luther Vandross's "Still In Love With Me" began to play. Sienna listened and cried. Cried and listened. When the song was over small wads of used tissue spattered the comforter.

Hawk had never done anything like that before. She didn't know he had it in him, and her heart spilled over with love, and it was because of that love that the ache was so deep. "My heart is broken too, Hawk, but I've got to face the truth. If you wanted me, wanted to marry me, you would have by now. I wasn't shy about letting you know how I felt." Sienna reached for another tissue. "But you chose not to marry me. And for a while you had a good reason. You said it was because of all that we've been through. All that the Legend of the Stonekeeper brought into our lives. And I believed you. For years I believed you. But I don't anymore." She looked at the crumpled, damp tissues. The next thing Sienna said was the most difficult, and she felt the words deeply. Believed them deeply. "You kept me around because you believe I am the Last of the Stonekeepers, and you thought you needed me. But the millennium has passed, and it's obvious you don't need me any more. Pretending to want Sienna the woman isn't good enough anymore. It may have been for a foolhearted woman in love, but it's not good enough for my baby and me." Sienna lay down and cried herself to sleep.

Hawk did not come to The Stonekeeper the following day, and Sienna couldn't help but think about it as she locked up the shop. It was the first day since they returned from Costa Rica that he had not come into the store. That was more than five years ago. Sienna felt the loss as she walked down Blossom Street. She looked in the familiar shop windows, and watched people pass on the street. Anything to take her mind off of how deeply she felt it.

Sienna approached the Gold and Diamond jewelry store. She stopped to admire a particularly beautiful diamond on display. Through the glass door the motion of someone waving caught her eye. Francisco, the owner, was at the counter motioning for her to come inside. Sienna waved and shook her head to say she had to go on. Francisco responded with an exaggerated face of disappointment.

Sienna felt guilty. She didn't have anywhere else to go. She simply wanted to sulk in her sadness over Hawk. *And why should I do that? Why? If I'm going to go on with my life, I am. I can't have it both ways.* Sienna nodded okay, walked over and went inside.

"Hello, Sienna," Francisco called as she approached. "It's been so long since I've seen you." He grabbed her hand as she placed it on the counter.

"I know. But it's not my fault. You and Gina have been living it up, I guess, off of all the money you're making down here. I stopped by about a month ago, and your son told me you two were on a cruise to the Mediterranean."

He laughed good-naturedly. "Part of that is true. We did go on a cruise." He spread his hands and looked at the cases. "But I don't know if it had anything to do with my making loads of money here."

"Don't tell me that," Sienna teased. "I see how Gina is always dripping in jewelry."

"She drips because she has to advertise them." Then his eyes sparkled. "But I can't say I refuse my wife when she comes across a few pieces she can't live without." He smiled his broad engaging smile. "What about you? How are you?"

"I'm okay." Sienna wished she could have smiled as broadly, lied and said, "I'm great."

"Okay?" Francisco lowered his thick eyebrows. "Okay isn't good enough for a woman like you. You better tell that eccentric man of yours to get in here and buy you one of these." Francisco pointed toward the engagement and wedding ring sets.

Sienna looked down at the diamonds that sparkled at her almost teasingly. She gave a small smile. "If it was only that easy." Tears stung behind the words. *My God. Am I going to cry again? I hope the entire pregnancy isn't like this.* But it didn't matter how Sienna felt about the unshed tears, they continued to press against the back of her eyes which she batted over and over, not wanting her fellow merchant to see her cry. But Sienna knew that if she stood there a minute longer he would. "Wow." She looked up. "I'm glad I stopped in. You have a restroom, don't you?"

"Certainly." He started toward the back of the store. Sienna followed "Right here." Francisco pointed. "And while you're doing that." He looked at his watch. "I'll lock up the store. It's past closing time."

"Thanks." Sienna entered the tiny, plain room. She crossed her arms and looked in the mirror. "You are pitiful. Do you know that? Do you think Hawk cries every time he thinks of you?" She shook her head dramatically. "No. No way." Then Sienna sighed. "But Hawk's not the one carrying the baby." Sienna waited a minute or so longer, dabbed at her eyes, and took a deep breath. "Okay." She opened the door and threw her shoulders back.

"Put all of the diamonds in the bag," Sienna heard a strange voice bark as she emerged into the short hallway.

Seven

Sienna froze.

"I'm trying," Francisco replied. His voice shook.

"Don't try. Do it. Or I'll blow your head off."

Sienna's hands went to her face. *The store is being robbed!* She couldn't believe it. Her body jerked when she heard something drop.

"Don't play with me, old man."

There was a whimper and Sienna guessed the armed gunman had hit Francisco. *What should I do?* Her arms reached out beseechingly, and the silver bracelet her Aunt Jessi gave her seemed to shimmer.

"Please. Please don't shoot me," Francisco pleaded. "I've got a wife and a son and—"

"I don't give a good goddamn what you have," the crook retorted. "You won't have a head if you keep wasting time."

I've got to help him, Sienna thought. Anxious, she looked around, but the only thing near was a pile of broken-down boxes sitting in a corner. Then Sienna spotted a two-by-four resting in some brackets against the back door. Without hesitation, as quietly as she could, Sienna moved toward it.

"That's enough of that. Give me some of those," the robber demanded.

Sienna eased the board out of the brackets, held it in both hands and tipped forward.

"You clumsy bastard."

"Aargh. Don't," Francisco pleaded.

"What the hell are you doing?" the bully replied. "I should kill you right now."

Sienna stood at the edge of the wall. Gingerly, she looked around the corner. The robber's back was to her and Francisco was struggling to rise from the glass counter. His head was bleeding. He appeared dazed when he looked up.

"If you don't do something right quick, old man, your life is over," the crook threatened.

Francisco wove a bit until he saw Sienna. Quickly, she gave him a glimpse of the two-by-four and made a motion for him to do something to occupy the robber.

"Okay. Okay." Francisco's eyes widened. "I've got my single diamonds in this drawer, but I'm so dizzy." He took a couple of steps back.

"Open the drawer." The gunman switched the gun to the opposite hand. "And remember if you try anything, you are gone."

Francisco did as he was told, and the gunman leaned over the counter to reach for the gems. Sienna knew that would be her one and only chance, so she took it. She rushed forward, swung the two-by-four over her head, and brought the wood down on the robber's head and back.

The gun fell from his hand, and he made a sound like the breath had been knocked out of him before his body collapsed on the counter. Quickly, Francisco picked up the gun.

Sienna and Francisco looked at each other, then at the unconscious would-be robber.

"I've never been so happy to see anyone in my life," Francisco said. "I forgot you were back there."

Sienna put her hand over her heart. Her breaths were heavy and fast. "We better call the police."

"Yes. Dial 911," Francisco agreed. "I'll keep the gun on him."

"Where's the telephone?" Sienna's heart continued to pound as she looked at the unconscious man.

"Over there. Behind that counter."

Sienna ran for the telephone and dialed emergency.

"911," a female voice answered.

"A man attempted to rob the Gold and Diamond jewelry store on Blossom Street. He's still here, but we managed to get the gun from him."

"You say the robber is still in the store?"

"Yes." Sienna swallowed. "He's unconscious."

"The robber's unconscious and you have his gun?"

"Ye-es! Francisco has the gun pointed at him right now."

"Who is Francisco?"

"He's the owner of the store. Please," Sienna pleaded. "Can you send someone over here right away, before he comes to?"

"Where is the store?"

"The eleven hundred block of Blossom Street."

"We're on our way," the officer informed her.

Sienna hung up. "They're on their way," she repeated as the masked criminal groaned and moved his head. "He's coming around," Sienna said as if Francisco couldn't see for himself.

"I want him to." Francisco shook the gun. "I want him to see how it feels to have someone hold a gun on you."

The previously armed man rose, slowly.

"I think you're going to get your wish." Sienna replied.

The man grabbed the back of his head. Sienna looked out the door to see if help had arrived. There was none in sight. "Is the door unlocked?" She was surprised at how panicked she sounded. Sienna did what she felt she had to do with the two-by-four, but now that she'd had a moment or two to think it over, she felt overwhelmed.

"No," Francisco replied. "He made me lock the door and then he took my keys from me."

"We've got to let the police in," Sienna said as the robber stood back and looked at Francisco, then over at Sienna. His eyes narrowed when he saw her.

"Give her the keys," Francisco commanded.

The criminal turned up his nose. "She's so big and bad, hitting me across the head with that plank, have her come and get them."

"Don't you talk to her like that," Francisco screamed as he pointed the gun in the man's face. His eyes were like fire. "I want to shoot you anyway. You say one more thing and I swear . . ." He began to sweat.

"Calm down, Francisco." Sienna said, but she sounded out of breath. "You don't want to do anything you will regret later." Sienna looked at the masked man. "Just throw the keys over here. Please."

The man looked at Francisco one more time, then down at the floor. He started to reach in his pocket.

"You better not try anything. If you've got a gun or knife in there, you're going to be sorry," Francisco warned.

Sienna looked at the man's pocket. She didn't think anything could fit in there besides a set of keys, but Francisco's adrenaline had gone over the top.

The man removed the keys from his pocket. He

tossed them on the floor toward Sienna. She picked them up.

"The police are here," Francisco shouted.

Sienna ran to the door and let them in. Two of the policemen grabbed the would-be robber by the arms, but Francisco continued to point the weapon.

"Are you the owner?" A third officer stood near the door.

Francisco nodded.

The policeman walked toward him, slowly. "It's okay. You can put the gun down now."

"I think he may be in shock," Sienna said as the officer advanced.

Everybody stood still until the policeman removed the gun from Francisco's hand. Afterward, Francisco closed his eyes.

"Get one of those EMT's in here." The officer shouted to a fellow policeman by the door. "You're going to be all right." He assured Francisco. The policeman grabbed a small chair. "Why don't you sit down?"

"I wouldn't be all right if it weren't for Sienna." Francisco slumped into the seat. "He hit me with the gun a couple of times, and all the while he threatened to kill me. If she hadn't hit him with the two-by-four, God knows how this would have ended."

The officer turned to Sienna. "Sounds like you're a hero, ma'am."

Sienna spoke to Francisco. "I'm just glad you're okay."

She watched them take the robber away, then they took a police report. Sienna was more than ready to go by the time the officer was done. She said good-bye to Francisco whose head had been bandaged, and was being taken to the hospital for a more in-depth examination. When Sienna stepped back out on Blossom Street she was still shaken. *I wish I could go to Hawk and tell him what happened. I need to feel his arms around me right now.* Sienna's heart sank as she walked rapidly toward her car. *But if I'm going to learn to live without Hawk, I guess there is no better time than now.*

Sienna climbed inside her car and drove home as her mind played and replayed the scene at the jewelry store. The sound of a dog barking ferociously as she stepped onto her front porch jolted her out of the mental trap. Sienna stopped short when she spotted a bouquet of flowers leaning against the door. She picked them up. A note lay beneath them.

Although there were times when we were physically apart, I have never left you emotionally. Never. We have been through too much to give up now.

Love, Hawk

Sienna raised the flowers to her face. She rested her cheek against their soft petals. Hawk was such a good man. Had always been. There was no way of denying it. But that wasn't what haunted Sienna. It was Hawk's ability to shut her out at the most crucial times. She simply couldn't stomach that anymore. He would go inside himself and simply close the door, no matter how badly Sienna needed to feel close. She didn't doubt, in his heart, Hawk may never have left her emotionally, but on the outside, in the only way that Sienna could know, Hawk had placed a barrier between them many times.

She went inside and sat in the first seat she saw, all the while fighting the impulse to call him. To tell Hawk how she loved the flowers, and that she wanted to see him right away. To be with him. But this was no longer the old days when they could tumble into bed and throw the future to the wind. They were no longer two young people with only themselves to consider. Those days were gone forever, and things would never be the same. Sienna was going to have a baby. Another life had entered the equation. A life whose needs had to be placed before her own. Sienna accepted that fully. She did not feel as if it was a sacrifice. She felt it was a privilege.

Sienna had spent the majority of her childhood in an orphanage. At sixteen years old, she'd gone to live with her Aunt Jessi. Sienna knew how important it was to be wanted. To have a family. To be a part of something bigger than herself.

She walked to the kitchen, took a vase from under the sink, filled it with water and placed the bouquet inside. As an afterthought she removed a rich purple peony before she headed out the door. "I've got to talk to somebody."

Eight

Sienna closed the car door and took out her cell phone. Her fingers knew the numbers well. "Hey, Dawn," she said. The phone had barely rung.

"Hey woman."

"You must have been waiting for my call. You answered so quickly."

"The telephone was right here, so I answered it as soon as it began to ring."

"Oh." Sienna hesitated a second. "What you doin'?"

"Nothin' much," Dawn replied. "Listening to a little relaxing music. Writing in my journal."

"Well, I just went through quite an ordeal. I need to talk to someone."

"Come on over, then."

"You sure?" Sienna knew Dawn. She could see her deep in relaxation mode with candles all around.

"Of course I'm sure," she replied.

"Okay. I'll see you shortly." Sienna hung up the phone.

It seemed like only a minute or two before she pulled up in front of Dawn's apartment building. Sienna took the elevator to the third floor. She got off and turned the corner. She saw Dawn standing with the door open, waiting. "I saw you drive up," she said, giving Sienna a hug.

"I thought you could *feel* I was on my way up," Sienna teased.

"I'm not that good, yet," Dawn replied. "You have to talk to Hawk about that."

Sienna's smile faded. She stepped inside the apartment.

"Welcome to Dawn's sanctuary," Dawn said as she closed the door.

Sienna took a deep breath. "Your place always feels so good. And smells good too." She inhaled the lightly scented air.

"Thanks." Dawn walked into the living room. Sienna followed and flopped on the couch. "Before you came I was burning incense. But considering your 'condition' I thought I'd put it out, until we determine what your constitution can and cannot take." Dawn smiled.

"That probably was a good idea," Sienna replied. "Yesterday, I felt like I was going to faint when I passed the scented soaps in the shop, but today I hit a man across the head with a two-by-four with no problem."

Dawn drew back. "Say what?"

"Yep." Sienna closed her eyes. "He was robbing the Gold and Diamond store. I had gone to the bathroom. When I came out, he had a gun pointed at Francisco. He was threatening to kill him."

"Oh my God!" Dawn's mouth dropped open. "So you just ran up and hit him with a plank?"

"I made sure Francisco had distracted him before I did."

"Distracted or not," Dawn replied, "I don't know if I would have the nerve to do that."

"When those kind of things happen, how do you know what you're going to do?" Sienna shrugged.

"You don't know until you're confronted with the situation." She exhaled again. "And that's how I handled it. But afterwards I was totally out of it. So was Francisco. Shoot. I still am." She looked at Dawn through heavy lidded eyes.

"Let me get you some tea." Dawn got up from her seat on the floor. "I've got some chamomile with lemon. I think that could be good for your nerves," she called from the kitchen.

"Excellent." Sienna forced her voice to carry.

"When did this happen?"

"About an hour ago." Sienna looked around at the mandala paintings, a statue of Isis and a clay dolphin sculpture.

"An hour ago! I would still be shaking in my boots." Dawn rounded the corner with two mugs.

"That's exactly why I'm here."

"You look pretty calm to me," Dawn replied.

"That's because I'm not wearing any boots," Sienna quipped.

They both laughed, a little.

Dawn took a sip of tea. "Did you tell Hawk?"

"No. I haven't seen Hawk today. But he left me a bouquet of flowers on my front porch with a wonderful note." She wriggled the peony.

"Really?" Dawn brightened. "So what are you going to do? Give him a call?"

"No," Sienna replied. "It's not that easy, Dawn." She looked in her friend's eyes. "There's much more at stake this time."

Dawn made a face. "What if you two haven't made up by the time we go to Hawaii? We need Hawk to lift all that stuff. Especially now." She glanced at Sienna's abdomen.

Sienna gave a slight shrug. "I guess he'll still have

to go. I'm sure we're not the first company who may have to complete some business in the middle of a breakup." Sienna stroked the flower. "And I'm sure we won't be the last."

"Well, if you ask me, I think you're cutting Hawk short. It's obvious he's trying to make up with you." Dawn put her mug down and crossed her arms. "This man has dealt with all kinds of things all around the world. Don't you think he could deal with knowing he's got a baby on the way? Maybe that will give him some insight into why you won't act right."

"*I* won't act right?" Sienna rolled her eyes. "Dawn, I didn't come over here for you to beat me up. I need some compassion right now."

"I'm sorry." Dawn looked justly chastised. She stuck out her bottom lip. "I just don't like it when you two aren't together."

"You think I do?" Sienna retorted. "I've been going crazy. So when this happened at Francisco's . . ."

"God." Dawn shook her head. "When it rains it pours, as my grandmother used to say."

"You can say that again."

Dawn's brows furrowed. "Although I think it's rather interesting timing."

"What do you mean?"

Meaningfully, she looked at Sienna. "You know there aren't any coincidences."

Sienna didn't want to hear it. "I-I-I don't know about that."

"Well, I do." Dawn's foot began to shake.

"And what do you know?" Sienna threw up her hands. "I find out I'm pregnant. Hawk breaks up with me, and I end up in the middle of a robbery. What in the world could be the connecting factor in all of that?"

"You," Dawn said softly.

"Du-uh. Tell me something I didn't know."

"It just seems like all kinds of things are happening . . . lately."

Sienna and Dawn looked at each other.

"And *you* know what I'm thinking," Dawn continued.

"Yeah, I know. But I'm not buying it." Sienna got up and walked over to the window. She stared out for a moment. Then she turned and looked at Dawn. "The millennium is here, Dawn. D-day came and went without a hiccup. So the legend is over with." Sienna stretched out her arm and pointed at the silver bangle. "Either Aunt Jessi's bracelet got canceled, or it was wrong in the first place."

"Well, we know it wasn't wrong," Dawn replied cautiously. "Too much happened for that to be true."

"Okay." Sienna began to pace. "So it was partially right. But that's behind us now." Exasperated, she stopped. "Can you see me battling with Michelle Fournier in Martinique or evading Paz in Costa Rica while I'm big and pregnant?"

Dawn shook her head. "Running would be more difficult." Then she stuck her finger in the air. "But it wouldn't be impossible."

Sienna pinned her with a stare.

"I'm just saying, things always pick up when the Stonekeeper's cycle is about to begin." Dawn placed her hands on her hips. "I should know, I was caught up in it the first time around."

"That's right. So don't be calling it up. You know how once you start saying stuff, it seems to happen."

"I'm not calling up anything. I was just making an

observation," Dawn replied. "So come on. Sit down. Finish your tea."

Sienna took a seat again, but what Dawn said stayed with her.

Nine

Sienna looked up from her paperwork. She thought she heard someone knocking on the shop door. *Who could it be?* she thought. *Not Hawk. It's Thursday. And Hawk teaches a special* hsing-i *class in the park after his workout.* Sienna continued to glance over the invoice as she got up. *It's probably a deliveryman. But he's kind of early. Normally they come later in the morning; The Stonekeeper doesn't open for another fifteen minutes.*

She left the back and entered the showroom. On her way, Sienna noticed the dwindling supply of essences. *I need to order more essential oils. We've got that aromatherapy workshop next week.* Afterward, Sienna looked at the door. She nearly tripped when she saw Hawk standing outside with a newspaper under his arm.

She opened the door. Sienna prayed he hadn't seen her reaction. "Hi."

Hawk stepped inside. "Are you okay?" His eyes were intense.

"Of course, I am," Sienna replied.

"I wasn't so sure after reading this." He unfolded the paper and pointed to a headline.

"Woman Foils Robbery Attempt." Sienna looked at Hawk. The concern in his eyes drew her in. "Oh-h. I didn't think they would put it in the paper."

"Seems like you made quite an impression," he said as he closed the door.

Sienna looked down. "You can believe that wasn't my intention."

There was a slight pause before Hawk said, "But I guess my radio dedication and the bouquet didn't."

Sienna looked up again. "They did," she said, softly.

"Enough for you to have dinner with me tonight? I've got some place special in mind."

"I don't know." She looked away again. "What would be the point?" Sienna felt Hawk's hand on her cheek. Gently, he turned her face toward him. "We would be the point, Sienna. We would be the point." His tone pulled at every aspect of her being. The words were clear, and so were his eyes.

"All right," she finally replied.

"Thank you," he said.

She barely heard the words. "That's not necessary, Hawk."

They stared into each other's eyes until Sienna looked at his lips. For a moment she thought he would kiss her. Instead, his fingers trailed slowly from her face.

"You'll need time to finish up here. So I'll pick you up at eight. You should be home by then."

He knows me so well. "That sounds fine," Sienna replied.

Hawk stepped back.

"Where are we going?"

"It's a surprise."

Sienna smiled slightly and opened the door.

"I'll see you at eight," Hawk repeated.

"Eight." Sienna nodded.

He went out and Sienna locked the door again.

She went back to her desk and sat down. Moments later the bell over the front door rang. It was Dawn.

"Good morning," Dawn sighed as she entered the room.

"Mornin'," Sienna replied, melodiously.

Dawn turned and looked at her. "What's up with you?"

Sienna turned innocent eyes on her friend. "What do you mean? I just said 'mornin'.'"

"I know what you said." Dawn unwrapped her breakfast biscuit. "But you said it kind of funny like. And look at you."

"What?" Sienna felt her mouth twitch at the corner.

"You're trying so hard not to grin that you're sucking in your cheeks."

Sienna's grin finally escaped. "You make me sick. You know that?"

"Yeah, I might, but for some reason I don't think your smile has anything to do with me." Dawn paused. "Hawk came over last night, didn't he?"

Sienna held her head high. "No."

"Then what is it?"

"He came by this morning and asked me to go to dinner with him tonight. He's inviting me to a special place."

"I knew it." Dawn took a big bite and chewed for a second. "You got to give it to the man. He knows how to work it. Flowers yesterday, and now a special dinner date."

"And a dedication on the radio, the day before that," Sienna bragged.

"You didn't tell me about that."

"No, I didn't. But I don't have to tell you everything."

Dawn made a face. "Excu-uz me." She paused. "Are you going?"

"We-ell." Sienna made a point of looking undecided.

"Sienna-ah." Dawn stared her down.

"You know you're funny." She chuckled before she confessed. "I'm going."

Dawn exhaled. "That's better. I don't know why you want to play with me." She broke off a piece of sausage. "You know how I feel about you and Hawk. You're my picture of the exciting, happy, loving couple. Give me a break." Dawn frowned. "I don't have nothin' else. So please, try not to mess up my fantasy."

Sienna laughed.

Dawn continued, "And this will be the perfect opportunity for you to tell Hawk." She leveled her gaze with Sienna's. "Everything."

"We'll see," Sienna replied. "If it feels right, I will. If not, I'm going to wait until a better time." She dug in her heels.

Dawn threw up her hands. "All right. I'm not pushing you or anything. It just sounds like perfect timing to me."

Sienna didn't reply. She started reading.

"Now she's ignoring me," Dawn said beneath her breath.

I sure am. I'm done talking about that. Sienna picked up a pen. *First things first, which means, I've got to see if Hawk and I still have a relationship before I bring in the baby.* She looked at the clock. "It's time to unlock the front door." Sienna stood up.

"I'll do it." Dawn walked toward the showroom floor. "Maybe I'll find someone who wants to talk to me out there."

Sienna smiled as Dawn went into the showroom.

She was as hopeful as Dawn when she thought of her date with Hawk. But for now, because of the baby, she couldn't allow her heart to make all of her decisions. Romantic dreams could not be the foundation for her actions. The baby was no dream, and Sienna was determined to balance the deep tuggings of her heart with logic.

Later that evening as Sienna dressed, she undulated between a girlish giddiness and a strict, unfeeling logic that reminded her of Miss Taylor, a forbidding worker at the orphanage where she lived as a child. When the doorbell rang Sienna glanced at the clock. It was five minutes before eight, and her stomach tightened as she thought of Hawk standing outside. She looked in the mirror one last time. Her upswept braids made her look cool and elegant, an image far from what Sienna was actually feeling, while the simple but form-fitted black dress added a hint of devil-may-care.

"I can't believe how nervous I am." She said as she crossed the room and took hold of the doorknob. *But this is different. During the last eight years that Hawk and I have been together, we never came close to breaking up. I almost can't believe it happened. But it did, and now we're trying to come together again with so much at stake.* Sienna looked down at her abdomen. *Our relationship is hanging in the balance, and tonight will determine our future.* Fear coursed through her as she opened the door.

"Hi." Sienna hoped her smile wasn't too broad or too scanty. The truth was her lips suddenly felt dry, and she had to force them to slide over her teeth.

"Hello," Hawk replied.

Their eyes met. Sienna was so aware of the tiny, brown locks cascading around his face and down onto his shoulders. She realized how rare it was, nowadays, to see Hawk's hair down. It was a powerful look. His golden eyes, trimmed with dark lashes, turned smoky as he passed her a single, red rose. The blossom was full.

"How beautiful." Tenderly, Sienna touched the petals. "Let me stick it in the vase with the bouquet you sent me. I'll be ready to go after that." She walked toward the dining area. She could feel Hawk's gaze following her. Sienna looked back. Hawk was still standing in the doorway. She gave him a slight smile which he returned, but even that was different. Normally, Hawk moved in her home as if it were his own, but not tonight. The dynamics of their lives had changed, and Sienna could feel it. She pressed the rose to her lips with a silent prayer. *Please God, don't take Hawk away from me.* She placed the blossom in the vase, picked up her purse and re-entered the living room.

"Ready?" Deeply, his eyes searched hers.

"Yes," Sienna replied.

Hawk stepped outside and Sienna locked the door. They walked to his car. Hawk opened Sienna's door, waited for her to settle in, then shut it behind her. Sienna watched him walk to the driver's side, open the door and sit down beside her.

"My goodness. Everything seems so formal," she said with a nervous laugh. "The rose . . . your opening and closing the door for me. . . ."

"Formal is one way of putting it," Hawk replied. "Or perhaps I haven't treated you the way you deserved until now."

"I wouldn't say that." Sienna looked down at her hands. "You've always been a conscientious man."

"Conscientious. That's probably true. But loving

. . . leaving no doubt in your heart about how I feel? In that area I think I could have done better." Their eyes met again before he started the car.

Sienna's heart rate increased. She could feel Hawk's sincerity, but there was something in his tone that made her think that he felt he might have come to that conclusion too late.

Sienna incredulous, in your life! I could feel it! And if you could feel it, I could sense it too! Not you couldn't I before he started to say the words, but I found them Sienna could feel it was time to lose perception for herself. Perhaps we got the perfect fit here. But then there's something lower and more sorrowing than his words.

Ten

Aware of a budding uneasiness, Sienna changed the subject. "Where are we going?"

"To a restaurant called The Abbey."

"The Abbey?" She thought for a second. "Seems like I've heard of it."

"That's highly possible," Hawk replied. "It's nationally known. The food is great and it's absolutely beautiful. Originally, it was a Methodist Episcopal Church built in 1915."

Sienna glanced at Hawk. Since she had known him they'd gone out to eat many times, but Hawk never expressed an interest in restaurants like The Abbey. He claimed to prefer simpler establishments. A familiar, nagging suspicion that she never really knew Hawk surfaced. "You seem to know it well."

"Pretty well," he replied. "Years ago, it was one of my favorite restaurants." Hawk drove past a sleek black Mercedes with sparkling rims. "I love the architecture. It has vaulted ceilings that are about fifty feet high and massive stained glass windows. Whenever I was there I felt transported beyond my everyday life. That was before my life changed. I was majoring in fine arts, remember?"

"Yes. You've told me."

He glanced at Sienna before focusing on the traffic again. "I felt safe there. I had carved out a kind of routine. The Abbey was a part of it."

She studied his profile as Hawk continued.

"I long for that homogeneity."

"Homogeneity?" Sienna's brows rose. Although she felt she understood what the word meant, whenever Hawk's well-versed side appeared it made her that much more aware of their differences. She had no college education. Hawk had just a few months left before receiving his Master's degree.

"Sameness. Consistency." Hawk explained.

Sienna thought of the baby. She looked out the window. "Life would be boring if things were always the same."

Silence came between them. Finally, Hawk filled it with something safe. "I think you'll like The Abbey. At least I hope so."

"I'm sure I will." Sienna was glad to agree.

The conversation continued in a light manner. Hawk did the majority of the talking. Sienna commented when she felt it was applicable, but was constantly aware of a distinct change in Hawk. A change she could not explain.

After about a thirty-minute drive they pulled up to the restaurant. A valet attendant came over and offered to park the car. Hawk agreed. The man opened both doors, and once Sienna and Hawk got out, he got inside and drove away.

Hawk took Sienna by the hand and walked toward the entrance.

"This is amazing." Sienna looked up beyond the precipice of the building to a lit window beneath a cone-shaped roof. She stopped to admire the eighteenth-century church, aware of Hawk's hand holding hers.

Gently, Hawk draped his arm around her waist and moved her forward. "Wait until you see what's inside."

Sienna allowed Hawk to lead the way, and by the time they were seated she felt she had been transported into an old world of medieval tapestries, towering pointed arches, monks chairs and linen tablecloths. Timidly, she smiled at Hawk across the candlelit table.

"Good evening." A quiet waiter in clothes that conjured up another time and space greeted them. "Welcome to The Abbey." Slowly and with an enticing lilt, he told them about the specials the restaurant offered before motioning toward the menu. "But, I must say, everything we offer is really good. Would you care for anything to drink?" He looked at Sienna.

"I'll have a glass of merlot," she replied.

"Any particular brand? We have our house merlot, which is—"

"The house merlot will be just fine," Sienna interrupted, her nerves getting the best of her.

"And you, sir?"

"A double martini," Hawk replied.

Sienna tried not to look surprised. She had seen Hawk drink wine on various occasions. But she had never known him to drink hard liquor.

"Very good." The man bowed slightly. "I'll be back with your drinks and to take your order." He walked away.

Sienna and Hawk studied and discussed the menu as a haunting piano tune played.

"That's live music," Hawk said, continuing to browse. "You can't see it, but it's being played on a baby grand piano."

"Really?" Sienna replied, impressed.

Hawk looked at her. His eyes seemed to beam. "Did you notice the hanging lamp?"

Reluctantly, Sienna removed her gaze from Hawk's face, and admired the huge dangling fixture far above them. "It's beautiful," she said softly.

"And so are you," Hawk replied.

Once again Sienna looked at Hawk. The emotion emanating from his eyes melted her heart.

"I've never loved anyone like I love you, Sienna," Hawk said as he continued to look at her. "And no matter what happens I want you to remember that."

Sienna felt as if she could barely breathe. "Forget that?" She shook her head with the impossibility. "I will never forget this moment, let alone that you love me." Sienna reached across the table and touched his hand. "From the time I realized I loved you, I knew I could never love anyone else as much." She smiled, almost in tears. "But we won't have to re-member this because we'll be together always. Until we're so old that memories are all we have." She gave a nervous laugh.

Hawk looked down.

It wasn't the reaction Sienna expected. "What is it?"

He showed a mournful smile. "I'm glad we have this night together."

"So am I," she said, but suddenly she felt uneasy again. Sienna sat back when the waiter appeared.

"Merlot." He placed the rich red wine on the table. "And a double martini." He sat the crystal clear drink before Hawk. "Are you ready to order?"

Hawk looked at Sienna.

She nodded.

"Yes," he replied. "The lady will have the duck

and I'll have the lamb. We'll both take one of your house salads."

"Excellent choices." The waiter took the menus. "I'll bring you your salads along with some bread." He turned on his heels.

Hawk sat back and raised his glass. "Here's to us."

Sienna was surprised again. She raised her glass too. "To us."

They touched crystals.

Sienna sipped her wine and tuned into the music. Every once in a while she could feel Hawk's eyes on her face. They would look at each other and smile.

Their salads and bread arrived, and soon after, their entrees. Conversation flowed smoothly between them. Hawk was more talkative than usual, and Sienna wondered if the quickly emptied martini glass had anything to do with it. When the waiter returned to check on them and Hawk ordered another drink, Sienna couldn't hold back.

"I didn't know you drank martinis."

"I used to," he replied. "Before . . . things changed."

"Oh." Sienna looked down. "So I guess coming here to The Abbey brings back all kinds of memories."

Hawk looked around. "Yes. It does." He took a swallow of alcohol. "Before I'd walk into a church and think nothing of it. Now the only way I can go into a church is to convince myself it's only a restaurant." He gave a mirthless chuckle, then paused. "This place is still more than a restaurant, but maybe I'm the only one in here who can feel that."

Sienna drew a deep breath. Although there were people laughing, eating and drinking, there was an undeniable feeling of sacredness everywhere. It was in the walls, in the air. "No, you're not the only one. I feel something too."

He looked at his fork. "So I've brought the woman I love to dinner, but in actuality I am killing two birds with one stone."

Sienna lifted the merlot to her lips. "What do you mean?"

"I get to show you what's in my heart, in God's house." He shrugged in a too-crafted manner. "If I still exist to Him. He stopped existing for me a long time ago."

Sienna put down her glass. "Don't say things like that, Hawk. Why wouldn't you exist to God like every other human being?"

He laughed inappropriately. "You know why." Then, into her eyes, he said it again. "You know why."

Sienna did not budge. "But I've never accepted that that's how it is. There's so much good in you, Hawk. You're special, to me and to God."

"And that is one of the reasons I love you." His mouth smiled, but his eyes were like hard amber.

When it came time, Sienna ordered dessert, but Hawk continued to nurse his martini as he talked excessively. She was glad he didn't order another drink because Sienna wasn't sure what might happen if Hawk imbibed more liquor. Secretly, she breathed a sigh of relief when dinner was over and they walked to the front door of the restaurant. Outside Hawk placed his arm around her waist as they waited for the attendant to bring the car.

"Will you come home with me, Sienna?" he whispered in her ear as his hand massaged the flesh above her hip. "I've missed you so much."

She felt a jolt of anticipation when she turned and looked into his face. "I've missed you, too."

"Then I guess the answer is yes," he replied as he pulled her close.

Sienna stroked Hawk's hand. "What else could it be?" she asked.

The car arrived and they climbed inside. Hawk placed his hands on the steering wheel. "From now on, Sienna, we must always show each other how we feel." He looked at her, his eyes rich with love and vodka. "Time is too precious to waste on holding back." With every part of her Sienna agreed, but there was something that made the promise bittersweet.

Eleven

Hawk stopped outside his apartment building. He switched off the car, and said, softly, "We're here."

Sienna nodded, but found it difficult to hold his gaze. She knew she and Hawk would go inside and make love, something they had done many times before, but Sienna knew this time it would be different. Maybe it was because they were making up. Or maybe it was the change in Hawk. Whatever the reason, Sienna felt as nervous as a woman who was about to make love for the first time.

When she stepped out of the car, Hawk was there, closing the door and taking her hand. Sienna followed him up the walkway to the door of his apartment. He unlocked it with ease. Afterwards, Hawk switched on her favorite oriental lamp. It emanated a soft, elusive light.

It didn't take much to light Hawk's studio apartment that held a stylish futon, a comfortable chair, a dinette set for two, countless books, and an assortment of articles Hawk had acquired during his worldly travels.

Sienna watched Hawk ignite a single thick candle, set in the middle of the dining table. She knew he lit it for them, but Sienna also knew it was simply his way. Once, Hawk had told her that for him, a single candle flame symbolized an ever burning hope. And without hope he didn't know how anyone survived. Something made her wonder how much hope Hawk had left as she sat in a familiar armchair. But Sienna did not want to go so deep so fast. "I don't know why it still surprises me to see how neat you keep everything."

"In a space this small, there's no other way," Hawk replied. "I couldn't function if I didn't keep things in certain places."

"I bet," she said. Sienna had heard similar words before, but the circumstances were quite different. They had discussed "Hawk's place" many times before and it had turned into a heated argument. Sienna didn't understand, after being together for eight years, why he chose to remain in the cramped quarters. She had made it plain to Hawk that he was welcome at her house right after they expressed an intention to get married. This time, Sienna let the controversial subject lie.

She watched Hawk flip through a collection of CDs. He extracted one and put it in the player. A soft classical piece filled the room. Sienna had definitely heard it before, but she could not think of the name. She knew that was something Hawk would never forget. He loved all kinds of music, and had opened Sienna's life to many things she had never considered. Hawk was a gift. A gift and an enigma.

He walked toward her and stopped in front of the chair. There Hawk leaned forward, lifted her hands from her lap, and pulled Sienna toward him. "Dance with me," Hawk said as he gathered her in his arms.

Dance! Sienna was surely surprised. She'd seen Hawk dance in Martinique and on two distinct occasions after that . . . but dancing was not something he did often, and before she could respond to his request, Hawk was gently coercing her body to move with his. His upper torso moved slowly, fluidly, but his feet remained in place. Sienna followed his lead, and she snuggled close, resting her face just beneath his shoulder. They danced in place, moving as one, listening to the melody as it bloomed.

"This music . . . it's so beautiful," Sienna said, her voice hushed. "I've heard it before. What is it?"

"Bolero," Hawk replied. "It was composed by Maurice Ravel, a French composer."

At that moment Sienna didn't care that she didn't know the things Hawk knew. It didn't seem to matter. The music and the moment created something deeper in her that had no room for insecurity. It moved her to be grateful for his presence, his love, and all the things he meant in her life, including the baby he had helped her conceive.

Sienna and Hawk were glad to be in each other's arms again. The music held them captive as they danced, but their love was the element that bound them into oneness.

As the repetitive phrase within Bolero continued to build, Sienna lifted her face from Hawk's chest and offered him her lips. He accepted them wholly, exploring the moist cavern within. Afterwards when Sienna looked into Hawk's eyes, they reminded her of a misty forest they had experienced together in Costa Rica.

He touched her face. "When you look at me like that, what are you thinking?"

"I'm thinking you are the most beautiful man in the world. Your eyes never fail to show how deeply you feel. They change, you know. As they've changed now."

A sad smile touched his lips. "My eyes have been a blessing and a curse. There's no way for me to hide.

But what about you?" Hawk asked as his eyes darkened. "I don't always understand you, Sienna. You're more of a secret to me than ever, and there's nothing so obvious about you that lets me know how I make you feel."

"Then let me tell you, Hennessy, you move me beyond words."

In response, Hawk lowered his firm lips slowly to hers. Languidly, he rubbed them against her softer ones before the tip of his tongue made itself known and invited Sienna into a mingling kiss. All the while they clung to each other, making sacred all their memories, and the ones they would create.

Before Sienna and Hawk knew it, wrapped in each other's arms, they were on the futon. Tenderly, he traced the shape of her face before his finger grazed her mouth that was still warm with his kiss.

"There was a moment today, when I realized there'll come a time when I won't be able to hold you like this," Hawk whispered, then paused. "Death is something that comes to all of us."

"But it hasn't come yet, Hawk," Sienna interrupted him. She kissed his fingertips. "And I don't want to talk about that now. Not now." Her eyes implored him.. "I want you to make love to me, Hawk." She placed his hand on her firm breast, and closed her eyes. "I want to feel you inside of me."

"Oh Sienna." Her name was thick on his tongue. "I can't think of anyplace that I'd rather be." Hawk reached down and pulled her dress over her head, before he removed his shirt.

Over and over their lips touched, moist and inviting as they removed the remainder of their clothes. When their bodies were totally free Sienna cupped her breasts and offered them to Hawk, her eyes swimming with desire.

"You are beautiful, Sienna." Hawk said before his warm mouth sucked the tip of each mound, and his tongue made them shine.

Sienna's body quivered with ripples of pleasure and her reaction seemed to fuel Hawk's vigorous motions. Aggressively, he lapped at her brown breasts while his hand traveled downward, smoothing her belly and touching her navel before it eagerly cupped the triangle below.

"You are so warm." Hawk whispered, leaving her breasts long enough to breathe in her ear. "So warm and . . ." His mouth covered Sienna's, and as Hawk's tongue entered her mouth, his finger slipped inside her.

Sienna gasped and her arms went around his neck.

"I love you, Sienna. I love you," he confessed as he played with the tiny bud within her that enlarged with his strokes. Faster and faster Hawk's finger vibrated until Sienna's womanhood ran with her affections, as her body eagerly moved against it, asking for more.

"No. No. You're going to make me . . ." Sienna tried to stop his hand before she reached over and embraced his hardness. "This is what I want, Baby. This is what I need." She directed his maleness to the focus of her desire and placed the tip just outside. That was more than enough for Hawk to understand.

He pushed Sienna back on the futon and straddled her. "You don't have to say another word," he announced as he filled her. "And I've got something that's going to help me do my talking." Slowly, he moved his maleness within her.

Hawk's strokes were gentle at first until his desire

proved it had a mind of its own and his body began
to move of its own volition.

"Yes," Sienna beckoned as she nibbled at his ear.
"You know what I want. You know what I want. No
other man but you." She enticed as she clung to him
with her legs open wide.

Already Hawk's passion was roaring in his ears, but
with Sienna's words it was almost blinding. Back and
forth he thrust with all his life. "I know you want me."
Came from deep within his throat. "But tell me you
love me, Sienna." His body moved like a frantic machine. "Tell me now."

Sienna could barely talk, Hawk's moves were so
powerful, but she managed, "Yes. Yes." Between her
staggered breaths: "I love you, Hawk. I love you."

It seemed to be all he needed to hear, because
Hawk drew Sienna closer as his body sought her love.
Caught up, Sienna felt as if she were on a mighty ride
and the nerves in her center vibrated with each
thrust. Hawk had made love to her before, but never
had his passion been so potent. It wasn't long before
Sienna's breaths came in tiny bursts and her body
filled with uncontrollable pleasure. It was obvious
to Sienna, because Hawk knew her body so well he
was able to meet her moment in a grinding thrust.

"Sienna. My Sienna," he said through a fulfilled
fog. "May it always be just you and me. You and me,
my love."

Through her own ecstasy, Sienna listened to his
words with a divided heart. She was thrilled with his
clarity about his love for her, but Hawk's claim of a
future with the two of them alone, wove a thread of
concern. As he held her, and their passion subsided,
Sienna knew she would not tell Hawk about the baby.
Not yet. She would wait until the fabric of their re-

constructed relationship had grown strong enough to support the product of their love.

"It will always be you and me, Sienna. Just you and me," Hawk said as he held her. "Nothing will ever come between us again. Nothing or no one."

Sienna closed her eyes as she felt Hawk's strength and his love, and it was most difficult to hold back on what she wanted to say, *But there is someone else, Hawk. Someone who won't be a wedge between us, but a kind of bond that we have never known before. Someone who will show the world our love.*

Twelve

The next morning, half awake, Sienna eased over in the bed. She anticipated cuddling against Hawk's warm body, but all she found was the sheet and comforter. Sleepily, Sienna opened her eyes and looked around. Hawk wasn't there.

She shielded her eyes and looked through the large sunroof that allowed light to pour into the studio apartment. Sienna recalled it was the sunroof that convinced Hawk to rent the tiny space. She sat up and leaned against the headboard. No. Hawk wasn't there in body, but certainly his presence was everywhere.

The front door opened quietly. Sienna's gaze met Hawk's as he stepped through the door carrying a white paper bag. "Good morning," he said.

"Morning."

"I couldn't sleep. So I thought I'd go out and get us something for breakfast."

Sienna smoothed the braids away from her face. "What did you get?"

"Some carrot walnut bread and some zucchini bread." He put the sack down. "And I thought I would cook us a couple of eggs."

"Sounds wonderful," Sienna replied.

Hawk walked over to the bed and kissed her. "Good."

Sienna and Hawk smiled the smile that said things were good between them. She watched him move over to the sink where he washed his hands.

"It's beautiful out there," he said without turning around.

Reluctantly, Sienna looked up through the skylight. She had wanted to hold onto Hawk, to pull him back in bed, but she could tell he was already in gear for the day. "I can tell."

"There were quite a few people at the coffee shop."

"Oh yeah?" She looked around for a clock. "What time is it?"

"It's a little after eight."

"So what time did you get up?"

"About seven." Hawk removed four eggs from the refrigerator. "I thought I'd have time to get some *hsing-i* in, but I got to talking to a couple of men at the shop."

Sienna stretched. "Oh, really?"

"Yep. They read the article about you in the paper."

"God. I bet everybody's going to be talking about it." She rubbed her eyes.

"That's what happens when you play heroine," Hawk replied.

She swung her feet over the side of the bed. "Well, it surely wasn't my intention. It just happened."

"You just kind of got caught up in it, huh?"

There was something in Hawk's tone that made Sienna look at him. But he continued to mix the eggs. Dawn's words echoed in her mind. *I'm just saying, things always pick up when the Stonekeeper's cycle is about to begin.*

"Yeah." She looked down at her feet. "Got a shirt or something for me to wear?"

"Look in the closet and take your pick."

Nude, Sienna plodded across the floor to the closet and selected a shirt she hadn't seen Hawk wear recently.

"I hope scrambled eggs are okay," he said. "I forgot to ask."

"Scrambled's fine," she replied.

"Do you have to open up the shop this morning?"

"Nope. Dawn's going to do it. I'll go in sometime this afternoon. What about you? What's on your schedule today?"

Hawk placed a bowl on the tiny counter. "Late this afternoon, I've got this guy who's booked a private *qi gong* session. I think he's a dentist, and he's having some kidney problems. He's heard that *qi gong* is good for the kidneys, so . . ."

"Is that true?" Sienna buttoned the last button on Hawk's shirt.

"Yes. It's very good for them. The body's life force, the *qi*, is deeply associated with the kidn—"

A catchy tune interrupted him.

"That's my phone." Sienna reached for her purse, opened it and took out a Nokia. She glanced at Hawk. "Speak of the devil." Sienna pressed one of the buttons. "Hello Dawn." She watched Hawk pick up an egg, crack it, and dump the insides into the bowl.

"Hi Sienna. Did I wake you?"

"No, it's okay. I'm awake."

"So how did last night go?" Dawn sounded as if she were whispering. "Did you and Hawk get together?"

"Yes." Sienna glanced at Hawk again.

"Great. Is he there right now?"

"Ye-es," Sienna repeated, trying to let Dawn know this wasn't the time for questions.

Hawk turned and looked at her.

"Well, I won't keep you, but I wanted you to know Francisco is here. He wants to speak to you."

"Okay." Sienna's brows knitted.

"Hello, Sienna." Francisco's accented voice came over the phone line.

"Hi Francisco. How are you?"

"I am very good this morning, thanks to you. I brought you some flowers. And I got a little something for you. But you're not here."

"Flowers. . . . You didn't have to do that, Francisco." Sienna and Hawk's eyes met.

"No-no. I wanted to. I wanted to show you how much I appreciate what you did the other day."

Hawk turned back to the eggs, but not before Sienna saw a resigned look in his eyes. "I know you appreciate it." She took a deep breath. "I'm just glad I was there and could make a difference."

"Are you coming to the store today?" Francisco asked, cheerfully.

"Yes, I'll be in later this afternoon."

"Let me know when you get here, and I'll come back with your gift."

Sienna laughed shyly. "Okay."

"See you then."

"All right. Goodbye."

"Goodbye."

She hung up and noticed an unnatural stiffness in Hawk's back as he beat the eggs. The sound seemed excessively loud. Sienna knew what was on Hawk's mind. It was the same thing that was on her mind as her fingers involuntarily went to the birthmark between her breasts, the mark of the crystal. *Is it beginning? Is this the start of the Stonekeeper's cycle?*

Sienna knew what the cycle had brought in the past. But in those days she had the luxury of ignorance. Sienna didn't believe there was such an event as the Stonekeeper's cycle. She truly didn't believe she was a Stonekeeper. She didn't know what it meant nor what would happen. But now, after experiencing two of the cycles, events that were beyond anything Sienna could have imagined, ignorance was a luxury she could no longer afford, no matter how she tried. Sienna thought of Hawk and all that he had been through, and she knew with every part of her that Hawk could not afford it either. She tried to bring a light feeling back into the morning. "I guess this is my week for flowers, isn't it?"

"Seems that way," Hawk replied as he stirred the eggs into the waiting oil.

"I'll get the plates." Sienna joined him.

They looked at each other once again, but neither mentioned what was heavy on their minds.

Thirteen

"Why don't you come in the shop for a minute?" Sienna suggested as they approached Blossom Street. "Dawn will be glad to see us together. Sometimes I think she's more concerned about our relationship than we are."

"Yeah, when you think about it, Dawn's been a part of us from the very beginning." He nodded slowly.

Sienna smiled, slightly. *Dawn was a very important part of the first Stonekeeper's cycle.* "Yes, she has," she replied.

Hawk looked at the clock on the dashboard. "All right. I've got a few minutes to say hello." He pulled into the first parking spot they saw. Together, they walked to The Stonekeeper. When the backs of their hands brushed accidentally, Hawk clasped Sienna's hand in his, just for a second, before they entered the store.

There were several customers milling around. Francisco's flowers, which sat on the main counter, were visible even from the door. They were a huge assortment of tropical flowers including bird of paradise, hibiscus and lantana. Sienna went over to the bouquet and gave it a closer examination as the bell over the front door chimed. Some of the customers were leaving. Only one woman remained.

"Hey!" Dawn said, chipper as ever. "You like your flowers?"

"Of course I do. They're gorgeous." Sienna touched one of the blossoms. She wished her heart felt as joyful as her voice.

"And what about you Mr. Jackson? How are you feeling?" Dawn smiled as if she knew more than she should.

"Pretty good, Dawn. Can't complain. And you?"

"I'm great. Looking forward to the day after tomorrow when we head for Kaua'i." She swiveled her hips.

Sienna had to laugh. "Are you going to Kaua'i to hula, or are you going to work?"

"Both, I hope." Dawn flashed a smile. "But you know I take care of business." Her chin descended. "So I am informing you that the boxes we shipped to Kaua'i are scheduled to arrive today. I will place another call this afternoon to make sure they did. And, the few things we plan to take with us, I have already begun to pack."

"You are so good," Sienna praised her.

Dawn made as if she were polishing her hand. "I know it."

"Just let me know," Hawk injected, "when you need me."

"We will," Sienna replied. "There'll only be a few boxes. We shipped everything else."

The front bell rang again. Sienna turned and saw Francisco hurrying across the floor.

"There you are," he said, smiling at her. "Hello, Hawk." He nodded, then turned back to Sienna. "I can't stay, but I wanted to give you this." Francisco presented a small velvet box.

"Wow." Sienna smiled, but it was obvious she was uncomfortable. "What is it?" She looked at Francisco. "I guess I don't do presents well."

"What's there to do?" Francisco asked. "Just open it."

Not having much choice, Sienna did as she was told. Her mouth dropped when she lifted the lid and saw the silver pendant.

"Do you like it?" Francisco couldn't wait for Sienna to respond.

"I don't know what to say." She continued to stare at the pendant. Finally, Sienna looked at Hawk, and positioned the box so he could see inside. Immediately, the color of his eyes shifted.

"My goodness, let me see." Dawn leaned over. "Oh my God. The markings remind me of your silver bangle."

Sienna glanced at the bracelet her Aunt Jessi had given her, although she didn't need to look at it in order to know there was a definite resemblance between the two pieces.

"I tried my best," Francisco said. "I knew you wore the bracelet all the time, so I thought, why not make Sienna a matching pendant."

"But the stones . . ." Sienna tried to keep her voice steady. "Why did you . . . is this a ruby?" She pointed to the red stone.

"It is." Francisco informed her. "And that is an emerald, and of course this," he smiled proudly, "is a diamond. The gems are not very big, but they are very good quality stones."

Sienna closed her eyes. *Another sign. This is another sign. There is no way to deny it. The cycle has begun, or it will begin very soon.* She thought of her baby, and Sienna prayed, whatever happened, that it would not put her child in jeopardy. "I'm sure they are," she finally said.

"What is it, Sienna?" Francisco looked at her

strained face. "If you don't like the pendant I can
come up with something else, but I thought this
would be perfect."

Sienna exhaled with resolve. She looked into
Francisco's eyes. "It is perfect, Francisco. More per-
fect than you could ever know." She glanced at
Hawk.

Francisco smiled broadly. "I am so pleased, that
you are pleased."

Overwhelmed, Sienna grabbed Francisco and
hugged him. When she let go, it was Francisco's turn
to look embarrassed.

"Well, I guess I should go now." He glanced at the
three of them, then looked down. "I just wanted you
to have something that would always remind you of
how much I appreciate what you did."

"How could I ever forget? Pendant or not," Sienna
replied. "But thank you for the flowers, and for the
pendant."

Francisco shook his hand as if to wave off her
words. "No. It was my *pleasure*. My pleasure." He
walked toward the door. "Have a good day."

"You too," Sienna replied.

Quickly, Dawn wiped a tear from the corner of her
eye. She hugged Sienna. "I guess I should get back to
work." She glanced at Hawk, and walked away.

Hawk stood next to Sienna as she looked back
down at the pendant.

"Do you want me to help you put it on?" Hawk's
question was almost a whisper.

"No. Not yet," Sienna replied. She looked at him.
"I'm not ready to wear it yet."

There was a moment of silence before Hawk
nodded.

Sienna knew he understood that she was not only

declining wearing the necklace, but she was also holding off donning the robe of the Stonekeeper. She would not hurry it. Sienna would not hurry what she could not fathom.

Hawk covered her hand that held the velvet box. He spoke slowly. "Perhaps we should try and see what is to come."

"What?" Sienna's brows knitted.

"Instead of letting it take us by surprise." Hawk's voice was steady. "Perhaps I could try to see what's in store for us."

"You mean . . ." Sienna couldn't believe Hawk was offering to use his gift for personal reasons. She knew how he really felt about the visions and the voices that flowed through him, that if he had his choice, they would not be a part of his life. For years Hawk reluctantly conducted readings for others, but as soon as he was able, he stopped the readings and began to teach martial arts classes to make a living. Initially, Hawk feared the powers that be might rebuke him. But nothing happened. That was four years ago and as far as Sienna knew he had not conducted a reading since.

"I mean tonight I will use my abilities to try and prepare us for what is to come. It's the least I can do, Sienna."

Sienna didn't know why Hawk's words brought tears to her eyes. Maybe it was the way he had said them. All Sienna knew was she felt a deep sorrow. "All right," she quietly replied.

"I'll come by your place at seven," Hawk said. "We'll order in some food and see what happens."

Suddenly, a part of Sienna wanted to say, "I don't want to know. Just let it happen, and we'll go with the tide, just as we've always done." But she could see the resolve in Hawk's eyes and instead replied, "I'll be ready."

As Hawk kissed her and headed for the front door, Sienna wondered if Hawk would be able to see their future, and the child that would play a huge part in it.

Fourteen

Sienna cleared away the last remnants of Chinese food from her dinette table and came back to the room. Nervous, she sat down across the table from Hawk.

"I've got to do this session somewhat differently than the readings I've performed in the past," Hawk said. "For them, I could just be near the person and the answers to their questions would come. But for us, for answers to questions that involve me, I sense I need to go into a deeper state."

"Into a hypnotic state?" Sienna asked.

"No." Hawk's brow wrinkled. "It's more like total surrender, a melding of myself with something else, something bigger. And there's something else." He paused. "Physically, I know I can't tolerate that state for very long, Sienna."

"What do you mean?"

He looked into her eyes. "I can't stay in that place for a long time. Letting go of my logical mind for that long . . . I could become totally lost, what some people call 'out of my mind.'"

"You mean, you'll be insane?" Sienna's heart quickened.

"That's one word for it." His lids shielded his eyes.

"But whatever you call it, I would be disconnected from the normal world mentally."

Sienna's eyes filled with concern. "That sounds dangerous, Hawk."

"Only if the session goes longer than we discussed," he assured her. "And I've told you what to look for. If my body begins to quiver and I begin to sweat profusely, know that you have no more than three or four minutes before we must stop."

"I remember," Sienna replied. "But I don't know if I like this."

"Do you understand?" Hawk held firm.

"No, I don't." Sienna crossed her arms. She was afraid. "And I'm not going to pretend that I do."

Hawk looked down. "Don't fight me, Sienna. This is something I need to do . . . for us." Gently, he touched her chin. "You ready?"

"I guess I have no choice," Sienna replied.

Hawk sat back. "Then let's begin." His gaze began to soften.

Sienna turned on the tape as they had agreed. Without trying, she felt her body stiffen. Sienna realized she had only seen Hawk prophesy once in her life, and that had been in Costa Rica. It was an experience that she would never forget. The voice that came out of him was so foreign, and the manner in which he spoke was more like poetry than normal speech. But most of all, Sienna recalled when Hawk allowed her to see his face. Hawk's handsome face had been. . . ." She gasped.

Hawk's eyes became focused again. He looked at Sienna. "You're afraid. Don't be. Don't be afraid," he implored. "We need to face our future, Sienna. Take control, somehow."

Sienna nodded.

"I need to know you're with me."

She drew a deep breath. "I'm with you, Hawk."

Their eyes held before Hawk sat back. Once again his gaze went soft. "The only way I know to bring this on of my own volition," he informed her, "is to become very relaxed. Very relaxed." His eyes closed. "Any other way my logical mind fights its intuitive double. It refuses to let me hear the voice that I am seeking now for us, for myself. So I must become very quiet," he continued, almost as if talking himself into the altered state. "I must surrender the thinking part of me to something that is beyond me." Hawk's breaths appeared to slow down. "Remember, when you see my breathing has slowed to the point where you wonder if I will take another breath, that is the time to start the questions."

"I remember," Sienna replied.

Anxiously, she continued to watch Hawk until, just like he said, his breaths were spaced in such a fashion that Sienna feared he might not take another, but he always did. She knew he was ready.

"Hawk?" Sienna said.

There was no reply.

"Hawk? Can you hear me?"

There was a slight pause, before Hawk said, in a voice that was not his own, "We are the one you call Hawk."

"We?" Sienna replied, shocked.

"Yes, we."

"How can Hawk be a 'we'? Who makes up this 'we'?" Her eyes narrowed as she studied Hawk's face.

"The physical body that you know as Hawk. The logical mind that allows the thoughts that We speak to come through. The spirit of Hawk that is always in contact with All That Is."

"All That Is, meaning what?"

"Meaning, God, Spirit, the Universe, there are various terms."

"So does this mean Hawk is special in the eyes of God, like his intuitive gift is special?"

"The 'we' known as Hawk is no more than any other human being. All human beings are a 'we'. How can The Creator create something that it is not a part of? How can a drop of water that flows from the ocean not be the ocean no matter where it goes or the form it takes?"

The wisdom that Hawk spoke was profound, but also confusing. Sienna wanted to ask more questions, but she and Hawk had already agreed on what she would ask. Reluctantly she read from the paper where the questions were written.

"Am I the one called the Stonekeeper?"

"You are." It was said with finality.

"But why?" she asked, although it was not one of the questions. "Why me?" Sienna demanded.

"Why is a blue jay a blue jay? Why does the moon wax and wane? You came to this life with this mission. You are only fulfilling what you and All That Is agreed upon."

"I agreed to do this *before* I was born?" Sienna asked, shocked once again.

"Yes."

Sienna wanted to debate the entire idea of reincarnation, but she went to the next question instead.

"And Hawk, why is his destiny tied to mine . . . tied to the Stonekeeper?"

"As twin souls you agreed to work together for the betterment of mankind. Hawk, We, agreed to be placed in a position where we would be driven to participate. You, The Stonekeeper, did not create such personal stimulus."

"You say we agreed to this . . ."

"Before you incarnated into your bodies. You agreed."

"Before we incarnated," she repeated, astonished. Sienna couldn't hold back. She asked another question that was not on the paper. "Does Hawk love Sienna the woman, or Sienna the Stonekeeper?"

There was a long pause before the voice spoke slowly. "Does one love the fragrance of the rose, or its velvety petals? They can not be separated."

Sienna glanced at the winding tape of the tape recorder. She wanted a clearer answer and Sienna wanted to ask about the baby as well. Would it be healthy? Would she and Hawk be married and raise the child together? But she dared not since Hawk did not know she was pregnant.

Almost imperceptibly Hawk's body quivered and Sienna looked at the clock. She knew she had to hurry. Sienna forced herself to ask the next question on the paper.

"Has the cycle of the Stonekeeper begun?"

"Now is like the clouds before the storm. You see the signs that are the forebears."

"Is this the last cycle?" Sienna asked, watching Hawk's face intently.

"It is the last one that was agreed upon."

"How can Hawk and I better prepare for what will happen?"

"Your soul is always prepared."

"Our souls . . ." She felt exasperated. "But how can we better prepare?"

"Become one with your soul."

She shook her head but moved on. "When will the Stonekeeper cycle begin?"

"Within the next seventy-two hours."

"Will Hawk's . . . will Hawk's face change?" She could barely ask the question.

"The blister is his resistance to what he knows, who he is. It is the resistance that brings it into being. The blistering of his face is the predecessor to the blistering of his mind if he does not honor his soul's intent."

"What do you mean?" she demanded. Although the words were coming from Hawk's mouth, Sienna did not feel as if she were speaking to Hawk. The Hawk she knew did not speak in parables, but the voice did. Sienna wanted answers she could understand, and although she believed the answers were being given, the voice seemed like an adult with a mind far beyond her own. She felt like a frustrated child.

Suddenly, Hawk's body quaked violently.

Sienna looked at her watch. "It's time to bring him back." Quickly, she read the words at the bottom of the page. "It is time to come back, Hawk. To feel yourself in your body. Totally integrated with your body. There is no separation, there is only the one."

Hawk's body stopped shaking, but he did not open his eyes.

"Hawk?" Sienna called.

He sat like a statue. Nothing moved, not even his chest that had risen and fallen with each extremely slow breath.

"Hawk!" she screamed, as she shook his arm. "It's time to come back now. Feel your body. There is no separation, there is only the one."

Fifteen

Hawk's eyes fluttered, then opened suddenly. *There's a mist in the room*, he thought, but as the objects in the room became clearer, he wasn't so sure. *Or is there a film over my eyes?*

"Are you okay?" Sienna drew closer. "Say something, Hawk." She grabbed his face with both hands.

"I'm all right," he replied, his voice a mere whisper. He felt drained.

Sienna shut off the recorder. "Do you want some water?" she asked, looking at him strangely.

Hawk nodded. "Water would be good."

She rushed into the kitchen.

Hawk drew a few deep breaths and looked around the room. In all the readings he had conducted he had never felt this drained before. It was taking all he had to remain awake. Hawk felt the distinct inclination to lie on Sienna's couch and go to sleep.

Sienna returned with a glass of water. She sat it in front of him.

"The tape." His words ran together.

"What?" Sienna leaned in close.

"Did you tape what I said?"

"Yes." She looked at the portable tape recorder. "But I want to warn you . . . it doesn't sound like you." Sienna gazed into his eyes. "Not really."

She's worried about how I will feel when I hear it. "Did I answer the questions?" His voice remained weak.

"Most of them." Sienna looked down.

"Rewind it." Hawk took several gulps of water. "And play it back. Please."

He watched Sienna press one of the buttons on the machine. A strange expression remained on her face. "What is it?"

"I just want you to know, you sound very different. It reminded me of Costa Rica." Sienna shook her head. "Hawk, in a way the tape creates more questions than it answers."

What she heard totally unnerved her. He studied her concerned features. *She says the tape creates more questions than it answers, but it has to have some merit. If this damn ability can't help us in a time of need, what good is it? Hell, I might as well go crazy now and get it over with.*

The tape stopped rewinding. Hawk leaned forward and pressed the play button. First, he listened to Sienna call his name. Then she called it again. Next, Hawk heard a booming, gravelly voice say, "We are the one you call Hawk." Shocked, he looked at Sienna. Her eyes were confused.

"See that's what I'm talking about. I don't—"

"Sh-sh-sh," Hawk said with more strength than he had shown since the session. "I want to hear it."

They listened in silence, their eyes meeting over and over again. When Hawk heard Sienna ask, "Does Hawk love Sienna the woman or Sienna the Stonekeeper?" he looked down. Hawk knew Sienna simply wanted him to love Sienna Russell, the shop owner, the woman who wanted to marry and have a family, and Hawk did love her, but he also loved the Stonekeeper. The Stonekeeper who was destined to bring back the fairness and balance that was stolen when he accidentally evoked the power of the hiero-glyphed crystal. There was no way for him to choose between them.

As the tape played, Hawk agreed with Sienna that it created many questions, but it also gave them the time frame in which the Stonekeeper's cycle would start. It would start within seventy-two hours.

Hawk breathed a sigh of relief. He had to believe the insanity that overtook him in his personal vision would wait until this last Stonekeeper's cycle had passed. That he would be there to help Sienna.

A click sounded on the tape. It was Sienna turning off the machine. Once again they sat together in silence.

Hawk did not want Sienna to know how unsettling it was for him to listen to the bizarre-sounding voice that came out of him. "I'm going to listen to the tape and write everything down." He willed strength into his voice in order to sound clear and determined. "We've got three days before the cycle begins."

"I know." Sienna rubbed her hands together. "It begins the day the gem show opens in Kaua'i." She looked at him with deep concern.

"Come here," Hawk called to her. He wanted to relieve her fears, but wasn't sure how.

Sienna got up and walked to the other side of the table. Tenderly, Hawk pulled her onto his lap.

"You're going to do fine," he assured her, wrapping her in his arms. She closed her arms around his neck, and held on tight. Hawk could feel her heart beating. It was beating much too fast.

"I thought I had put this stuff behind me, Hawk," Sienna said, with her face nestled in the base of his neck. "At least I hoped I had." She paused. "But here I am."

"Here we are," he assured her.

"We. It's such a good word when it's used like this." Sienna sat back and looked in his face. "But when you said 'we' during the session, it shocked me."

"Me too." *The powers that be claim all men are a we, but not all men are going through what I'm going through right now. All men are not being threatened with insanity. An insanity that might harm the one they love.* Hawk guided Sienna's face onto his shoulder again. "But as you and I know there are so many things in this world that are beyond what we even know to believe." He stroked her hair. "And I don't think right now is the time to delve into the why of it. I don't see how it could help. We've got enough on our plates. We surely don't need anything else."

Sienna sat up again. She looked at him as if she had something she wanted to say.

"What is it?" Hawk prodded.

"I was just thinking about everything." She sighed and laid her hand on the side of his face.

Hawk turned toward it and kissed her fingertips. "We must enjoy every moment we can, Sienna." He hugged her close. "We can't control tomorrow. We can only hope that we'll make it through."

Their lips were drawn together in a sweet kiss. Sienna softly rubbed her face against his until their mouths joined again revealing their fears and their hopes. As their tongues touched, for Hawk it was like a drug. A drug he feared he could never live without.

Hawk hugged Sienna and closed his eyes. Emotionally, her lips were more than satisfying, but his body could not be so close to Sienna without awakening. Hawk could feel his need rise and press against her through their clothes. "See what you do to me," he said close to her ear. Hawk looked deep into Sienna's eyes. "I can't help it. But I never want you to think this is the only reason I love you. My love runs much deeper than the physical. Much deeper." His voice trailed off.

"I know that," Sienna replied. She pressed herself against him before she leaned forward and offered her parted lips.

Hawk thrust his tongue deep within the moistness, and Sienna stroked his head as she moaned. He continued, covering her neck and her shoulders with tiny kisses as he removed her clothing below the waist. Hawk's passion catapulted when he saw Sienna's eyes light with anticipation before her underwear slid to the floor.

With long gestures Hawk stroked Sienna's body from her breasts to her hips, where he molded the plump area with his hands. "I love your hips, they're so round." Hawk spattered her breasts with succulent kisses. "I love all of you," he said as Sienna continued to straddle him before he lifted her onto her feet.

For a luxuriating moment Hawk closed his eyes while Sienna ran her hands through his locks, and untied the wrap that held them back.

"I'm glad I still appeal to you," her soft voice said through his trembling eyelids.

"Appeal to me." His smoky eyes opened and fixed on hers. "You do more than that." Revealing the tip of his tongue, Hawk leaned forward and traced the mark of the crystal between Sienna's breasts before he allowed it to slither down, where he circled the interior of her navel. "Appeal to me . . . Sienna, you consume me." He moved down in the chair and his eyes burned as his tongue swirled through the curly mound below.

Hawk felt Sienna's buttocks quiver, and his desire

grew as he slid his tongue into her valley where he explored it thoroughly before he sucked on the center.

With abandon Sienna moved against his mouth until his tongue sank deep within her and she cried out as her pleasure flowed. Inflamed by her wetness, the smell of her, her cry and the look on her face, Hawk quickly impaled her on his waiting hardness.

The warmth of Sienna made Hawk's body jerk, and he tried to bring her closer, to encourage her body to take all of him as he strove to join her at her peak. But Sienna dug her fingers into his back and whispered, "Slowly. Slowly, my sweet man. I want to enjoy you, at my pace."

"Whatever you want," Hawk replied, and with unbelievable control he willed himself to relax.

Slowly, Sienna began to gyrate, and his eyes clenched as the blood pounded in his organ.

"Yes. Right there, Hawk. Right there." She situated herself with long, rhythmic strokes.

With each descent of her tight moistness, Sienna engulfed more and more of Hawk until he was fully sheathed and quivered with pleasure.

"Nobody knows me like you, Sienna. Nobody," Hawk said as he grabbed her face with both hands and nibbled her lips. But by then Sienna was not interested in his kisses. Her body had reached a syncopation that cried for an ecstatic release, and it was the signal Hawk had been waiting for.

He clasped her around her waist and held her to him tightly. Gone was the need to hold back, gone was the ability. Hawk gave all that he could until Sienna's body shook as she began a slow, mounting wail. *"E-eeeeee-ah-hhh!!!"* And he knew he had her there. Hawk was blinded by the pleasure and he drove into her again and again until he quaked and spilled over with love.

"Nothing will ever part us." Hawk's voice quivered as he spoke and their bodies slumped. *Nothing but death, or my inability to recognize the one I love,* he thought as they remained locked together on the chair.

When he was able, Hawk kissed the top of Sienna's head, tenderly. He hoped, since he could not pray, that he would never live to see the latter.

Sixteen

"Isn't this something?" Dawn said as she stepped into the lobby of the Kaua'i Coconut Beach Resort. She looked at the trees, flowers and vines that tumbled from balconies above. "Would you look at that," Dawn exclaimed, over the forty-foot waterfall that topped off the tropical ambience.

"This is great," Sienna said.

"It is." Hawk looked around slowly.

"I didn't expect all this," Sienna remarked as she studied a huge bas-relief that rambled through the lobby telling the story of how the Hawaiian people arrived in the islands.

"Well," Dawn exhaled. "With the balmy breeze, aqua blue ocean, and this . . . I think I've finally died and gone to heaven. When you two"—she wagged her finger between them—"leave here, you're going by yourselves."

Sienna laughed. "You need to quit."

Dawn lifted an eyebrow. "I'm not playing. You've lost an employee, honey."

"And what are you going to do in heaven to survive?" Sienna continued to laugh.

"Sell coconuts or something," Dawn quipped.

"Yeah, I'm sure." Sienna eyed her. "That won't last for long. You like your Gucci sandals too much."

"Let me tell you something." Dawn stood her ground. "If I lived here, I wouldn't even wear shoes. I'd barely wear clothes."

"You hussy," Sienna hissed before the hotel clerk interrupted.

"May I help you, please?"

"Yes, you can. Two rooms have been reserved under the name of Sienna Russell." But Sienna continued to laugh at Dawn. "We're here with the International Gem Trade Show."

"Oh yes." The woman smiled pleasantly. Her fingers tapped over the computer keyboard. "Russell." She scanned the computer screen. "Right here. You have two oceanview rooms. And you will be staying with us for five nights." She looked at Sienna for confirmation.

"That's right."

The woman returned to the keyboard. "Now, the two rooms are beside one another, but your lanais will face different directions because one of the rooms is a corner room."

"Private lanais?" Dawn batted her eyes as she looked at Sienna. "That will be fine by me."

Sienna laughed. "As you can see you won't get any argument here."

"Wonderful," the attendant replied. "Do you need help with your luggage?"

Hawk shook his head as if he was going to say no, but Sienna stopped him. "Yes, we do."

The woman nodded. "I'll get someone to help you." She walked to the other end of the counter.

Sienna took Hawk's hand. "I'm taking my cue from Dawn." She batted her eyes as Dawn had done. "Let them do it. It's their job."

Hawk almost smiled. "You two are pitiful."

"We might be, but I can say I'm pitifully happy," Dawn replied. "And I'm going to be waited on hand and foot."

The hotel clerk returned with the keys. "Here they are. Are you planning on joining us at the *lu'au* tonight?"

"There's a *lu'au* here, tonight?" Sienna asked.

"From six to nine. It's really a wonderful affair. The *imu* ceremony starts at six fifteen, so you can see the pig taken from the pit and prepared for the meal. There's all kinds of food for everyone, we'll be doing the hula and hopefully, if you come, you'll join in."

"Sounds like fun," Dawn exclaimed. "And it's free?"

"No." The woman looked a little embarrassed, but she recovered quickly. "It's only fifty-five dollars for adults, and the food and specialty drinks alone are worth it, without even thinking about the music and the performance. Plus, tonight, some Hawaiian spiritual elders will be attending. One of our grand Kahunas, Elikapeka, will be here. You know what a *kahuna* is, don't you?"

"I think so," Sienna replied.

"It's a Hawaiian spiritual teacher, who works with herbs and the ancient Hawaiian medicine-way, *huna.*"

"Sounds like it's right up my alley," Dawn said.

"Interesting." Sienna looked at Hawk. His expression was unreadable.

"Interesting and fun." The clerk leaned on the counter. "Now to find your rooms, you simply go to the elevator and up to the third floor. When you get off, go to the right. Your rooms are at the end of that hallway." She smiled. "Enjoy your stay."

"Thank you," Sienna replied. She gave one of the card keys to Dawn.

"If the room is anything like the lobby, I'm going to be more than pleased," Dawn said, pressing the elevator button. "And it's still early. We've got the entire day to explore the island and fraternize with the locals." They got off the elevator. Sienna and Hawk walked down the hall listening as Dawn chattered. "So what are we going to do?" Dawn asked when they reached their rooms. "I think we should wait for our luggage and put everything away, then meet back out here in, say, fifteen minutes."

"Fifteen minutes." Hawk repeated. "We need to rest a bit."

"Who needs rest? We've been sitting on an airplane for hours," Dawn reminded him, "and we slept the majority of the time."

"Just because you are the ever ready rabbit, doesn't mean everybody is," Sienna remarked.

"You two don't fool me." Dawn stuck her key in the slot. "That stuff you want to do can wait until later on tonight. You've got all your lives for that, but you won't have but one first day on Kaua'i." She opened the door. "Call me when you're ready to do something. And if you wait too late, I might be gone, all by myself." She closed the door.

Sienna and Hawk entered their room. It was decorated in pastels and earth tones. Artwork with Hawaiian themes gave it a personal touch.

Sienna watched Hawk walk out onto the lanai. He appeared pleased as he reentered the room.

"This is nice, isn't it?" Sienna sought Hawk's approval.

"Real nice," he replied. "And look at that." He

pulled her in front of him and wrapped his arms around her waist. They gazed out at the ocean.

"Despite everything, I feel so lucky," Sienna said.

"Why?" Hawk asked softly. "Because you're in Hawaii?"

"No, because I'm in Hawaii with you." She snuggled closer and pressed her buttocks against him. She was happy with the hotel, the ocean, and her life at that moment. Sienna hoped it was a promise of good things to come.

"See there?" he said in her ear. "Dawn knows you well."

"Like she doesn't know you." Sienna's voice turned sexy. She closed her eyes and felt the hardness and strength of Hawk's body behind her.

A rapid knock interrupted them. "I've got your luggage," a cheery voice boomed.

"One minute," Sienna called back. Reluctantly, she stepped out of Hawk's arms and crossed the room. She opened the door.

"Where do you want them?" a bellman in a Hawaiian-print shirt asked.

"You can put the boxes here." She pointed. "And the luggage over there."

The bellman did as he was told. When he was done, Hawk handed him a tip.

"Thank you." He smiled. "Enjoy the resort."

"So much for our moment." Hawk placed his suitcase on the bed and opened it. "But, you know, Dawn is probably right. We only have today to get out and explore. Maybe we should make the best of it."

Sienna unzipped her bag. "You're turning down my invitation," she accused.

"C'mon now, don't do that." Hawk placed some

belongings in a drawer. He looked at her. "You know I—"

"That's one thing about you that hasn't changed in all these years." Sienna hung a group of clothes in the closet. "You have no clue when I'm kidding. And you know why?"

"Why?" Hawk continued to unpack.

"Because you're far too serious." She walked over and pulled his locks.

"Well." A shadow crossed his features. "We'll see what changes I can make in the future."

"That's the spirit." Sienna smiled. She liked it when Hawk referred to the future, a future that included her. "I guess I'll give Dawn a call and tell her we'll be ready in about fifteen minutes.

"Good idea," Hawk replied.

Sienna called Dawn and finished unpacking, and in less than ten minutes they were sitting in the resort lobby.

"Since we're in Wailua . . ." Dawn looked in her guidebook. "I don't know if I pronounced that right, so, better still, since we're on the southeast shore, we've got to go to the Fern Grotto and Smith's Tropical Paradise. But I also want to see Wailua Falls. They're in the Wailua River State Park. And we're very near every one of them."

"I don't know if we'll have time to do all of that, Dawn," Sienna said. "Plus I want to go to a re-created Hawaiian village that I read about."

They looked at Hawk.

"I'm open to everything," he replied. "But first I think we should check out the Coconut Marketplace so we can see where the show is going to be held."

"Hello." Sienna made a face. "I should have thought of that."

"Yeah," Dawn sighed. "It must be the Kaua'i air. We forgot, it should be business before pleasure."

Seventeen

Sienna, Dawn and Hawk walked out of the lobby, found the rental car and climbed inside. Hawk took the driver's seat, Sienna, in the passenger's seat, opened a map of Kaua'i on her lap, while Dawn leaned between them from the back.

"We'll take Highway 56 toward the airport, and the Coconut Marketplace should be on our left," Sienna said.

"All right. Don't get us lost now," Hawk teased.

"I won't. I'm good at this," Sienna replied.

They arrived at the Coconut Marketplace in a matter of minutes. Many people were out shopping in the large collection of stores situated in a somewhat unorthodox manner.

"How are we going to find it?" Dawn asked, looking around.

"There's got to be a map of the place somewhere," Hawk replied, as they approached one of the stores.

Sienna took a different approach. "We're looking for the Ship Store Gallery," she said to an elderly man who looked like he'd been around long enough to know everything.

"Ship Store Gallery." He shook his head. "Mo' bettah. You looking for scrimshaw?"

"Excuse me?" Sienna replied. Confused, she

glanced at Hawk, then said to the man. "I'm sorry, I didn't understand."

"Scrimshaw." He made a motion like he was scratching with his hand. "Pictures."

"Scrimshaw," Hawk repeated with understanding. "No, we're not. We're just looking for the Ship Store Gallery."

"That way." He pointed a puffy hand.

"Thanks," Hawk replied.

After they had walked away, Dawn looked at them. "What the heck was he saying?"

"Scrimshaw," Hawk said. "It's a Hawaiian form of art. They etch or carve figures and scenery on bone and ivory."

"Oh yeah. I read about that," Dawn acknowledged.

"Me too," Sienna added. "But I couldn't understand him to save my life."

"Me either," Dawn replied.

"He had a pretty heavy accent, as accents go," Hawk said nonchalantly. "But when you've traveled as much as I have, your ear adjusts to the nuances very quickly."

Dawn slipped her arm through Hawk's. "You're just special all around, aren't you?" She winked at Sienna.

"You better watch it, Baby. When Dawn gets too nice you know she wants something," Sienna teased.

Sienna was the first to see the Ship Store Gallery. "There it is." She pointed.

They walked up to the store. It sported a sign which read "International Gem Trade Show" and gave the days and times and pointed to the building next door.

"So the trade show is going to be over here," Dawn commented as she walked to the entrance.

They wandered inside the building. There were shelves and shelves of carved objects.

Dawn turned to Hawk. "Is this scrimshaw?"

"Yes, it is. And I must say I'm impressed." Hawk examined a knife with a finely carved handle. "This is museum quality artwork. There's some of everything here from scrimmed letter openers to fine jewelry."

"I've never seen anything like it," Sienna remarked.

"Me either," Dawn said. "But that's not important. Where is the trade show going to be held? This looks like a store."

They continued to ramble until they saw a man arranging the scrimshaw on the shelves.

"We're with the trade show," Hawk said. "Can you tell us where it's being set up?"

The elderly man looked up with a scowl. Finally, he thumbed toward the back of the building.

"So much for a kind welcome," Dawn remarked as they walked away.

"Yeah," Sienna said. "You would think he'd be a little more hospitable."

Hawk simply shrugged.

Eventually, they reached a large area filled with tables and chairs. The walls were decorated with Hawaiian artwork and the sun beamed through the window creating a pleasant atmosphere. Although nothing had been set up, Sienna could see it could work out very well. "This isn't bad at all," she said as Hawk walked over to one of the tables.

"No, it isn't," Dawn replied. "I guess there is some saving grace to the place, excluding the sourpuss out there."

Sienna turned when she heard rapid footsteps. A tall, young man, possibly of Hawaiian descent, was headed straight for Hawk. He too wore a scowl. The man stopped a few feet in front of him.

"Is there some kind of problem?" he demanded in a confrontational manner.

"Excuse me?" Hawk stepped back.

"You talked pretty roughly to my—"

"No. No. That's not him." The first man hurried in behind the younger one.

"It's not?" the confused man said.

"No. The man I told you about left no more than a minute ago."

"Oh." The younger man turned to Hawk. "I am very sorry. You see, my father had some trouble a little earlier, and I thought it was with you."

"We both apologize," the father spoke up. "Another man asking about the gem show was very rude. He complained that we had too many exits and the place would not be very secure. He wanted to know how many security guards we were going to have." His hands moved constantly. "Would there be someone posted by the doors? And I told him that things would be very secure, but I was not going to tell him all the details. The things that came out of his mouth were awful." The man shook his head. "But to look at him, you would think he was a well brought up man." He looked pensive. "So, I am so sorry that my son thought you were him."

"It's okay," Hawk replied, but his eyes did not match the calmness in his voice.

"Perhaps I can make it up to you," the oldest man said. He offered his hand. "By the way, my name is Keoki, and this is my son, Phillip."

Greetings were exchanged.

"Are you going to do any touring while you're here?" Keoki continued.

"Yes," Hawk replied. He appeared a bit more re-laxed. "We plan to do some touring right after we leave here."

"Well I have something for you." Keoki beckoned for them to follow. He went to the front of the build-ing where some boxes and papers were stacked. "I don't know if you were planning to go to *Kamokila*, but it is a good experience." His eyes brightened. "*Kamokila* is a re-created original style Hawaiian vil-lage. It is very near the location of the first of seven ancient villages in this valley."

"We were talking about it earlier," Sienna piped up. "I am very interested in going."

"Good. Because I have passes for you to get in." Keoki smiled as he gave each one of them a pass. "It is a wonderful way to learn about the roots of Hawaiian life. I am one of a very few pure-blooded Hawaiians. We are less than a thousand now." He tapped on his chest, then pointed at Phillip. "Even I married outside of my people." Then he shrugged. "Hawaii has become a place of many people. Still it is important to me to remember my ancestors, and to never forget how they lived and the things that they believed. So, because of my son's mistake and my poor attitude, I would like for you to have these passes."

"Thank you," Hawk said. "I'm sure we'll enjoy the village."

"*Kamokila* is on the way to the Fern Grotto, but be careful, the road is very steep," Phillip warned. "It is on Route 580. You will get to the turnoff before you reach Opaeka'a Falls Lookout."

"Thanks for the information and the passes." Dawn flashed a smile.

"I will see you again, tomorrow." Keoki bid them goodbye.

Farewells were exchanged before they left the store and headed for the car.

"That was nice of him," Dawn said as she slid into the backseat. "And now it makes sense. Keoki was mad at somebody else."

Hawk started the vehicle.

"Sounds like somebody has brought some very expensive stones to the show," Sienna replied.

"Seems that way," Dawn said. "But if they're that concerned about getting ripped off, they should have brought their own security."

Hawk drove, getting a few words in edgewise, while Sienna and Dawn talked about one thing and then another. They talked about the hotels, the beaches, and the landscape as they progressed. When they turned off at the sign that marked the village, Sienna realized why Keoki had warned them. The Toyota was making a steep climb on a one-lane road that skirted a very high ridge.

"I am not looking down," Dawn proclaimed. "As a matter of fact I'm going to make sure I sit behind Hawk to weight the car on this side." She closed her eyes. "Oo-wee. Just tell me when it's over."

Sienna didn't react as rashly as Dawn, but it only took one glance down the slope to make her realize how quickly she wanted to reach the village. She looked at Hawk, who appeared as calm as ever, and Sienna was more than happy for his quiet reassurance.

Finally, they reached *Kamokila*. There were several vehicles parked near a group of thatched roof buildings. Hawk, Sienna and Dawn got out of the car and walked toward the entrance where a small admissions building was set up.

"Aloha," the young man inside greeted them.

"Aloha." Sienna smiled as she returned the Hawaiian greeting.

"You want to see the village?" he innocently asked.

Silently Sienna gave the guy a hard time. *What else would we be doing up here?* But she replied, "Yes. And we've got passes." She placed her pass on top of the counter.

The young man looked uncertain. "Passes?"

"Yes. A man name Keoki at Coconut Market Place gave them to us," Sienna replied.

"Oh." He stood there with an indecisive look on his face. Finally, he said, "Wait a moment please. Let me check on this." He went over to an older woman, and Sienna could tell he was explaining the situation. She watched the woman say a few words then bow her head affirmatively. The young man hurried back.

"You can use your passes." He smiled broadly. "I'm new here and I haven't seen any passes before."

"That's okay," Sienna replied. She took Hawk and Dawn's passes and placed them on the counter.

"Now this is clear. . . ." He visibly relaxed. "There is a guide who will take you around and explain *Kamokila* to you. You see that group of people over there?" The young man pointed.

"Yes," Sienna replied

"They are waiting for the tour. It won't be long." He looked at a large clock on the wall. "I suggest you join them."

"Okay," Sienna replied. "Thank you."

They wandered toward the restless group that included three children and seven adults. The kids pestered each other after a woman chastised them for pulling leaves off of some of the plants. Other than the children's voices, there was an intense calm about the place. Sienna slipped her arm through Hawk's as she wondered what their child would be like.

"It seems so quiet up here," Dawn remarked. "I mean, if it wasn't for the children can you imagine how quiet it would be?"

"It really isn't," Hawk said. "It feels unusually quiet because we're in the middle of a clearing, and the natural habitat has been pushed beyond the settlement. It's your perception. Because we're in the middle of a forest you expect forest sounds," he continued. "But believe me, nature is doing its thing all around us."

"And you are right." A beautiful woman appeared from behind them. "Perhaps we should keep you here as one of the guides." She placed a *lei* around Hawk's neck.

Eighteen

"Welcome to *Kamokila* everyone. I am Wila, and I will be your guide today." She surveyed the group. "As you can see the village is being renovated. This is a constant effort on our part because we want *Kamokila* to be as authentic as it can be. It was destroyed in 1982 by Hurricane *Iwa* and was hit again, but not as badly by Hurricane *Iniki* in 1992. But we are determined to keep it going so visitors like you," she said, smiling, "and our islanders will have a place where they can come and experience what island life was like for ancient Hawaiians. Now let's begin the tour." Her hips swayed gently as she began to walk in front of them. "Follow me, please."

Wila pointed out fruit trees and medicinal plants. She explained the ancient Hawaiian approach to agriculture and took them to locations where crafts and everyday activities were being reenacted. She was a wealth of knowledge and Sienna could appreciate that, but she couldn't appreciate the special attention Wila gave Hawk, and his quiet acceptance of her ministrations.

"Next, I will take you into *hale koa*. It's the warrior's house, where big, strong men like you reside. What's your name?" she asked.

"Hennessy Jackson." He replied

"Hennessy, like the whiskey?"

He nodded.

"Only warriors like Hennessy, here, were allowed in these quarters." Wila's eyes brightened as she entered the structure.

Sienna and Dawn looked at each other. Dawn made a face and silently mocked Wila so that only Sienna could see. Once they exited *hale koa* Sienna deliberately walked a couple of feet behind Hawk, to see if he would notice, and just as she suspected he continued with the group oblivious to her absence.

"Now this is *pahoku hanau,* the birthing house," Wila explained. "Only females were allowed in here, and all the babies were born in *pahoku hanau.* Afterward, the mothers rested here until they felt strong enough to rejoin the village."

"I'm sure there are plenty of mothers now who wish there was a birthing house they could go to after having their babies," a woman commented. Several others agreed.

Sienna thought about how it would be once her baby was born. She was certain Dawn could manage the shop, but Sienna wondered how well she would manage without having her mother or some other woman around to help. She believed Hawk would be there, but how much would he be willing to do?

Sienna watched Hawk. All of his concentration appeared to be focused on Wila's explanations. She couldn't help but wonder if Hawk would be there for her and the baby or if he would allow something else, some foreign travel, or a woman even, to take him away from his family.

Sienna looked around the birthing house. In size it was very similar to the others they had toured. Still the everyday tools made her think of women working in harmony, supporting one another because of the sisterhood they had been born into. Sienna listened as Wila talked about some of the tools and how they were used. As an orphan, she had never experienced that kind of support, and Sienna decided that her baby would always have a family.

"The next building we will visit is a very important one." Wila led them outside. "It is the chief's sleeping quarters, *hale noa*. In ancient times you had to be of a certain stature to even approach his quarters, let alone enter them," she explained as they walked toward it.

Sienna noticed another group of people led by the woman who approved their passes, approaching it as well. They were the first to reach the chief's sleeping quarters. The woman connected with admissions stepped aside so another extremely large woman could enter. But before she went inside this woman stopped as if something was wrong, then turned toward their group. Sienna noticed her facial features were gentle, but there was a rare kind of strength beneath them. She was also certain the woman was looking directly at her.

Their eyes met and held before she looked at Hawk, then turned and entered *hale noa*. Three men followed.

"It seems like we may have a change in plans." Wila made a motion with her hand for the tour group to stop. "Let me see what's going on." She smiled. "I'll be right back." She joined the woman who continued to stand outside the chief's quarters.

"I wonder what's happening," Dawn said.

"I don't know," Sienna replied, "but I got the distinct feeling that the woman who went inside the chief's quarters purposefully turned to look at me."

"Really?" Dawn's brows furrowed.

"Did you see how she looked at you, Hawk?" Sienna asked.

"I saw her look this way," he replied. "But I didn't notice that she looked at either one of us."

Sienna smarted. *Perhaps if your mind wasn't on Wila you would have.* "Well I know what I saw," she retorted before Wila returned to the group.

"I'm sorry," Wila began, "but it appears we will not be able to go inside *hale noa* at this time. A very important delegation, including a revered Kahuna, *Elikapeka*, will be using it. She, along with several other spiritual elders, have gathered on Kaua'i."

"What's a *kahuna?*" one of the tourists asked.

"They are like a Hawaiian spiritual leader." Wila smiled a smile that Sienna thought Ultra Brite toothpaste would kill for. "But let's continue on. There is plenty more to see."

Sienna slipped her hand into Hawk's. She wondered if the woman who had singled her out was the kahuna, and why the spiritual elders were meeting on Kaua'i. Did it have anything to do with the Stonekeeper's cycle? Sienna squeezed Hawk's hand, seeking his reassurance in a situation that only the two of them really understood. But when he looked down at her his eye contact was brief, as if he were oblivious to the things that were on her mind. Sienna felt at a loss, and that nagging uncertain feeling about Hawk resurfaced.

The tour lasted a while longer and by the time Sienna, Hawk and Dawn were on their way to the Fern Grotto, Sienna felt resentful toward Hawk for his silence, and things went downhill from there.

They toured the grotto and, to their surprise, the misty fern-filled rock amphitheater was a favorite site for weddings. Several brides and grooms exchanged vows in choice picturesque spots, then paraded about in their wedding wear, while musicians played a Hawaiian wedding song. The ceremonies reminded Sienna of her dream of marrying Hawk on Kaua'i. She could tell Dawn was very aware of her feelings, but Hawk appeared to be in a world of his own, polite beyond measure, but distant. It was like torture and Sienna could barely hold her tongue.

By the time they left Fern Grotto even Dawn had fallen silent beneath the building tension between Sienna and Hawk, a tension of which Hawk seemed to have no clue. The tour had taken more time than they had anticipated, so they cut their visit to Smith's Tropical Paradise short in order to get to the *lu'au* on time. That was fine with Sienna. Touring had lost its appeal. She couldn't wait to get to the room and let Hawk have it.

Nineteen

"What in the world has gotten into you?" The hotel room door had barely closed before Sienna launched her tirade.

Hawk looked into her eyes, but Sienna didn't feel any connection. "I don't know what you're talking about."

"You've barely spoken since we left that village."

"I haven't?" He seemed to contemplate the situation. "It wasn't on purpose." Hawk removed a shirt and some pants from the closet. "I guess I didn't have much to say."

Sienna stood watching him with her arms crossed. It was as if he wasn't getting it, that this was a confrontation. But from Hawk's actions Sienna could have said "pass me the salt" and, emotionally, it would have affected him the same way.

Hawk laid the clothes on the bed, then looked up at her. "Are you okay?"

Sienna had to grit her teeth to keep from screaming. *He knows he and that woman had some kind of thing going. He knows it! Now he's asking me if I'm okay. . . .* Sienna grabbed a dress from the closet. *Since my feelings are so inconsequential to him, I refuse to be the only one who's upset. I can be as detached as Hawk, even more than Hawk can, but he better not expect me to be hot and ready in bed tonight.* "I'm just fine." She spaced out each word as she closed the bathroom door.

By the time Sienna and Hawk were dressed for the *lu'au,* she was steaming. Hawk hadn't initiated one conversation, even after she had mentioned his silence, and Sienna had had enough. She was about to walk out of the room and leave Hawk behind when Dawn knocked on their door. Sienna opened it.

"You two ready?"

"I am," Sienna said, stepping out into the hall.

The door had nearly closed when Hawk caught it and joined them.

Dawn looked at Sienna. She took a deep breath when Sienna narrowed her eyes and cut them in Hawk's direction. "I'm starved," Dawn said quickly. "That fish sandwich I had earlier is long gone and I can't wait to dive into the food at the *lu'au.*"

"Mm-hmm," Sienna replied as they started walking up the hall.

"I read some information in the room about it," Dawn continued. "And it seems like there's going to be so much food that we will be stuffed for days, if we do our fair share." Dawn looked from one of them to the other.

Sienna tried to put on a smile, but it wasn't working, and she refused to look at Hawk, who was still in his own world.

"Are you hungry, Hawk?" Dawn asked.

Sienna knew Dawn was trying her best to smooth things over, but from where she saw it there was nothing Dawn could do. The damage had been done. Hawk was going to have to do some major sucking up to get back in.

"A little," he added. "The truth is, I'm not very hungry."

Sienna wanted to retort, *"Then why are you going?"* but she continued to silently steam instead.

They arrived outside just as the *lu'au* master was removing the pig from the pit. A wonderful smell of pork having been roasted in an underground oven layered with hot stones and banana stalks filled the air as the *lu'au* master passed by. The *imu* ceremony had drawn a huge crowd, mostly tourists, and Sienna wondered how many of them would be participating in the trade show.

"I thought we were pretty timely," Dawn said as the attendant led them inside. "But it looks like most of the tables near the stage are already taken."

"Seems that way," Sienna replied.

"Those people bought stage-side tickets," the attendant informed them.

"Oh. I see," Sienna said as they continued to look around. At least Sienna and Dawn did. Hawk appeared almost indifferent to the surroundings. Sienna was beginning to wonder if something was seriously wrong with him.

The attendant gestured. "This is your table."

"Thanks," Sienna replied.

"Welcome." A razor thin woman wearing a colorful kaftan greeted them. "It's good to have some company."

"Why thanks," Sienna said as they took a seat.

"I got here real early." The woman appeared very excited. Her bright blue eyes with pronounced crows-feet in the corners sparkled. "By the way," she said, leaning forward, "my name is Miriam."

"Hi Miriam, nice to meet you. I'm Sienna."

"I'm Dawn." The introductions continued around the table.

"My name is Hennessy," Hawk said without projecting his voice.

Sienna glanced at him. He looked at her and looked away.

"Nice to meet all of you." Miriam smiled. She touched the large moonstone hanging around her neck. "Are you here for the gem show?"

Sienna and Dawn practically said yes together. Hawk nodded.

"How did you guess?" Dawn asked.

"I'm here for the show too, but I can also pick out people who are into stones." Miriam leaned in again. "Just between you and me, I'm very good at that kind of thing. I've been working on it for years now."

"Working on recognizing people who work with stones?" Sienna asked.

"No. Knowing things. Sharpening my intuition." Miriam's brows went up.

Sienna glanced at Hawk. His eyes were on Miriam, who appeared to glean a lot of pleasure from sharing her special talent with them.

"Oh, I see. Actually, I own a natural products shop in Atlanta," Sienna informed her. "We sell all kinds of things, including stones, natural body care products, and quite a bit of semiprecious jewelry set in silver."

"You have a shop. How industrious of you," Miriam replied. "I have a kiosk at one of the malls in St. Louis, Missouri. And I love coming to these shows." She showcased her moonstone. "Most of the stuff I buy will probably be for me, but I don't care. I love the stones and they love me." Her eyes twinkled. "What about you Dawn? What do you do?"

"I work with Sienna at The Stonekeeper and I teach a little yoga on the side."

"Really?" Miriam looked please. "I love yoga. I've been doing it for years, but recently I stopped. Maybe my talking to you is a sign that I should start back."

Dawn's shoulders lifted a bit. "Could be."

Miriam looked at Hawk. "And you Henn— What was your name?"

"My name is Hennessy," Hawk replied. "I was cursed by one of those damn stones that you love so much. Now I teach some martial arts, but before that I was forced to give readings with the same ability that you claim to have, but actually have very little of." He concluded, showing no emotion.

"Hawk!" Sienna was surprised. She looked at Dawn, who looked like she had swallowed an egg. Then she looked back at Hawk. He appeared to be more interested in the courtyard than the damaging words he had just dropped. When Sienna looked at Miriam, the woman was obviously upset.

"I'm sorry." She looked from Hawk to Sienna. "Did I offend him by forgetting his name?" Her hand was over her heart.

"I remember his name," Wila said as she approached their table. "He's named after the cognac which matches the color of his skin. His name is Hennessy," she announced.

"Oh. Hennessy," Miriam repeated, but it was obvious from her expression she didn't know what to make of Hawk or Wila.

"I saw you all from across the courtyard, and I had

to come over and say hello," Wila continued. "Are you staying here at the resort?"

Sienna chose not to respond. Hawk gave an almost imperceptible nod.

"We are," Dawn said with a placating smile.

"Excellent choice," Wila schmoozed. "The food here is absolutely wonderful, and they have *kahiko,* which is a refined, dignified ancient hula, as well as *awana.*" She shook her hips so rapidly Miriam gasped, and Hawk looked up at her for first time. "Which is a modern hula."

"My, you look like you can do that very well," Miriam said.

"I should be able to. I've studied it for a long time." Wila smiled at Hawk.

"So, Wila," Sienna pronounced her name in a fashion that clearly expressed how she felt, "you work at the Kaua'i Coconut Resort as well?"

"No. I don't," she replied. "Several of us from *Kamokila* decided to come here tonight because the Kahuna, Elikapeka, and the spiritual elders are attending this *lu'au.*"

"I see." Sienna stared at her.

"Well." Miriam cleared her throat. "Thank you for coming over here and sharing your knowledge with us. We probably never would have known any of that if you hadn't told us."

"Huh," Dawn sounded.

Once again Miriam's blue eyes were taken aback.

"Well, I thought I'd come over and say hello either way," Wila concluded. "And Hennessy?" She placed her hand on his shoulder.

"Yes." His reply was lifeless, monotone.

"I'll be back to get you when they call for the visitors to dance the *awana*."

Hawk paused, then replied, "That could be quite interesting."

"Believe me," Wila leaned closer to Hawk but it was obvious she wanted everyone to hear, "it will be." She walked away.

Twenty

Miriam cleared her throat. "They called our table. I think I'll get in line to eat."

"Me too," Dawn said.

Sienna rose from her seat. "How about you, Hawk? You ready to eat?" His bizarre behavior was becoming even more of a concern. In all the years Sienna had known Hawk, even during times when it could have proved useful, Hawk had never been rude to anyone. It was so unlike him to address Miriam as he had.

Hawk looked at her, and for the first time since *Kamokila* Sienna felt he really saw her. He touched her hand. "Maybe in a little while."

Sienna smiled and breathed a sigh of relief. *Maybe he was simply reacting to the island.* Sienna could relate. Kaua'i's tropical atmosphere had definitely dredged up memories of other Stonekeeper cycles. But Sienna kept telling herself, according to Hawk, they had another twenty-four hours before this cycle began. Deep inside, Sienna held on to the hope that it might not happen. That the millennium had passed and the time of the Stonekeeper's cycles had, too. "We'll be back," she reassured Hawk, then joined Miriam and Dawn in the buffet line.

When they reached the buffet table, scores of dishes were at their avail. Sienna picked foods with tiny identification cards that ranged from *pu pu,* finger foods such as fish kabobs, tempura and cracked crab to *limu,* an edible seaweed. She filled her plate with the smaller fare and some of the more serious dishes including a beautifully prepared *mahi mahi* and a chicken dish smothered in a mango chutney. Sienna got plenty, thinking she might be able to entice Hawk to share her plate.

They returned to the table, and Sienna saw Hawk had made some choices of his own. He had two drinks sitting in front of him. One of them, a blue concoction, was already half empty.

He's drinking again! I can't believe it. Slowly, Sienna sat down. She tried not to be judgmental, but she didn't think it was a good idea for Hawk to consume so much alcohol before he had eaten a decent meal. Especially since he wasn't a drinking man.

"I got plenty of food because I thought you might want to have some." She placed the plate between them. "Even . . . Even if you don't want anything heavy to eat, there's lots of fruit. Papaya, guava, br—"

"I've got plenty of fruit right here," Hawk replied, pointing to his second drink that was served in a carved-out pineapple, with cherries and papaya shooting out of one section of the rim.

"That's the kind of fruit that can get you in trouble," Sienna said teasingly, but she was very serious.

"I'm already in trouble," she heard Hawk say before he finished the blue drink.

In trouble? What does he mean? Is Hawk seriously attracted to Wila? Sienna picked up a cracker and took a tiny bite off of the end. *Or does he mean he's in trouble with me?* She wanted to ask, but it wasn't the proper place or time so she forced herself to keep quiet.

Sienna, Miriam and Dawn chatted while they ate. They sampled some of the fancy Hawaiian drinks, while Hawk seemed to consume as much alcohol as possible. He didn't appear to be interested in the food, although from time to time he would pop a *pu pu* in his mouth, before he took another swig.

Sienna's appetite suffered as a result of Hawk's drinking. She could tell Dawn was trying not to act surprised at Hawk's behavior, but Sienna knew she was. As a result, Sienna found herself watching every swallow Hawk took.

It was only after a group of Hawaiian musicians began to play that she began to relax again. The music was soothing and conjured up images of lazy days in the sun and making leisurely love on the sand. After the musicians played for a time, an accomplished troupe of dancers joined them. Men and women performed the ancient hula, while their hand movements and bodies called up the past.

Sienna's gaze fell on Hawk's familiar features over and over again. She wondered what was going through his mind, if his thoughts were on her, Wila, or the things that might come. She looked for signs of inebriation, and although she didn't see any, Sienna was certain Hawk was well on his way.

Suddenly, the music changed. It was no longer refined and smooth. Now, aggressive drums propelled the rhythm and the dancer's bodies echoed the static beats. It wasn't long before the troupe had worked up a kind of joyous frenzy and began to encourage audience participation. Wila was one of the first chosen by a male dancer.

If Sienna hadn't known better, she would have assumed the dance troupe had planted one of their own, Wila, in the audience. Wila was such a good dancer that she gave the professional female dancers a run for their money, and the men a reason to shout and dance with renewed vigor.

It was obvious Wila was enjoying herself, and she continued to dance alone after her partner pursued a new inductee. It appeared to Sienna that Wila had been waiting for that moment, because she wasted no time in making a beeline toward Hawk.

Sienna's first instinct was to jump up and cut her off at the pass, to tell Wila to keep away from her man. But in her mind's eye, Sienna could see how foolish she would look, and how embarrassed she would feel afterward. So with all the resolve Sienna had, she sat there while Wila danced up to Hawk, her hips moving like an old-fashioned washing machine, and with her arms outstretched in invitation. At that moment, the only thing that gave Sienna solace was knowing, during their entire relationship Hawk had danced only four times. She was certain he would turn Wila down. But to Sienna's utter surprise, Hawk stood up and followed Wila into the center of the courtyard.

Wila's hips began a double time and the stretch-fitted pants she wore left nothing to the imagination. Maybe that was what inspired Hawk, because moments later he too was shaking his hips, slowly at first, but as the seconds passed Hawk seemed to lose himself in the rhythm. It seemed to Sienna, the more Wila shook the wilder Hawk became, until he was jerking and shaking as if he was in a spasm. Dancers and visitors alike gave them room to perform although Hawk appeared to be in his own world, oblivious to the admiring crowd. After a couple of minutes Sienna could take no more. She had had enough. Sienna couldn't watch Hawk make a spectacle of himself with Wila, albeit a robustly attractive one.

She put her napkin in the middle of her food. "Dawn, I'm going back to the room."

"Sienna . . . don't," Dawn beseeched her.

"I've got to." She shook her head. "This is crazy."

Sienna stood up and had only walked a few yards when the woman from the admissions office at *Kamokila* took hold of her arm. Surprised, she looked into the woman's dark eyes.

"I've got a special request for you. Kahuna Elikapeka says it is important." She motioned toward a table that was sitting in a protected alcove. "She would like a private audience with you and the man who dances as if there is fire in his soul."

Alarms went off in Sienna's head. *Does the Kahuna know something about the Legend of the Stonekeeper?* But when Sienna looked at Hawk gyrating and grinding in front of everyone, a wave of embarrassment washed clear through her. At that moment, to Sienna, it all seemed so far away. It might as well have been a joke. "Fire in his soul. That's as good a description as I've ever heard." She looked down. "Why does the Kahuna want to see us?"

"You must ask her," the woman replied.

Sienna cut her eyes in Hawk's direction. "Well, I guess you will have to ask him if he is interested. I have nothing to do with what he does."

"He is with you," the woman replied.

"Is he now? I'm not so certain about that."

The woman glanced at Hawk and Wila. "Elikapeka says he is your partner," the woman pressed. "Will you bring him?"

Their gazes held.

"I'll bring him, if he wants to come," Sienna finally replied.

"Then meet us at the small house at the end of the wharf."

"When?" Sienna asked.

"After the dance, of course." The woman gave a slight smile and walked away.

Sienna looked at Hawk and Wila before she crossed her arms.

Twenty-one

Hawk threw his body into the music. It was intense, just like the feeling inside of him. Hawk wanted to be the rhythm, needed to be the drum. Breathlessly, he found release in every thrust, every jerk. It did not matter to Hawk how it looked, only how it felt.

The crowd around him was a blur, but the energy that gushed up his spine, flowed through his heart and burst out of the top of his head was very real. More real, and intense than his body could handle. *If I can only keep moving, I might rid myself of it. Rid myself of this fire that is burning my insides. That is traveling upward with the intention of burning my brains.* As strange as it seemed, it was a moment of clear thought. A moment when his mind and his body were not enemies. But Hawk knew it would not last for long.

The first time he felt the tingling at the base of his spine, they were still at *Kamokila*. It was a subtle buzzing, but as it grew in intensity it drew Hawk deeper and deeper within his own mind, to a place where it was difficult to relate to others. It was as if the sensation was forcing him to see his own soul, and to speak nothing but the truth, be it ever so harsh about others. It was because of the thoughts that Hawk ordered the drinks. He hoped it would stifle them, and douse the energy that was filling his body.

"In all my life I have not seen a mainlander move like you." Wila said gazing into his face. "It is such a pleasure to see someone so free."

As Wila's voice touched Hawk, he saw a light in her eyes . . . eyes that were full of lust, full of the need for momentary pleasure. They were not the familiar brown eyes he loved so much. They were not . . . Sienna's caring eyes, eyes drenched with concern and confusion.

"I'd love to see you again, Hennessy," Wila continued. "Perhaps we can lose your girlfriend and get together later tonight."

Hawk stared at Wila's face until it faded into darkness, and once again he was mainly aware of his body. Shut off from the woman who shimmered and shook in front of him, she was merely a stranger with her own agenda. "You are ruled by your sexual appetite," the words came from his mouth of their own volition. "One day your body will wear that badge, a loveless badge of sexual abandon and promiscuity, a badge of illness and decay."

"What!" Wila stopped dancing but the drums continued to roll. She glared at him before she shouted "You *stink face*. You must be *lolo buggah*. A crazy person." She continued to rage at him until the drums came to an abrupt halt.

The crowd burst into applause oblivious of the disruption before them. A semiconscious Hawk saw Wila walk away and, without a second thought, he headed in the opposite direction, as an inner knowing led him to Sienna's side. "Sienna, I—"

"Finally had enough?" she asked.

"Too much," Hawk replied. He tried to focus on her face.

"I'm not talking about the alcohol." Sienna clarified.

"Neither am I." Hawk squeezed his forehead.

"Look at you, Hawk," Sienna said, her voice lowered.

"Sienna—" Hawk attempted to communicate through his dilemma.

"I've never seen you like this." She shook her head before she continued. "We've been invited to a private audience with the Kahuna. It's an honor, but of course that word couldn't mean very much to you right now." She paused. "Or perhaps you would prefer to go with Wila. I'm sure she would be more than happy if you did."

"Wila isn't important," Hawk managed to say as he rubbed his eyes. "Not important."

Sienna looked around to see if anyone was watching. *He's absolutely drunk,* she thought. But it didn't seem as if anyone cared. Hawk and Wila had provided some extra entertainment, and now everyone was on to something else. "She's waiting for us in the beach house at the end of the main walkway," Sienna said through stiff lips. "We need to go."

Hawk stepped forward but he teetered and accidentally bumped into the table beside him. He was barely aware of what had happened. He could make out the surprised faces of the people looking up at him, but all Hawk could give them was a mumbled: "Not important."

"We're sorry," Sienna said quickly, before she walked past Hawk. He fell in step behind her. *Why is he doing this? He's got something going on inside of him that I just don't understand. Lately, I've been through so many mood swings with Hawk, I can't count them anymore.* She looked back at a barely coherent Hawk. Sienna shook her head in dismay. *Is he sick and tired of his life in general? Or is he sick and tired of me and doesn't know how to let go? All I know is, we can't continue like this. We can't.*

When they were clear of the courtyard and almost to the beach, Sienna's frustration flared. "I never thought I'd see the day when I'd feel like this, but I don't want to be seen with you." She threw her hands in the air. "How can we go see someone when you can barely stand up?" She looked at the beach house where the Kahuna was waiting. "You know I'm not into telling you what to do, but you can't go in there like this." She tried to get her thoughts together. "I'm going to go down there, apologize, and tell them we simply can't make it tonight. Hopefully, they'll accept it. After that, I'll take you back to the room so you can sleep this off." She tried to see his eyes whenever his droopy eyelids would allow. Despite Sienna's anger her heart went out to him and she added softly, "And I pray that you'll have the mother of all hangovers tomorrow to warn you never to do this again."

She started down the walk. Sienna could hear Hawk walking behind her. "No, Hennessy." She used his formal name to break through the fog. "I'll be right back."

She started off again, then turned to see if Hawk was behind her. To Sienna's relief he was leaning against the rail, looking up at the sky, so she hurried onto the beach. Sienna looked back at Hawk as she arrived at the beach house door. He was still there.

She drew a deep breath and knocked softly. The door opened on her third rap. The woman who told her of the invitation stood in front of her.

"Hello," Sienna began. "I came to let you know we won't be able to visit with the Kahuna tonight." She looked away and tried to think of what she should say. All Sienna could come up with was, "It's just not a good time."

"There will be no better time," a strong female voice said from within. "Tell her to come in."

"Elikapeka asks that you come in." The woman continued to hold the door ajar.

Sienna glanced at Hawk. Now, he was leaning on the rail with both elbows. Satisfied he would be okay, she stepped inside and allowed the woman to close the door. "I can't stay but a moment," she warned.

When Sienna advanced beyond the tiny entranceway, she saw the Kahuna sitting in a large, ornate chair. The woman's size was impressive, and Sienna felt it was an important aspect of who she was, a visible symbol of her power.

"Time is very important, isn't it?" Elikapeka said when their eyes met.

"Yes," Sienna replied as she thought there was something special about the Kahuna's eyes. "I've got a busy day tomorrow, and some important things to take care of tonight."

The Kahuna's eyes softened before she closed them and nodded. But despite her show of understanding Elikapeka motioned for Sienna to take a seat.

Sienna shook her head, "I can't. The man that I was with is—"

"He's standing at the beach house door." Elikapeka completed Sienna's sentence. "Kenike, let him in, please."

Shocked, Sienna watched as the woman disappeared inside the entranceway, then reappeared with Hawk.

"Now both of you may have a seat," Elikapeka instructed, smiling serenely.

Sienna walked over to Hawk and put her arm through his. She guided him to the couch. They sat down together.

Twenty-two

"How did I know he was standing outside?" Elikapeka asked the question that was on Sienna's mind. "His *aumakua*, his spirit-self, let itself be known to me. His is very powerful, and although you may look at him at this moment, and not see it, I can feel it."

Sienna laughed nervously. "Really?" She looked at Hawk. "That's something to be thankful for because he's not normally like this." Sienna felt the need to explain.

"I can believe that," Elikapeka replied. "The islands, especially Kaua'i, can have a very powerful affect on people. And if they are spiritually sensitive, it is even more the truth."

Sienna nodded and looked around. She returned her attention to the Kahuna. "Why did you want to see us?"

Elikapeka laid her head back against the chair. "There is no coincidence that the spiritual elders of the islands and I gathered on Kaua'i at this time. It was in the wind that something special was on the horizon, and that it would take place on Kaua'i. We did not know what that event would be, but we all agreed that we would gather at this time, and the answer would be given to us." She paused.

"And was it?" Sienna asked with a lump in her throat.

"Yes. When I saw you at *Kamokila* I knew you were part of the answer. When I saw the two of you."

Sienna folded her hands in her lap and looked down.

"May I ask, what are your names?"

"My name is Sienna Russell, and this is—"

"My name is Hennessy Jackson." Hawk lifted his wobbly head. "But I am known as Hawk."

Gently, Sienna placed her hand on his thigh. She gazed at him, her eyes full of concern.

"Why are you here on Kaua'i?" the Kahuna asked.

"We're here for the gem trade show," Sienna replied. "It's called the International Gem Trade Show."

"That is not the only reason you are here," Elikapeka said.

Sienna could feel Hawk forcing strength into his spine. "We are here because she is the Last of the Stonekeepers. The very last one." His voice weakened again.

The Kahuna's eyes brightened. "Stonekeepers. Here in the islands we have many stories, legends, and one of them involves the Legend of the Stonekeepers. Are you saying you are a part of this?" She looked at Sienna.

Reluctant to speak about it Sienna said, "I have been in the past."

Elikapeka's wise eyes studied her face before she did the same with Hawk.

"How did you know about Hawk and me? That we would be a part of what takes place here?" Sienna felt compelled to ask.

"The islands are alive," the Kahuna said. "Literally alive. The earth is constantly being born here, and new land is formed. Because of this life force energy Spirit is very strong in Hawaii, and those of us who have made spirituality a way of life are made aware of many things." Elikapeka lifted two delicate hands and placed them together. "When I saw your faces, the voice inside of me said you were important to our mission here on Kaua'i. It was that simple."

"Well, we might be," Sienna replied, uncomfortable. "But the truth is we don't know what's going to happen any more than you do."

"Then that must be the way it is to be." A peace blanketed Elikapeka's eyes. "If you were to know, you would know. I am certain it is perfect just the way it is."

Frustrated beyond words, Sienna replied, "That's not how I see it, and that's not how I feel."

"And you Hawk," Elikapeka paused, "how do you *see* it?"

Sienna watched their eyes connect and hold. To Sienna's surprise Hawk appeared to pull himself together, to almost be himself again.

"I see this as a fight for my life," he said slowly, as his visual connection with the Kahuna continued.

Elikapeka nodded. Finally she said, "And all I can say to you is, you will be given the weapons that can allow you victory. The victory itself is not a given."

Hawk slumped back on the couch and closed his eyes.

"I think we need to leave now," Sienna said, looking at Hawk. "I need to get him to bed."

"Yes. He needs his rest. I can see that," Elikapeka replied.

Sienna helped Hawk to his feet.

Elikapeka did not stand, but she sat up straight. She seemed to expand as a result of it. "Know that the hearts of the spiritual elders and my heart is with you here on the Garden Island. Know that you can seek me out if you are in need of help."

"Thank you," Sienna replied.

Hawk nodded and gave a barely audible "Yes. Thank you."

Sienna and Hawk walked to the door and exited the beach house. The walk to their hotel room seemed long, and when they closed the door behind them, Sienna helped Hawk undress. She watched him climb into bed. It was only a matter of seconds before he was in a deep sleep.

Sienna sat on the bed and watched him. Hawk didn't move a muscle, and eventually his breathing became heavy and laborious. Sienna hung her head. *What is happening to Hawk? He told the Kahuna he was fighting for his life. Have his experiences with me and the Stonekeeper cycles been so traumatic that in anticipating the last one Hawk has turned into a drunk?* She laid her hand on his cheek, to try to quiet his snoring. *In this state he is no good for himself or me, and he definitely would not make a good father. Tomorrow, I'm going to talk to him about it, make him tell me what has disturbed him so badly that he would come to this.*

Twenty-three

Sienna awoke to the sound of Hawk closing the bathroom door. She lay there for a moment, then looked at the clock. The red numbers displayed 6:30. Sienna opened and closed her eyes several times. It felt extremely early, but she knew they had a busy day ahead of them. They had to get the booth ready for the trade show.

Sienna swung her feet off the bed and sat on the side. She felt tired as she thought of the *lu'au*, Hawk and the Kahuna. The more Sienna thought about it the more drained she became. *My day hasn't begun and I'm already tired. This isn't going to work,* she moaned. *I've come all the way to Hawaii for this show and I've got to get it together. Our future depends on it.*

Sienna pressed her thumb and her finger against her eyelids. She heard the bathroom door open. Slowly, she removed her fingers from her eyes, not knowing what to expect.

"Good morning." Hawk stood near the bathroom door. His locks were tied behind his head in his customary ponytail.

"Hi," Sienna replied.

"I tried to hurry because I know you need to get in here." He motioned behind him.

"Yeah. I do." But Sienna didn't move.

Hawk walked over and stood beside her, and Sienna continued to look straight ahead. The next thing she felt was Hawk's lips against her temple.

"I know we've got to talk," he said. "There's something I've got to tell you. I've wanted to but I just couldn't bring myself to do it."

"What is it, Hawk?" She gazed into his eyes.

"We don't have time to discuss it this morning."

"But you can't say something like that and expect me not to want to know right now," Sienna replied, but she felt a little guilty because she had not told Hawk about the baby.

"I'd be doing myself and you a disservice if I try to explain this in a hurry. I promise you it can wait until after the show."

Sienna looked into his familiar eyes. "I'm not going to want to shoot you after you tell me, am I?"

Hawk looked down. "No. I don't think so."

"Are you sure?"

"I'm positive," Hawk replied.

Sienna looked uncertain. *What does Hawk have to tell me?*

He looked into her eyes. "And believe me, a few more hours won't make that big a difference. At least I don't think it will, because it's not about you or us, it's about me."

If he can look me straight in the eyes and say that, I guess I can trust him enough to wait. "How do you feel this morning?"

Hawk sighed. "I feel much better."

"You do?" Sienna searched his face. There was some puffiness beneath his eyes, but other than that he was as handsome as ever.

"Definitely," Hawk replied.

With Hawk's reassurance, and feeling as if she

would finally get to the root of his actions, Sienna stood up. "I guess I'll get ready then."

"All right," Hawk said. "And I'll make good use of the time by putting the boxes in the car."

Sienna nodded. "Okay." She wanted to kiss him, to grab his hand and say everything was going to be fine, but she walked over to the bathroom and closed the door instead.

By the time Sienna was dressed and ready, Hawk had bought coffee and pastries for the three of them to eat on the way to the trade show. It was a short drive, and Sienna was grateful for the food because she knew once they started setting up the show, eating would go on the back burner, and she needed the energy to perform the work.

This morning, unlike the first day they visited the Coconut Market Place, there was plenty of activity in the trade show room. Vendors were setting up their wares and some people in food booths were making whatever preparations were necessary to cook and sell their products.

"We have Booth 43," Dawn said, turning in a circle. "You would think it would be over here." She pointed. "That's where it was on the paper they sent us. But it's not there."

"Well, it's got to be here somewhere," Sienna said, rising onto the balls of her feet.

"There it is," Hawk said over the box he carried.

Sienna followed him as he made his way past several booths. She watched his confident stride and capable back as she walked behind him. This was the Hawk she knew. This was the man she wanted their child to know.

"Here we are." Hawk handed Sienna the car keys, and placed the box on the empty table. Behind it were stacks of boxes that were shipped earlier. "I'm going to get the others from the car."

"This is a pretty good location," Sienna said. "We're not too far in the back and we're not in a corner." She was feeling better every moment, seeing Hawk was back to his old self.

"Good," Dawn replied. "Because I hate getting stuck in some remote corner. Not as many people come over." She bent over and ripped the tape off of one of the boxes. "Oops, I need to count these before I get started, just in case something's missing. When you ship stuff like this, there's no such thing as checking too many times."

"I know," Sienna replied. She looked at the booth next to theirs. "No wonder we couldn't find it."

"What?" Dawn said, continuing to count.

"Find our booth. Our name card is on that table over there."

Dawn made a face. "It sure is. Not that it would have helped. It's too little."

"Little or not, it's ours," Sienna replied as she walked over to the other table. "And we brought our banner, so people will have no problem knowing who we are." Sienna picked up the small sign, and was reading the name of the placard beneath it when she turned around and collided with a man.

"I'm sorry," they said in unison.

Sienna stepped away.

"Is this your booth?" he asked, looking at the other table.

"No," Sienna replied. "I'm in Booth 43. I was over here because my sign was on this table."

"That must be my table," the man said. "We're in Booth number 44."

"It probably is," Sienna replied as she rejoined Dawn.

When Hawk returned and they had three sets of hands working, the booth took shape quickly. The more elaborate art and jewelry pieces were placed in plexiglass cases, but the majority of the display was made from natural articles. Hand-woven cloths from various cultures were used as display boards, while dangling pendants hung from driftwood, and birds' nests with colorful stones as eggs were ongoing themes.

As a unified team they worked for hours, and eventually Dawn, who at first appeared to be a little uncertain about Hawk, was back to her old playful self. "I just have to ask, did you have a hangover this morning?"

"A little," Hawk replied.

"A little," Dawn chuckled. "Yeah I bet. With all you drank, and you don't normally drink . . . your body had to be in shock."

"Not really," Hawk said.

"Well, if I had—" She stopped abruptly, her gaze fixed on the booth next door. Dawn walked over to Sienna and whispered, "Did you see that deep blue necklace they put in that case?"

Sienna glanced at the booth that initially wore their sign. "I couldn't help but see it."

"Girl, they've got some money over there. They've been pulling out all kinds of expensive-looking jewelry. I wonder if they were the folks who were saying we needed more security."

"Could be." Sienna coerced a string of turquoise and red coral to fall into a decorative pattern on a piece of batik.

"What kind of stone is that?" Dawn asked.

"It's too far away to tell," Sienna replied. "I'll go over there and get a good look at it later."

"Whatever it is, it costs some money." Dawn gave her the eye.

Sienna put her hand on her hip. "If you don't stop, I'm going to feel as if we are out of our league at this show."

"I'm not saying that." Dawn paused. "They just seem so elaborate. Look at some of the other booths. They're selling some really fancy stuff too, but they're not like those folks." She tried to act as if she wasn't staring. "Like what is that big, black container that's sitting on that stand? What can they use that for? Nobody can see inside of it the way they've got it situated. And it's got"—she counted—"one, two three . . . about eight sides to it."

"Your guess is as good as mine, Dawn," Sienna replied. "So why don't you go over there and ask them about it since you want to know so bad." Dawn had gotten on her nerves.

"I'm just curious." Dawn hung some malachite strands on a piece of driftwood.

"Well, I feel like they can do whatever they want to do over there. They paid for the booth." Sienna had her back turned. "What time is it anyway?"

"It's ten after twelve," Hawk replied. "The show starts in about twenty minutes. Do you want me to see what kind of food they're selling? I could bring some to the booth."

"I'm all for that," Dawn replied.

"Yeah. Me too," Sienna said. She found herself searching Hawk's eyes, trying to make sure he was okay. "You know what we like, so just bring something back."

"All right," Hawk said before he walked away.

Sienna and Dawn arranged a few more items. Finally, Sienna crossed her arms as she looked around the booth. "I think we're just about there."

"It looks good." Dawn straightened one of the cloths. "Better than most of them," she added conspiratorially.

"I agree," Sienna whispered back as she looked over Dawn's shoulder. "Un-huh, I guess the mystery of the black container has been solved."

Twenty-four

Dawn turned. They watched the men in the next booth struggle with an extremely large quartz crystal.

"Oh-h." Dawn crossed her arms. "So that's what they're going to put in there. I've never seen a crystal that big."

"Neither have I," Sienna replied, then suddenly she called out, "Watch it!" but it was too late. The men hit one of her tables as they maneuvered the crystal inside the container.

"We're so sorry," the man who collided with Sienna earlier said. "I hope we didn't break anything."

Sienna looked over her display. "It's okay," she replied, satisfied nothing was damaged. "Everything looks fine."

"We were wondering what you were going to do with that." Dawn pointed at the black stand.

"Yes, it is rather odd looking. It's custom made," the man explained. "We use it at these shows. A Herkimer diamond this size is a great attention getter. It's like our mascot." He wiped his brow. "But as you can see, it's not an easy task putting it in the stand."

They all stood back quietly and admired the stone.

The man rubbed his hands on his pants. "By the way, I'm Steven Adler."

"I'm Sienna." She shook his hand. "And this is Dawn."

Dawn gave a playful wave.

"So it's a Herkimer diamond," Sienna said. "That makes sense. Because I thought it was exceptionally clear for a quartz crystal."

"It's a beauty though, isn't it?" Steven replied. "We like to say it's the biggest Herkimer diamond in the world."

"And you may be right." Sienna admired the large crystal.

"Wow. Since that's a Herkimer diamond, and they are good for helping a person just 'be' who they really are inside"—Dawn made a floating motion with her hands—"everybody around here should be well attuned when this show is over."

"Yeah." Steven wagged his head. "That is if you believe in that kind of stuff." He looked down in a skeptical fashion. "But, you know, you can't believe everything you hear or read. If you could, by now, with this around"—he pointed to the Herkimer diamond—"I should be clairvoyant, clairaudient and everything else." Steven laughed. "Because it's supposed to stimulate that kind of thing as well."

Dawn looked disappointed. "You mean to tell me you sell all this beautiful jewelry, with some of every kind of stone, and you don't believe they have certain kinds of energy?"

Steven shrugged. "Who am I to say?" He attempted to look diplomatic, but it was obvious where he stood. "As they say, whatever floats your boat."

Dawn turned on her heels and walked back into their booth. "That's what's wrong with this business now. Too many people getting in it who just want the money. They don't believe in anything, they just sell the stuff."

Sienna heard her, and from the look on Steven's face he did too.

"What did she say?" he asked.

"She's just talking to herself," Sienna replied, stepping back. "Well, it looks like your booth is ready and I guess I'd better get back to work so we will be ready too. The show will be starting in a few minutes." She attempted to make her getaway. "Nice to meet you, Steven."

"You too," Steven said. "And you can tell your friend, I don't know if she's naïve or what, but we're all in it for money. Her too." He had a dangerous glint in his eyes. "Money makes the world go round, and she shouldn't forget it." Steven turned and started talking to one of two men who had helped with the herkimer diamond.

"Oh my goodness," Sienna said as she crossed the booth and bent down as if she was looking in a box. "Dawn, can you give me a hand?"

"Sure." Dawn bent down beside her.

"He heard you," she whispered.

"Did he? I didn't mean for him to, but what I said was the truth."

"But sometimes you need to watch what you say." Sienna made a face. "He wasn't too happy with you, and he let me know it."

"What did he say?" Dawn's voice went up, slightly.

Sienna decided not to tell Dawn the whole truth for fear that she might confront Steven. "He said that everybody's in this business for money. You too, and you shouldn't forget that."

"What? He doesn't know me. And yes, I make a living doing this, but I actually believe"—she got a little louder—"No, I know some of these things are true. So—"

"What are you two doing down there?" Hawk towered above them.

Dawn stood up. "I was being told off for having a big mouth."

"I didn't tell you off," Sienna denied.

But Dawn continued. "I told Sienna those folks over there are making money off of this stuff, and couldn't care less about what any of it means. And it's true."

Hawk looked at Steven's booth and suddenly, the color drained from his face.

"What is it?" Dawn asked, but Hawk didn't seem to hear her as the food slid from his hands onto the box below.

Sienna tried to catch it, but it was too late. Something that looked like curry spilled down the side of the box, while freshly fried taro chips tumbled onto the floor.

"Hawk." Sienna stood up, but he did not answer.

Although Hawk was standing upright, his body looked as if it was vibrating, and in a matter of moments it reached a rate that was convulsive.

"Oh my God!" Dawn squealed. "What's wrong with him?"

"I don't know," Sienna cried. "Hawk, can you hear me?" She tried to hold him, but his movements were too erratic. She stepped back at a loss as to what to do.

Hawk's face became fixed in a stare, so when his mouth began to move he resembled a puppet. "Ma-ma-ma-ma," he said over and over again, until it sounded like a hum. Next, his body stiffened like a board but continued to shake, and Hawk's speech mirrored the sounds of people speaking in tongues.

Frightened that he might hurt himself, Sienna tried to get her arms around him again, but his body moved in a way that made it impossible. She stumbled backward into a bewildered Dawn. Alarmed, Sienna looked at her friend.

"We need help," Dawn said, and she hurried out of the booth.

Sienna continued to try to contain Hawk's movements, with little success. "Hawk! Hawk! Stop, Hawk!"

As quickly as it commenced, his body ceased to vibrate. But next, the vibrating was replaced by abrupt jerks, and Hawk began to say things that made little to no sense. "4460 Nehe . . . 4460 Nehe. Nehe. Not later, now. Now." His head flipped from side to side. "Know now. Diamonds. Diamonds!"

Sienna's fears mounted. He seemed so unreachable. "Hawk! Hawk! Please stop. Please. You're frightening me."

"Crystal Alley. The smuggler's alley. Crystal Alley."

Sienna looked around at the small crowd that had gathered. Some were asking if they could help. Others simply stood by amazed.

Desperate, she grabbed hold of him with all her might. "Hawk. It's Sienna. You've got to come back. You've got to come back to me."

Suddenly, his body stopped shaking. Their eyes met, and just for a moment Sienna saw clarity there, before she heard Dawn say, "I've got some help. A security guard," from somewhere nearby. In a matter of seconds, the clarity in Hawk's eyes transformed into anger.

Through clenched teeth Hawk said, "I cannot live this way, Sienna. I will not."

Sienna glanced over and saw Dawn with a man in

a uniform close on her heels, just as Hawk's body began to quake again. This time instead of standing still Hawk took off at a run.

"Hawk!" Sienna ran a few feet behind him, but when she saw him leap over one of the tables and nearly collide with an elderly woman who screamed at the top of her lungs, she stopped. Feeling helpless Sienna watched Hawk run toward one of the exits and with a mighty push, thrust open the doors. He disappeared outside.

Twenty-five

"Where is he going?" the security guard asked.

You saw Hawk just leap over a table and nearly knock an old lady down and I'm supposed to know where he went! Her mind screamed but Sienna tried to remain in control. "How would I know?"

He seemed surprised at her brusqueness. He looked around as if embarrassed, then he cleared his throat. "Is he your husband?"

"No," Sienna said, quickly. Not because she was denying her relationship with Hawk, but because she didn't see how the question helped the situation.

"But he is with y—"

"He is my boyfriend." Sienna tried to stay calm. Things were slower on the island, and the people's attitudes reflected that. "And yes . . . we are here together."

"Does he take medication?"

Sienna's brows knitted. "What kind of medication?"

"For this, or anything else."

Sienna noticed some of the onlookers had walked away, but there were a few who were trying their best to hear the exchange between Sienna and the guard. "No. Never." She shook her head. "Hawk would never take anything unless he absolutely had no choice."

The guard donned a superior look as he focused on her. "He looks to me as if he should be on medication."

"But he's not." Sienna had tired of the guard's approach. She wanted someone to help Hawk, someone who could give some answers, not ask twenty million questions. She extended her palms. "I don't see how this is helping. We need to go after him."

The man shook his head. "I'm not going after him." He tried to mask his fear. "I'm not authorized to. What I am going to do is call the authorities and notify them of the situation."

The way he said authorities put Sienna on alert. "What kind of authorities?"

"The police," he replied. "And I'm sure they will turn him over to one of the mental health facilities."

Sienna looked at Dawn, who was obviously upset. "The police and a mental health facility," she repeated.

"Yes." The man straightened his back as if he were reestablishing his power with the decision. "I'm going to call them now and I will need you to come with me so that I can give them the proper information."

Sienna stared at the security guard. From the look on his face, she was certain he was determined Hawk should be locked up, and that he would convince the police of the same. *I'm not going to help them lock him up. And I've got to get to him before they do. See if there is another way to handle this.*

The security guard beckoned for Sienna. "Come with me, please."

She ignored him. "Dawn, you stay and take care of the booth. I'm going after Hawk." She started toward the door through which Hawk disappeared.

"Where are you going?" the guard called. "Come back. We need more information."

But Sienna ignored his cries as she opened and closed the door. Once she was outside, Sienna tried to remain calm as she took stock of the surrounding area. But there were stores everywhere, and Hawk was nowhere in sight. Part of her wished that he were. But another part of Sienna was relieved that he had continued to run or had taken cover. That way he was safe from the guard, or anyone, who would have him caged.

Which way did he go? Sienna tried to decide but she knew one guess was as good as any other. So she stayed away from the entrance to the marketplace, something she figured Hawk would do if he were in his right mind. But from the way he leaped over that table, like a fleeing animal, Sienna wasn't sure.

She looked over at the next building, then looked down at her feet. A wave of massive sadness washed over her. "God, I need your help. I need you to help me find Hawk. You say I'm special. You say that I'm this Stonekeeper." She scuffed the ground with her shoe. "Then help me," she pleaded. "But I tell you this right now, if you let anything happen to Hawk, the father of my child," Sienna paused because the words seemed to burn her insides, "I will never forgive you. Never in all my living days."

Sienna wiped away her tears as she ran without knowing where to go.

The security guard looked at Dawn, "Well, since you are the only one left, I need you to come with me."

"I can't leave the booth," Dawn replied. "The show is about to start."

"I understand that. But we're going to need you

to answer some questions, so I want you to come with me."

Dawn shook her head. "I'm not going anywhere. If you need me to answer questions you can tell anybody who wants me that I'm right here." She gave him a look that said she meant business.

The security guard squinted, "As I recall, you were the one who came to me and asked for help, and now you're not going to cooperate?"

"Cooperate? Instead of going after him, you just let him run out of here." Dawn tried to get a hold of herself. She crossed her arms. "So, I'm willing to cooperate as much as you are. Anything you might want to ask me, I will answer to the best of my ability. But I'm simply saying, I've got a job to do. I will answer your questions as long as it doesn't interfere with that."

The guard's mouth tightened. "I'll be back." He turned on his heels and walked away.

Dawn sighed, but she could still feel a trembling in her chest. Quickly, she rolled off several sheets of paper towels and wiped up the food that had spilled on the box and onto the floor.

Dawn cleaned up the mess while several gawkers continued to watch from the aisle. She tried to hold her tongue, but the longer they stood there the more difficult it became. Finally, she said, "I think the show starts in a few minutes. I suggest you go back to your booths because this is not a part of it."

Slowly, the people walked away but they talked among themselves as they glanced back.

"Can I help you with anything?"

Dawn looked up at Steven Adler. "No." She stood up. "I think I have everything under control."

"Okay," Steven replied. "I could get you some more food."

"No. I'm fine." Dawn picked up a bottle of water. "I'm just going to drink some water and try to calm down."

Steven looked as if he wanted to say something. "I'm truly sorry about your friend. What's his name?"

"His name is Hawk." Dawn took several long, slow swallows.

"Hawk," Steven repeated. "I don't understand. He seemed fine earlier. I hope everything goes okay."

Dawn glanced at him. "Me too," she said softly.

"What do you think happened?" Steven moved in closer.

"I don't have the slightest idea," Dawn lied, but how could she tell a stranger about Hawk and his connection to the cycle of the Stonekeeper. She stared at the Herkimer diamond. Dawn was certain it had something to do with what happened to Hawk.

"And he was saying some of the strangest things. Did any of that stuff make sense to you?"

Dawn took another deep breath. She vowed to herself she would not go off, but the truth was Steven was proving to be more of a pest than the security guard. "None at all," she replied as a man entered Steven's booth. He began to talk with the men who helped Steven mount the Herkimer diamond.

"Well, I'm going to go now and let these guys do their part," Steven announced. "But if you need anything, just let one of them know. I'm sure they'll give you a hand."

"Thanks," Dawn said before he walked away. She watched Steven say a few words to the group before he and the newest man strolled out of the booth.

At that moment, the doors to the show opened

and people began to pour in. Dawn glanced around the booth one more time. Everything was ready. She tried to concentrate on the people who were coming through the doors, but her gaze kept straying to the door through which Hawk and then Sienna had disappeared. Silently, Dawn prayed that Hawk would be fine and that Sienna would find him. She had never seen that kind of fear in Sienna's eyes. Dawn had seen many things before, but never that. It was the look of a woman who feared her life and her dreams were crumbling around her; a woman who loved a man, and in his darkest hours had no clue how to help him. Dawn could see in Sienna's eyes that she wondered if she would ever get the opportunity to tell the father of her child about their baby, and if Sienna did, if Hawk would be of sound mind enough to recognize his own child.

Quickly, Dawn wiped away a tear that had crept into the corner of her eye, and she forced herself to smile at a blond woman who eyed one of their tables. "Hello," Dawn said. "And welcome to The Stonekeeper's booth."

Twenty-six

Now that Hawk was certain he wasn't being watched, he sped up his pace again. He had no idea where he was going, but what Hawk longed for was to shut out the images that played in his mind. Sienna's frightened look when he was present enough to see it, the shocked faces of the small crowd that had gathered, and the desperate sound of Dawn's voice when she said, "I've got some help." Hawk didn't remember a thing before that except for the brilliance of the huge stone in the black container. It had been blinding.

I don't know what that stone was but it did something to me. The light entered my eyes and it felt like it was scrambling my brain, before everything went dark.

Hawk rounded a corner where a large tour group was pouring out of one of the stores and boarding a bus. He shuddered uncontrollably as a police car buzzed by. Hawk guessed it wouldn't be long before someone like the police would be looking for him. *What else would they do? Even if Sienna were against it, with all the people who witnessed what happened to me on the tradeshow floor, who else would they send to "help" me? But I can't be locked up. I may be going crazy, but if they lock me up . . . I will go crazy for certain.*

Hawk looked over his shoulder one more time before he slipped into line with the tourists boarding the bus. He didn't know where they were going, but it didn't matter. What he needed was time to think, and he couldn't do that around Sienna or Dawn, not after what they saw and how frightened they became. No. Hawk knew he would have to handle this alone. *And if I can't, I'll find some place out in the wild to go crazy and die, like any other mad animal.*

Hawk looked straight ahead as he walked to the back of the bus. Nobody seemed to notice that he didn't belong with the group. He thought one woman looked at him questioningly, but then he realized she was reading something behind him through the window.

Relieved, Hawk made his way to a seat and sat down. Most of the tourists sat near the front of the vehicle, a few sprinkled themselves in the center and near the back. For Hawk, that was ideal. He slouched down as another convulsive wave shook his body and he counted his breaths as he closed his eyes. Hawk hoped focusing on his breathing would take his mind off of the erratic energies that were pulsing inside of him.

"Bo-bom-bom-bom-bom. Bo-bom-bom-bom-bom." A young male voice belted out an African rhythm.

Hawk opened his eyes, slightly. It was a boy about fifteen years old. His eyes were closed, earphones were stuck in his ears, and his short pants hung on his hips. Hawk watched a dark-haired woman who could have been the boy's mother turn toward the back of the bus.

"Daniel. Daniel," she called, trying not to yell too loudly. But the boy did not hear her. Frustrated, she cast one more look in his direction before she turned around.

Daniel's head continued to bob and weave. Finally, he opened his eyes long enough to take the seat across from Hawk. He nodded a greeting. Hawk managed to give one back before he lowered his eyelids again.

Hawk sighed as the bus took off and he tried to shut out the talking. The voices sounded louder than normal, and many of the tourists were excited. Hawk knew it because he could feel their excitement. It pricked him like hundreds of tiny pins. He rubbed his forehead and opened his eyes slightly when he heard what sounded like an open mic. A man, wearing a Hawaiian-print shirt, stood at the front of the bus holding it.

"Everyone is back and we are on our way again," he said in a let's rally together voice. "The next stop we will make will be Opaeka'a Falls. Make sure you look out the windows because we'll be traveling through a beautiful area. You will really get to see how lush Kaua'i is and understand why Kaua'i is the Garden Island."

Hawk saw the tour guide strain his neck and look at him. He could feel that the man felt he had never seen him before. The guide continued to watch him as he said, "Enjoy the ride." He turned off the mic and started toward the back of the bus.

Hawk had no idea what he would do or say if the man confronted him, but for the moment he remained very still as he watched the guide approach. The man was in the middle of the bus when a small, arthritic hand reached out and touched his arm. "Yes," Hawk heard him say before he nodded his head adding another, "Yes, ma'am," as a little old woman took out a map and began to point. After a few moments more the guide took the seat across the aisle from her. Hawk could tell she had roped him into a time-consuming explanation. Thankful for the reprieve, Hawk was on the verge of closing his eyes again, when he saw Daniel remove his headphones.

"How's it going?" His eyes were eager as he spoke.

Hawk let go a long breath. "Could be better." *Could be much better*, he thought, as the scene in the tradeshow room replayed in his mind.

"Yeah. I know that's right," Daniel replied. "Kaua'i's beautiful and everything, and I appreciate my parents bringing me here, but you know there's not that much here for somebody my age to do."

"I can imagine," Hawk said before a pulse riveted through him.

"Are you cold?"

Hawk shook his head and looked out the window.

"I've been admiring your dreadlocks, man," Daniel continued to talk. "How long did it take for you to grow them?"

"There's nothing dreadful about my locks," Hawk replied in a low but audible voice. He turned and looked at Daniel. "I've been growing them for eight years."

"I want to grow some, but my parents are against it." Daniel shrugged. "They're against anything I want to do, tattoos, piercings, dreadlocks."

Hawk stared at Daniel's naturally straight chestnut hair. "Don't you think locking your hair would be rather difficult." *Why must we as human beings choose the most difficult routes? Why must we fight what is inevitable. Like me, why am I fighting the madness? Why can't I just give in and be done with it?*

"It wouldn't be as easy maybe as it was for you," Daniel said quickly, "but I know some white people with dreadlocks."

Once again Hawk nodded. He could barely concentrate on the mundane chitchat, and as he turned his face toward the window a familiar burning surfaced on the right side. Hawk gritted his teeth at the pain. *It's happening. I've lived four years without it, but now it's happening again.*

As Daniel continued to talk, other sounds and voices inside his head vied for his attention. But Hawk tried to focus on the foliage that flew by, and he wondered if the horrible blister would overtake his face before they reached the falls. It seemed just the thought of it caused the burning to deepen.

"Sir," Daniel's voice sounded strained.

Hawk slowly turned his eyes in the boy's direction.

"I don't know if you've gotten into something"— Daniel seemed to draw back toward the window—"but there's a rash coming up really fast on your face."

Hawk stared into the boy's eyes until the young man looked down, then he covered the burning area with his hand before he turned toward the window again.

And so I have my answer, he thought trying to think through the rising voices. *The rash is well on its way, and my ace Daniel there didn't appear too eager to continue a conversation with me. Daniel looked as if he wanted to disappear into the side of the bus if he could.*

Hawk felt the inappropriate desire to laugh. Laugh at his life, laugh at the powers that be who couldn't let him live it like a normal human being, laugh in the face of all of it to show he didn't care. That he had given up on caring and was ready to let it do whatever it pleased with him. But then Sienna's face rose in his mind. Sienna would care. Sienna would definitely care.

Suddenly, the noises inside Hawk's head leaped in

volume. He sat forward quickly and grabbed his forehead. Hawk tried to press through the noise, to hear his own thoughts, but the others drowned them out and he felt sucked into a sea of thoughts that were not his own. Everything was accelerated. The voices and noises continued as a roaring blur, and the burning on the side of his face felt as if it were spreading.

"Excuse me, but I don't remember seeing you on this bus earlier," a thin voice asked from above him. "Are you sure you are with the right group?"

Hawk remained bent forward.

"Sir? Did you hear me?" He felt tapping against his shoulder. "I think you are on the wrong bus."

When Hawk looked up, it was as if he were in a blaze of fire, his body, his mind and his soul. He didn't really see the man in front of him when he sprang to his feet, and at that moment all he wanted was relief—release maybe was a better word—from the scorching heat that engulfed him.

"Shit!" the tour guide yelled as he stumbled back, away from Hawk who had entered the aisle. "What in the world . . . ?"

Hawk tried to open his eyes but the skin around them was swollen from the outbreak and he could barely see. His hands returned to his face, and when Hawk touched it all he could do was cry out. "Ughhhh." Once in awhile he could hear as the people reacted around him. "Oh my God. Look at him!" A woman screamed. Moments later, a male voice cried, "Why in the hell do you have us on the bus with somebody who's infected like that?"

"Open the back door!" the tour guide suddenly yelled.

Hawk heard a confused "What?" float toward them from somewhere far away.

The tour guide was almost yelling in Hawk's ears. "Open the back door right now and let this man off here!"

The bus came to a screeching halt and the door swung open. Hawk felt a cool, balmy breeze against his ravaged face and he went toward it. Suddenly, he fell down the bus stairs. Hawk had forgotten they were there. Bruised in body and spirit, he picked himself up and moved as fast as he could toward the foliage. But before the door closed Hawk heard Daniel say, "Mama, did you see that? The only time I've seen someone look like that is in my comic books and in the movies. I've never seen anybody look like that in my entire life."

Twenty-seven

"Jason, you won't believe what went down in here," Steven said as they strode casually across the trade show floor.

"Try me," Jason Truman said, adjusting the bottom of his sleeveless designer tank top.

"It was bizarre. The guy in the booth next to ours started shaking like a leaf on a tree before his eyes went all strange, and he started saying stuff that—"

"Maybe he's an epileptic and was having a fit." Jason courteously allowed an elderly woman to pass.

"I thought about that." Steven hated when Jason acted as if he lacked reasoning skills. "But what epileptic do you know that remains standing during convulsions and doesn't need a spoon or something put in his mouth?"

"I don't know," Jason replied impatiently. "But what's the big deal? Haven't you seen someone have a fit before?"

"I've seen folks have fits, and worse," Steven said. "But while this guy was in that state, he called out the address of our condo and started mumbling about diamond smuggling."

Jason stopped walking. "What?"

Steven lowered his voice. "The man said 4460

Nehe, and he mentioned diamond smuggling. But do you know what else he said?"

Jason's eyes bore into Steven's. He shook his head.

"He said Crystal Alley."

Jason's velvety brown eyes narrowed.

"Yes, he did." Steven pulled out a pack of cigarettes.

Jason looked around, before he said, "Let's get out of here because I'm not believing this."

Jason and Steven stepped through the front door and walked through the crowd of shoppers in silence until they reached a nearby parking lot.

"Now let's start from the beginning," Jason said. "You mean to tell me this guy that was almost convulsing rattled off our address and talked about diamond smuggling?"

"I heard it with my own ears," Steven said. "He said the address, and he mentioned diamonds and smuggling." Steven removed a cigarette, lit it and took a drag while Jason watched. "I also heard him say Crystal Alley."

Jason remained quiet as he tried to think things through. It just didn't make sense. "Well, who is this man?" he demanded finally.

"All I know is he's connected with the booth next to ours. And I questioned the woman that you saw." Steven thumbed toward the trade show. "But she seemed clueless about the entire thing."

"Yeah. Right." Jason paced a few steps, then turned back to Steven. "Somebody knows something or he wouldn't have known our business."

Steven did a slow shrug.

"Was there anyone else in the booth?"

"Yes. A woman named Sienna. I think she's the owner. We talked a little bit about the Herkimer when we were setting it up, but that's all. She appeared to be pretty regular as well."

"So do we for all that's worth," Jason remarked.

"I hear you." Steven took another drag.

Jason felt a pounding in his head. He didn't know what was going on with these people, but he wasn't about to allow them to mess up his operation. Not being able to hold back his anger any longer, Jason smacked the car next to him. "I want to know how this guy knows our business, and the motivation behind that crazy stunt. Somebody's playing with our minds. They had that guy fake a fit and give out our information."

"I'm going to be honest with you, Jason." Steven licked his lips. "He didn't look like he was faking to me."

"So what are you saying?" Jason leaned forward. "He just knew it?"

Steven remained calm despite Jason's accelerating emotional state. "I'm saying maybe he got the information somewhere, and he wasn't expecting to go into convulsions and tell everything he knew."

"And it just happened to happen in the booth next to ours." Jason's eyebrows lowered with distrust.

"Yeah . . . that's a lot of coincidences," Steven replied.

"And that's what I'm saying." Jason rubbed his hands together slowly. "There isn't that much chance in all the world." He paused. "So what did they do? Take him to the hospital?"

Steven shook his head. "No. They didn't get a chance. He leaped over one of the tables like he was in the movies and ran out of the door. The woman, Sienna, eventually went after him."

"This is unbelievable." Jason ran his hand over his

expensive haircut. "This is un-damn-believable." He exhaled. "So you know what you need to do."

Steven raised his brows and waited.

"We've got to find out what we can about these folks. Find out what they really know. I'm too close to retiring off of this crap for some unknown elements to creep in and monk up everything."

"Yeah." Steven rubbed his eyes. "I feel the same way."

"But we've got to be extra careful with the diamonds now." Jason's mind was going a million miles a minute. "I don't want anybody stealing them from us, before we can get rid of the them. I've got to think of something. A place no one would ever look in case they've got some tricks up their sleeves."

"I know that's right." Steven nodded.

"Well, I'm heading back to the condo. See what you can find out," Jason instructed. "And I'll do the same. Because no one is going to steal our stolen ice from us. It just ain't happening."

Not knowing what direction to take, Sienna simply stood in front of one of the buildings. She looked up as a tour bus passed by. Through the windows she could see people chatting happily, and it mirrored to her how complex her life felt at that moment. She wished she were one of them, just a tourist on the island of Kaua'i enjoying the sights and sounds, and not a woman desperately looking for the man she loved.

As her gaze scanned the faces on the bus, it stopped when she saw Hawk ease down into a seat and lay his head back before the vehicle moved on. On instinct, Sienna ran toward the bus, but when she realized that would do no good she ran toward the parking lot and their car. "Where in the world is he going?" she said as she jumped inside the car and started it up. "And why is he on that bus? He doesn't know those people." She backed out of the parking space and into the driving lane. That's when it hit her. *Perhaps he doesn't know why he's on the bus. Perhaps he doesn't know what he's doing at all.*

By the time Sienna pulled out onto the street the bus was nowhere in site, but she knew the direction it had taken. As she pressed the gas pedal, Sienna tried to be aware of everything around her, all the people, all the cars, any bus within viewing distance. She felt as if she were being stretched in a thousand directions. *Why is Hawk doing this? Why is he doing this to us? How can I ever have a future with this man? I'm tired of the erratic ups and downs. If they don't stop, it's going to kill me.*

But even with that thought, Sienna continued up Highway 56, her body tense, her eyes missing nothing. Finally, she saw the tour bus. Sienna followed it as best she could, although the cars in front of her seemed intent on being obstacles to her progress. As the bus continued up the highway, which was no more than a four-lane road, traffic continued to be a problem, not because of congestion, but because of the slow pace that many of the drivers adhered to.

Sienna kept her eyes on the bus and again she wondered where it was going, and whether Hawk knew, or if he was in a state in which he did not know or care. Anxious, Sienna hoped she could maneuver and get behind the vehicle, but before she could the traffic came to a gradual halt. It didn't take long before Sienna knew why. When the traffic started up again she was shocked to see Hawk running into the foliage beside the road. "My God! What is he doing now?" Her breath caught in her throat.

As soon as Sienna could, she pulled over and got out. She tried to run but almost fell because of the underbrush. "Hawk," Sienna called. "Hawk. Where are you going?" But he continued without turning around and disappeared into a thicker grove of trees.

All of a sudden she caught a glimpse of him. He was about thirty feet away. Apprehensively, Sienna went deeper into the forest, but she had to stop when she reached a wire fence hidden within a profusion of hibiscus, philodendron, and plumeria. Sienna realized that Hawk had run into the fence too. "Hawk," she called again, but only the birds answered.

Sienna searched the area using the fence as a guideline but with no result. "I've lost him," she said as she turned in a circle, aware that she had no clue where she was. "I've lost him out here. I hate to think what might happen to him if he's not in his right mind."

Afraid of just that, Sienna continued her search, until she came to a fast-running stream. Rocks and boulders bordered the moving waters and Sienna knew the stream could be dangerous for anyone who might cross it without care. Her anxious gaze searched the water and the opposite bank, but there was nothing there beside the raw beauty of Kaua'i.

"I've got to go back and get help," Sienna decided as she climbed over a fallen branch. "Hawk can't be that far away. I've got to get someone to help me search this entire area. But I'm afraid to leave. What if he's hurt?"

Without warning, all of the dreams she had of Hawk, all the plans of a life with them together surfaced in her mind. Sienna placed her hand on her abdomen and the baby that lay within. "We've got to find your father. I won't leave here without him. I can't go back. I can't take that chance."

She turned around and faced the direction where she believed the road was. All the while her eyes continued to search the landscape, and just as Sienna had given up hope, she caught a glimpse of something in her peripheral vision.

She turned and walked toward it. As Sienna drew closer, and even closer still, her heart sighed when she recognized Hawk's sleeve. It protruded from the opposite side of a large palm tree as he sat propped up against it. "Hawk?" she called. "Hawk!" He did not answer. Apprehensively, Sienna reached the tree. She circled it, slowly. When she stopped in front of Hawk, she saw his head was bowed. "Hawk," she said again.

Sienna descended to one knee. "Hawk, it's me." She spoke as if she were speaking to a frightened deer that might run away. Carefully, Sienna reached out to place her hand on his face. She wanted to lift it and look into his eyes. But as Sienna's hand lightly touched the surface of Hawk's skin his head jerked up, and the eyes that looked into hers were as wild as any animal's. But the face, the face that she had loved for eight years, was pockmarked and blistered beyond recognition.

Twenty-eight

"Oh no-o-o," Sienna cried, and Hawk seemed to re-coil from the abrupt outcry. Sienna just knelt there and looked at him with tears streaming down her face. "Is this what the Stonekeeper's cycle has brought us to? You can't even speak to me and I barely recognize you? Is this what being special means?"

Hawk stared at Sienna with eyes that could not see her, but yet seemed to see beyond her, beyond anything that any normal human being could or should see.

"You can't hear me can you?" she said through her tears. "And that's okay. You don't have to hear me." She sniffled and gave a false chuckle. "Because I'm the Stonekeeper. The one who's going to bring you justice." Sienna paused. "Is this the justice that you have been seeking all these years that you've been with me, Hawk?" She spoke through her pain and anger. "Were you supposed to end up here like some mangled animal in a forest on Kaua'i?" Sienna looked down. "A madman with a face not even a mother could love?"

She tried to think clearly. "Well . . . I got you into this, and I'm going to get you out." She stood up slowly and looked around. For a moment the forest seemed to fold in around her, and Sienna wanted to scream. She wanted to scream at the top of her lungs and continue screaming until there was no more voice inside of her. But she held back from the beckoning edge of falling apart. "I'm going to get us out of this, Hawk. I'm going to get us off of this island."

She looked down at him. "But how am I going to do it without them wanting to lock him away?" Her hand went to her mouth as she stifled a sob. "I've got to get him home. I don't know how I'm going to do it, but I will."

Sienna pulled up the determination that was needed to go on. "I'll be back, Hawk," she said to him. "Don't worry." She reached out to touch him again. This time she did not try to touch his face, yet longing for the contact, she reached for his shoulder instead. Still Hawk withdrew. Sadly, Sienna did as well. "I'll be back," she said through the lump in her throat.

She ran toward a lookout point, as again tears streamed down her face. Hawk would not let her touch him. He would not, and Sienna wondered if he ever would again.

Sienna's heart hurt as it had never hurt before as she climbed to the top of the stones. Yet Sienna knew she could not give in to that feeling. If she did, she too would be like Hawk, sitting against a palm tree, her mind in another place, her spirit broken. *Hawk's spirit broken?* The tears streamed again. *My strong, handsome man broken?* A part of her wanted to die from the thought of it.

Sienna forced herself to stand when she reached the top of the boulders, and the landscape spread out before her. But all she saw was trees, flowers, brush, and beauty beyond any she had ever seen. A beauty that was overpowering and terrifying in her present circumstance.

Still Sienna continued to study the landscape. She spotted the stream that was not far from the road and then her eyes narrowed as she focused toward the west. There, curling out of the mass of green was a small wisp of smoke, a singular vapor that rose above the trees. *Anyone with the courage to live out here by themselves may have the courage to help Hawk.* A spark of hope broke through. *I've got to take a chance that they will. I have no choice.*

She scampered down the boulders and went back to Hawk. "I've found a place for us to go, Hawk. You've got to come with me because we can't stay here," she said with authority, but there was a tremor in her voice. She reached out her hand, but Hawk simply stared at it.

"Come with me, Hawk. Come," Sienna pleaded. "You've got to come now." She tried to take his hand, but again he pulled away. "God, tell me what to do." She looked up at the sky as more tears escaped. Sienna took a deep breath and wiped her eyes. She looked back at Hawk. "Okay, I will not touch you, but you've got to come with me. You've got to follow me. So, I'm going to walk away and you can follow as far behind as you need to, but you must come."

Sienna turned and began to walk. She walked a few feet before she looked back again. Hawk was still sitting by the tree. "Like I said,"—her heart pounded but she continued to walk—"you can follow me at any distance, but you must follow me," she repeated. This time Sienna advanced several yards before she turned around. Hawk was nowhere in sight. Slowly, she looked to her left and just inside a thicker part of the brush, she saw Hawk standing at a distance behind a veil of foliage.

Relieved, Sienna forced herself to walk with confidence, and she prayed Hawk would buy into her ploy. That he would believe she could lead them out of the forest. Sienna also hoped that he was not able to sense the truth. That she was scared beyond compare. *I have no idea how to get down there. How do I reach that small stream of smoke in this? All I can see is trees.* Again she felt as if the forest might swallow her, but she pushed the feeling away. *If there is a house or something out there, there must be a path, a way to get to it. And I will find it.*

Sienna looked down. *I'll mark this spot, and I'll use the thread from my belt to keep me oriented.* Quickly, Sienna gathered four stones and three banana leaves. She stacked the stones on top of each other and placed the leaves between them. Next she untied her loosely woven belt and began to unravel it. Once Sienna had a sufficient amount of string, she tied the loose end to a branch near the marker. *Every once in a while, I'll build another marker to help me mark my way back to the lookout point.*

Sienna walked slowly, searching the ground, looking for anything that seemed like a human path, but there was nothing. Every once in a while she would catch a glimpse of Hawk's clothing in the brush. Strangely enough, even his silent presence lent a sense of support.

Sienna had no idea how long she walked, but it seemed like an awfully long time, but when she arrived again at one of her markers, she knew their situation was graver than she had been willing to accept. At that moment Sienna dropped to her knees, leaned forward and placed her face on the earth. "I can't take much more of this. I can't. If there is a God, then you will hear me now, because I am at my human end."

Her tears mingled with the moist soil as she huddled there, exhausted of spirit and heart. When
Sienna opened her eyes and sat back on her
haunches, she could see Hawk staring at her from
the brush, closer than he had been the entire time,
as if, even through his mental haze, he was reaching
out to her.

"You haven't completely left me, have you?" She
knew he could not hear her, because she spoke so
softly. But yet, his unblinking stare cut right through
her, and Sienna gave a laugh that was more like a cry
before she looked at the ground again.

"So . . . it is you," a voice said from behind her.

Startled, Sienna turned and was shocked to see
Elikapeka. The Kahuna looked different. She was
not dressed in European clothes as she had been the
first times Sienna saw her. Sienna's gaze traveled
from her feet that looked like an outgrowth of the
earth, up her brown legs which resembled strong
tree trunks that disappeared under a floral *mau mau.*
But there was one thing that was the same, even
among the huge trees, the Kahuna was massive.
"Elikapeka," Sienna said. "What are you doing out
here?"

"The question should be . . . what are you doing
here?" Elikapeka replied. "This land belongs to me.
This is my home."

Sienna gazed at the thick foliage around her, then
looked back at the Kahuna.

"I am waiting for an answer," Elikapeka pressed.

Involuntarily, Sienna's gaze strayed to Hawk, who
was still visible in the brush.

Before she could reply to Elikapeka's question the
Kahuna said, "I see."

Sienna continued to look at Hawk. "I don't know

what's wrong with him," she said as if Elikapeka had asked for some kind of explanation. "We were inside our booth at the trade show, then all of a sudden Hawk went into a kind of fit. The next thing I knew he was running through the room and jumping over tables until he ran out of the door. A friend of ours had gone and gotten this security guard to help us, but I knew from the questions he asked, his solution would be to lock Hawk away. So I left the gem show and I went after him." Sienna looked down. "And then I saw him on this tour bus. God knows how he managed to get there. So I got into my car and followed the bus, and the next thing I knew, I saw him running through the brush not far from here."

"You followed him to this place." There was a knowing behind her words.

Sienna knew one of the lessons the Stonekeeper's cycle had taught her was there was no such thing as a coincidence. Everything in life happened for a reason, and when the Stonekeeper's cycle was underway, that was truer than ever. "Yes, I followed him here," she replied.

The Kahuna's eyes bore into her and Sienna found herself rattling on. "I didn't want him to be caught by the police or the authorities because I'm sure they would have sedated him and locked him away, even if only temporarily." Sienna paused. "And you are the only person that I know, here on this island, that might be able to help him. That knows who Hawk is."

Their eyes locked.

"That knows who the two of you are," Elikapeka corrected her.

"I don't matter at this point." Sienna shook her head. "I'm not important."

"But you are important," Elikapeka cut her off. "This is part of the message, the understanding, that the two of you must have before either one of you can heal. Hawk is simply your male reflection, Sienna. There is no coincidence that he is in the state that he is in, and he is your mate. He is showing you there is a part of yourself that you are fighting against. That you have not accepted. You must take responsibility as well, Stonekeeper."

Sienna closed her eyes. Once again she wanted to shout. She didn't want to hear about responsibility. She didn't want to hear anything of the kind. She simply wanted someone to help Hawk. At that moment, Sienna felt as if she might burst, but when she looked at the Kahuna, the peacefulness of Elikapeka's countenance seeped into her.

"What do we need to do?" Sienna heard herself ask.

The Kahuna slapped at an insect that landed on her meaty arm before she looked over at Hawk. "We need to go to my *hale*, my house."

"Do you think he will come?" Sienna looked at Hawk.

Elikapeka studied Hawk through the brush. "Yes, he will come. He will come because he knows." She began to nod. "You walk with me. And don't worry about Hawk, he will follow." The Kahuna turned and began to walk away. "Although his mind is no longer present, the core of him is still there. He will follow because it is the core of him that has brought him here. Has brought him here to be healed."

Twenty-nine

Sienna followed Elikapeka further into the brush. The Kahuna walked through the foliage as if it were water, easily parted, but for Sienna it was another story. The branches that spread easily for Elikapeka, recoiled, striking at her face, arms and legs.

"Stay close," Elikapeka advised. "That way you won't be the victim of my backlash."

"All right." Sienna moved closer, and managed to block a healthy bush before it struck her.

"Yes," the Kahuna continued, "I am aware that I am a very large woman. How else would I carry all this wisdom inside without a body like this?" She laughed from her gut and it vibrated out into the forest.

Sienna couldn't help looking behind them to see if Hawk was following, but there was no sign of him.

"I told you not to worry," Elikapeka reminded her, not missing a stride. "Believe me, I know he is there, just like I knew that you two were here in the forest."

"You knew that we were out here?" Sienna replied, once again surprised.

"Why else would I come looking for you?"

They walked in silence before Elikapeka spoke again. "The truth is, I did not know it was you, but I knew someone had entered my land. I could feel it in my feet. The vibration was there, coming out of the Mother. We are one, you know. She and I."

"The Mother, meaning the earth," Sienna said to herself as memories flooded in from previous Stone-keeper cycles.

"Most definitely. The earth is my mother as she is the mother of all of us who are allowed to live upon her."

Sienna thought of everything that had happened since that morning and there was no doubt in her mind that the cycle had begun. Her heart beat faster with the acknowledgment, and the uncertainty of what it would bring.

It wasn't long before Sienna and Elikapeka reached a cleared area where a small house sat surrounded by palms and large hibiscus trees. Blossoms of yellow, red, pink and white billowed happily within a variety of greens, and the smell of plumeria dominated the air.

"This is my *hale,*" Elikapeka said, standing in the doorway that she seemed to fill. Sienna went through the doorway after her and was about to step into the room when the Kahuna turned and said, "No shoes."

"What?" Sienna asked.

"No shoes." Elikapeka shook her hand. "No shoes in this *hale.* This house is built on sacred ground, and although I can not keep you from walking upon the earth around it, I can ask you to remove your shoes in respect of its sacredness."

Sienna looked down at Elikapeka's brown, weathered feet. There was a deep dusting of earth around the edges and between her toes.

"Do not mind my feet. Mind your own," Elikapeka chastised her. "Yes, mine are covered with the Mother. But don't worry, I understand the meaning of washing with water, maybe better than you." She smiled slightly. "But I also understand that the more I gather, that is of the earth, the more it feeds what is sacred inside of me. I will sweep tomorrow, but today, I welcome her in, but not as plain dirt on the bottom of shoes." The Kahuna smiled again. "She knows I honor her, and I am honored to mingle with her."

Quietly, Sienna removed her shoes as requested. She looked around the house as she did so. It was very much like any other house, consisting of four rooms: a kitchen, a sitting area, a bedroom and a bath. If there was anything special about the Kahuna's quarters, it was the dried herbs that hung in the corners, the wooden objects that Sienna had no name for which sat on a table carved with fish, birds and flowers, and a large collection of Hawaiian art that covered the walls with barely a naked spot between them.

"Let us sit down and enjoy some *haupia,*" the Kahuna said. "And you can tell me the story. We, Hawaiians love to talk story. And I want to hear the story of what happened to Hawk. Do you like *haupia?*" Elikapeka leaned toward Sienna.

"To be honest I don't know. What is it?"

"It is my favorite dessert." She smiled easily. "It's a custard that we make out of coconut. I've eaten it since I was a little child."

Sienna shrugged. "Sure. I'll have some." Although dessert was the last thing on her mind.

With the grace of a dolphin swimming in familiar waters, Elikapeka walked over to the refrigerator and removed a bowl. Sienna was amazed, considering her bulk, how beautifully she moved. She watched the Kahuna dish up the custard. She gave herself a large helping, and Sienna a much smaller one.

"You may start at any time," Elikapeka said without looking up.

Sienna sighed. She didn't want to go over it again, but she did not want to offend the Kahuna. "Well . . . like I said, Hawk simply began to act as if he was going through some type of convulsions and—"

"Wait. No." Elikapeka stopped her. Purposefully, the Kahuna turned, and Sienna found herself looking into the depths of her smiling eyes. Smiling, but underneath the smile was a wealth of experience, a richness of life, that told Sienna this woman would be able to help her and Hawk find clarity, if nothing else. "That is not the beginning. You must really feel where this started, Sienna. When did it start? I must know it all."

Sienna looked down, and her mind began to tumble backwards. *When did this start with Hawk? When?* she asked herself. "It was several months ago," she said. "It was as if he was pulling away from me and I knew he was, but I didn't understand why. We even had what I would call our first official break up over it. I just couldn't handle his being with me and not being with me, not being present." Sienna hesitated. "He just wasn't there."

"Were you?" Elikapeka asked.

"Of course I was."

"Don't answer so quickly," the Kahuna warned. "Were you present in heart, mind and body when Hawk began to pull away? You must answer that question honestly, because the truth is, there is no separateness between you and Hawk. There is no separation. He is your reflection as you are his. As we all are reflections of one another. How else can it be when we all come from one Great Spirit?"

Elikapeka's way of talking made Sienna feel confused. "I thought I was there for him. There was nothing that kept me from it." She tried to think. "I was happy tending the store and I knew we were coming to Kaua'i. I even had this vision, this dream, of our getting married here."

"You say vision . . . dream," Elikapeka cut in.

Sienna nodded.

"So for you it was not a reality, this marriage. It was not something that you knew would come into being."

"No, it wasn't. I . . . always thought that Hawk would . . . might not go through with it," Sienna stammered. "That he might not want to marry me. He had shown reluctance until that point so . . ."

"And so there was a split," Elikapeka replied. "There was a division between you. You had begun to withdraw as well on some level, and Hawk was simply mirroring you in his own way. It is almost impossible to say which came first." The Kahuna paused. "So if you remember nothing else, Sienna, remember there is always the oneness, especially with those who we love the deepest. They are the clearest mirrors of our deepest fears, our deepest desires."

Frustrated by the way the Kahuna seemed to make her the source of Hawk's dilemma, Sienna retorted. "But how is that going to help Hawk?"

"When you acknowledge yourself, when you embrace your reason for being, it is helpful for not only yourself, but for those you love." Her eyes beamed. "It is most powerful, like balancing a scale. It is justice."

Sienna's eyes opened wide. "Justice."

Elikapeka nodded slowly. "Justice."

Sienna saw the Kahuna stop for no apparent reason with a spoonful of *haupia* near her mouth. Slowly, she placed the spoon back in her bowl, and without saying a word, walked to the front door.

"What is it?" Sienna asked as Elikapeka put up a quieting hand before she opened the door and closed it behind her.

Hawk looked up into the white blooms of the hibiscus tree, then over at a leafy philodendron that wrapped around a large aloe vera plant, before it climbed up a monkey wood tree. *Where in the world, am I?* he thought. He focused on the clearing that was beyond the brush, where a lone, small, wooden house sat in the middle of a plethora of flowers and short pineapple palms. Confused and feeling waves of nervous energy course through him, Hawk watched smoke curl up out of the stone chimney. *What is this place? How in the world did I get here?*

All of a sudden the front door of the house opened, and a large woman stepped over the threshold and into the yard. Hawk squinted as he watched her. For a moment she looked familiar, but then his mind, like an overloaded computer, failed him, and he wasn't certain of anything. He shook his head and tried to focus as the woman deliberately turned toward him. Hawk stooped down inside the foliage so he would not be seen.

"I know you are there," he heard her say, speaking as if she were addressing him. But Hawk remained quiet, his eyes watchful like that of an animal on the alert.

"I said, I know you are here, Hawk. I can feel you," the woman spoke again.

She called my name! Hawk's mind grasped at the thread of clarity that wove through. *She called my name!*

Hawk watched the woman proceed in his direction.

She walked slowly and purposefully, until she reached the edge of the clearing several feet in front of him.

"Last night the rumblings inside your soul were as volatile as that of the volcano Goddess Pele. I had no idea when the eruption would be," she continued, "but there was no doubt in my mind and in my heart, that it would be soon. I knew because I am so much a part of this island of Kaua'i, and she is deeply connected with the Mother Hina. Pele, the spirit of the fire that has been burning inside of you, is Hina's daughter. With their help, and *Aumakua,* I offer a way of healing to you. I am not saying that I can heal you, Hawk," her voice got stronger, "I am saying I know a way to open the door for your healing. But you must step forward to enter it. You must be ready. And you must let me know. Now."

For a moment Hawk remained crouched in the vegetation, but as he listened to the woman speak, his heart seemed to vibrate with her words, and something deep inside him said that she could do exactly what she promised. *She mentioned last night. I knew I had seen her before.* With Hawk's concerted effort to understand, to remember, clarity was once again his. *It's the Kahuna. The woman, Elikapeka, that I met at the beach house, and she is offering to help me. But can I trust her? Does she have the kind of wisdom that I need?* For a moment Hawk studied Elikapeka's wise countenance. *But the truth is what choice do I have?*

With that conclusion, Hawk slowly rose to his feet. "You say that you can help me?" he asked, his voice foreign to his own ears.

"Yes. I can help you, but I cannot heal you." The Kahuna repeated. "The healing of your *aumakua,* your spirit, Hawk, is totally up to you. Although Sienna is a key part, the final decision is yours."

"Sienna?" he said, and once again Hawk could feel his heart, but this time it constricted.

"Yes." The Kahuna looked back at the house. "She is here with me."

Hawk stepped back into the brush.

"Wait. Where are you going?" Elikapeka asked.

Hawk continued to back up into the plants. "I don't want her to see me like this."

"But it is too late for that," Elikapeka informed him. "That deed is done."

"Then I'm thankful I don't remember." He grabbed his head with both hands. "Thankful I didn't see the repulsion in her eyes. With how I feel right now, I could not have taken it."

"Taken what?" the Kahuna asked. "Have you considered your mind may be playing tricks on you? How do you know Sienna was repulsed?"

"I know," Hawk replied. "All these years I've tried to hide from it, but I've known all along. For her I have always been a reminder of things she'd rather forget." His hand touched his tormented face. "And this is worse than it has ever been before." Hawk's voice dropped. "I just can't face her. I wouldn't make it through seeing her rejection."

"So what would you have me tell her?" Elikapeka asked.

"Tell her to leave. Please." He closed his eyes. "Just go. Go back to the hotel. My thoughts are cluttered enough, and I simply can't think knowing that she is here. That she has seen me like this, weak and hideous. I know, through the years, she has tried to love me, but it was always a struggle." Hawk smarted from his own truth and his anger rose. "There is no way she can love me now." He added, harshly.

"Love is not based upon beauty, Hawk. What is

that old saying on the mainland? Beauty is in the eye of the beholder."

"Well . . . if that is true, perhaps Sienna doesn't love me." He paused. "Perhaps she never could."

"I don't believe that," the Kahuna replied. "But it is not for me to believe or disbelieve. What I should do, I am clear about. I will ask Sienna to go, and then you can reveal yourself to me. We have work to do." Her gaze pierced the vegetation. "But you can be certain, you two will be reunited on this island. It's important to this land, and everyone on it. It's important for all of humankind."

Hawk watched the Kahuna walk back to the house where the door closed silently behind her.

Thirty

Sienna didn't know what to think. One moment she and Elikapeka were having a profound conversation, the next the Kahuna had simply left her alone. Sienna looked around the house and waited. But as the minutes passed she became more and more restless. *I can't just sit here. Maybe Elikapeka left so quickly because of Hawk.*

Sienna rose from her seat as the door opened and Elikapeka stepped inside. "What happened? Where did you go?"

The Kahuna lifted her chin. "I think it might be better if you were to go now. You left your car, I assume, on Highway 56?"

Surprised, Sienna said, "Yes. But . . . what about Hawk?"

"Hawk's outside. It is because of him that I suggest you leave." Elikapeka rested her folded hands on her abdomen. "There is anger beneath this relationship that neither one of you have acknowledged. It is only now, when Hawk is being forced to acknowledge every part of himself, that he is also being forced to recognize the anger that he has toward you."

Sienna stiffened. "Hawk is angry with me? I can't— What have I done to him?"

"It is not what you have done, Sienna. It is what you have not accepted."

Sienna felt her anger rise. She looked at Elikapeka and shook her head. "I am not going to stand here and be the brunt of this entire situation," she counted off on her fingers, "everything that has ever happened to Hawk, and anybody else. I have done nothing but love him, and I am not the reason for all this. And if he believes that, and if you believe that . . . and if he's angry with me." Sienna could barely speak she was so enraged. "I am furious at him." She walked toward the door and opened it.

The Kahuna ignored her rampage. "When you go outside, if you look to your left, you will see several plumeria trees with reddish-orange blossoms. Beside them is a path that will lead you back to Highway 56."

Sienna was so angry she did not want to thank her, but she felt she had no choice. "Thanks," she said curtly and closed the door.

Sienna stepped outside and looked around for Hawk. Obviously, he had spoken to Elikapeka but now he hid from her. *I am the one who came after you. Not Elikapeka. No one else but me.*

Suddenly, Sienna realized that for years she had been carrying a lot of guilt when it came to Hawk. Somehow she did believe she was responsible for his condition. Responsible for the horrible outbreak on his face that changed him so drastically. Even for the visions that haunted and taunted him, changing his life from the respectable one he had lived before. *Well, I am done carrying all this guilt,* she thought as her eyes stung with held back tears. *Until now, I thought justice could only be found with the Stonekeeper, but it seems even I, plain old Sienna, am responsible for everything that happened*

*to Hawk. And if that is true, I don't know if there will ever be
any justice, because I am through.*

She started to enter the path but Sienna stopped
suddenly. Hawk's name rose inside her throat and she
almost called out to him. *I won't do it. I've done all I can.
Hawk is calling the shots now and I'm going to abide by them
even if it kills me.* She stepped into the foliage.

When Sienna reached her car, she climbed inside
and headed back up Highway 56. As she drove up the
road, she knew the trade show was over for the day,
and a part of her was grateful, because Sienna didn't
know if she could have manned the booth as if nothing was wrong. Drained, she turned into the hotel lot
that was laden with palms. Sienna hadn't been in the
room a minute before the telephone rang.

"Hello."

"Sienna!" Dawn's worried voice came over the
line. "You're back. Is Hawk with you?"

Sienna sat down on the bed. "No."

"Oh no. You couldn't find him? What are we going
to do?"

"No," Sienna replied. "I-I found him."

"You did? So didn't he come back with you?"

"He could have come back, Dawn. It seems he
didn't want to."

There was a pause.

"What are you talking about?"

Sienna didn't feel like explaining, but she knew
there would be no getting around it. "He . . . he,
never spoke one word to me after he ran out of the
trade show. I ended up following him several miles
away from here—"

"How did Hawk get several miles away?" Dawn in-
terjected.

"He got on a tour bus, and then the next thing I

knew I saw him run into the forest next to the road. So I followed him. But when I finally caught up with him, Dawn, I could not make him say one word to me." Sienna rubbed her forehead. "He just stared as if he didn't know me . . . as if he didn't know where he was." She sighed. "And then that Kahuna showed up."

"The one that we saw at Kamokila Village?" Dawn asked.

"Yes," Sienna replied. "Believe it or not, she lived nearby and we ended up going to her place."

"But what about Hawk?" Dawn pressed.

"Elikapeka suggested that I go with her because she knew Hawk would follow. It ends up she was right." Sienna paused. "And that's why I'm here and he's there."

"Sienna, you're not making any sense at all," Dawn said.

Sienna's short fuse went off. "What doesn't make any sense to you, Dawn? I'm here. Hawk's there. He didn't want to come. He chose to stay there, and as a matter of fact he told the Kahuna that he wanted me to leave. That he felt I was the reason for his problems. I was the root of everything bad that has ever happened to him."

"Oh-h, Sienna. You know that Hawk doesn't believe that. He's just not thinking properly right now," Dawn tried to console her.

"Well, perhaps for the first time in his life he is thinking properly. Or at least for the first time since he's known me."

"So now you're simply going to leave him with that woman?"

"What else would you have me do, Dawn? You have any grand suggestions?"

"No, I just thought that . . . I don't know. This is just . . . bizarre."

"Well, has my life been anything but bizarre since you've known me? No," Sienna answered her own question. "But I am not going to wallow in this. I am not going to just"—she hesitated—"become a victim of this. I am going to do what any other woman would do."

"And what's that?" Dawn's skepticism was clear.

"I am going to get dressed up and go out. Have a drink somewhere. I know if I stay in here I am going to go crazy."

There was a pause.

"Okay." Dawn's uncertain voice floated over the line. "Where do you want to go?"

"Probably downstairs to the bar. But you know, Dawn," Sienna sighed again. "I know you don't drink. It's just not you, so you don't have to go because I'm going."

"But I want to, I-I'd love to go," Dawn assured her. " I—you know, I don't have to have a drink, I can ask for some cranberry juice with lemon, or a twist of lime."

Dawn's words made Sienna remember the baby. *He's got me so crazy I forgot all about you.* She held back a sob. Finally, Sienna said softly, "We'll both have juice."

"That might be a good idea." Dawn's voice was soft too.

They each held the phone in silence.

Sienna felt the little energy she had drain out of her. "On second thought, maybe going out isn't such a good idea at all."

"Uh-uh," Dawn sounded. "Now you've gotten me all excited. You can't back out."

Sienna knew she was trying to lift her spirits.

"So you better hurry up and get pretty. And hey. We're in Hawaii. Even if the Devil himself shows up, we're not going to let him spoil this trip," Dawn declared.

Sienna just held the phone.

"So I'll see you in forty-five minutes," Dawn instructed. "And if you're not ready, you're going to man that booth all by yourself for the next two days. And that's a promise."

"Okay," Sienna replied. "Forty-five minutes."

Thirty-one

Hawk waited until he knew Sienna was gone before he ventured out of the forest. He grimaced as the scratches made by branches and prickly palms added pain to his ravaged face. With an almost steady hand he tucked his torn shirt into his pants and removed as much debris as he could from his hair. Hawk wanted to make sure he was as presentable as he could be, before he knocked softly on the Kahuna's door.

"It is unlocked," he heard Elikapeka say from inside.

Gingerly, Hawk opened the door. His eyes scanned the room. They stopped when he saw the Kahuna.

"I wondered how much longer you would remain out there," she said as she sat back in her chair. "I'm sure Sienna reached her destination long ago. Or did part of you hope that she would not leave without you?"

Hawk could not deny the thought had entered his mind, that Sienna might refuse to leave him behind. That she would not obey Elikapeka's request that she leave because he had asked her to. That with her love, Sienna would see through his pain and embarrassment. Hawk's jaw felt rock hard. But it was only wishful thinking. Sienna had left, and there was nothing he could do about it.

"Facing reality at any given moment is a powerful thing. Because perceptions can be tricky," the Kahuna said. "Can you imagine how much energy we human beings use pulling up the past and projecting into the future? We are so unaware that it is the now moment that is the key to everything. I will tell you this from the very beginning, Hawk, and it will save you a lot of misery. If the past or the future does not come to you of its own accord, do not waste your *mana,* your life force, bringing them into the present."

"That's easier said than done," Hawk said as he remained by the front door.

"For most people." Elikapeka looked at the objects on the table before her. "But once you master living in the present, you will never go back to the old way of being. You will see how it does not serve you." She smiled. "But most important of all, you will be space for others to live in the present as well."

Hawk leaned against the wall. "I don't know how I can help anybody else when I can't even help myself."

"Self-pity is not allowed in this *hale.* It does not empower anyone," the Kahuna said with authority, then she softened her tone. "Come take off your shoes and sit at the table with me. You've wasted enough time already. I told you we have work to do." She moved her hand like a graceful hula dancer. "I have assembled some tools that will help us." She placed a *lei* of plumeria flowers around her neck as she waited.

Stung by her remark about self-pity, despite his marred face, Hawk removed his shoes and strode defiantly across the room and sat across the table from Elikapeka. Hawk held his chin steady, and his eyes dared her to even flinch in response to his appearance. Still his heart pounded as he waited for her reaction. But instead of focusing on his countenance the Kahuna looked straight into Hawk's eyes.

"*Aloha*, Hawk," Elikapeka said with meaning. "This *aloha* means my heart goes out to you in welcome."

The simple words reopened his vulnerability, and Hawk's gaze clouded with emotion.

"This *lei* is for you." The Kahuna leaned forward and placed it around his neck. "It is made of *kukui* nuts. They are a symbol of *Aumakua*, Great Spirit. Your *lei* has been washed in a sacred spring. When you wear it on your body, *unihipili*, it reminds your body of its sacredness. It is an olive branch between your body and your mind, helping both to remember that *unihipili*, body, is not your enemy, but a special partner in Spirit." Elikapeka smiled sweetly. "But right now your body is rebelling."

"Rebelling?" Hawk studied her wide face. "You could have fooled me, I thought I was cursed."

"In a way you are." She sat back. The chair creaked under her weight. "Cursed by your own thoughts, your own limited views of who you are."

"But how can that—"

The Kahuna put up her hand. "Wait. Before we go any further, I must give homage to *Aumakua* for allowing us to share this knowledge, for allowing us to be. Do you mind?" Her eyes bore into his.

Hawk wanted to say he no longer believed in the Great Spirit or any loving deity. His life's experience had taken that away, but he kept that to himself. "No. I don't mind."

"Good." Elikapeka nodded. "Then I will offer a Huna chant to the Great Spirit." Slowly, she closed her eyes and raised her hands. "*O ka Maluhia . . .*" she begun.

To Hawk the Kahuna's voice filled the room like

a burgeoning cloud. A cloud filled with emotion and genuineness. At first he sat and watched her, but the sincerity in her tone, and the sound of the Hawaiian words soon drew him in. It was almost as if he understood their ancient meaning. Somehow Hawk knew the chant called for peace, peace within every world, no matter how small, be it the single life of a human being, or all the lives of every being, human and nonhuman, on the planet.

Hawk knew that Elikapeka was appealing to the highest source that she believed in, and he could almost feel a vast line of ancient Kahunas behind her raising their voices to join in the prayer. At that moment Hawk wished he knew Hawaiian. He wished his voice could sing out with the same vigor as Elikapeka's. For the first time in years, Hawk wished he had as much faith in a superior, benevolent being as the Kahuna had.

When Elikapeka's prayer tumbled into a vibrating *"wale no"* Hawk felt the salt of his own tears sting his face as silence filled the room.

The Kahuna's strong hand covered his. "There is no purer form of purging for a man, than for the ocean to pour from his own eyes," Elikapeka said softly.

This time it was Hawk who could not look at the Kahuna. He was embarrassed. Even when his eyes dried, he kept his gaze on the table.

"Before you go to bed this evening, Hawk, I promise you will have the keys to believing in and accepting every part of yourself," Elikapeka continued to speak softly.

He looked into her dark eyes.

"Your body, your mind and your spirit," the Kahuna continued. "Your good and your bad."

Hawk bowed his head.

"Have you ever looked inside a cut diamond?" Elikapeka asked.

Hawk raised his head. "A diamond?"

"Yes. A diamond."

His eyes narrowed. "Why do you ask? I mean, why . . . a diamond?"

"Because it is easy to see all the facets of a cut diamond," she replied. "There is no denying its many sides." Her warm brown eyes stared into his hazel ones. "You, like every other human being, are like a diamond, Hawk. There are many facets to your being. Many parts. Without experiencing, or accepting different parts of themselves, a person would never be able to grow. They would be cut off from their roots, and it is the roots that reach down into the rich dark earth, that determine the size of the blossom the world is able to see." She paused and smiled. "So for now I want you to put aside everything you've ever felt about yourself. We are going to begin your life again. I want you to be like a newborn baby, without a past, a baby who knows only now, this moment. Together, with the ancient Hawaiian spirits to aid us, we will examine the world, and through this microscope we will rebuild your identity. Because all of this"—she circled his face with her hand—"means you have forgotten who you are."

Elikapeka picked up a *kukui* nut suspended on a piece of twine. A small pointed, quartz crystal hung beneath the nut.

"What is it?" Hawk asked as the nut and the crystal swung in front of him.

"It is a pendulum," the Kahuna replied. "With its help you will reunite *unihipili*, your body, *uhane*, your

mind, and your higher self, *aumakua,* your direct link
to God, Great Spirit."

Hawk looked at the primitive-looking tool and re-
membered a time in his life, when, as an intellectual,
he would have dismissed its worth in the blink of an
eye. But that felt like eons ago. "I am ready to try
whatever you think is necessary," Hawk said.

"Good," the Kahuna replied. "We will start by asking a question and you will hold the pendulum as
steady as you can. If it circles to the right, that means
yes. If it circles to the left, that means no."

"But how can a pendulum truly answer any question?" Hawk asked.

"It is about the oneness, Hawk. Your body is one
with your higher self. One with Spirit. This pendulum will be your body's voice without your mind
intervening. The body holds all your memories from
the first moment of its birth. It is conscious. With this
pendulum, your body can tell you what it knows, and
believe me, before the morning comes, you will truly
understand the value of everything that has ever happened in your life, even that which you would chose
to hide or forget."

Hawk took the pendulum from the Kahuna's
hand. He did not know if he believed her or not. All
Hawk knew was he was tired of running from himself
and the powers that be that had destroyed his life. *If
what I hold in my hand will help me close the door to all
that has tormented me, I am more than ready. And who am
I to second-guess the power of any object, when it was what
appeared to be a harmless crystal that got me here?*

Thirty-two

"Lor-rd," Dawn wailed. "Here she comes stepping out here in a Hootchie Mama dress." She looked Sienna up and down. "I told you to get pretty, not go crazy. I didn't even know you owned one of those."

"Don't we all?" Sienna replied, as she pulled at her skin-tight black dress.

Dawn shook her head. "There's no need to tug on it now. It's not going to come down any further."

"I'm not trying to pull it down." Sienna rolled her eyes. "I'm smoothing it out."

"Well, it's smooth all right. Smooth enough to catch anything and everything that might happen by."

"You've made your point, Dawn," Sienna said. "But I figured, in a few months I won't be able to wear this dress. And after I have the baby I may not ever be able to wear it again."

"So all of a sudden you're trying to become something you've never been before. Like making up for lost time, that you haven't lost yet," Dawn needled.

"Not really." Sienna's thoughts strayed to what had happened between her and Hawk in the Kaua'in forest; how he never spoke to her, that he couldn't even see her. "I just need to feel—" Sienna closed her eyes. "I just want to feel like a woman."

"Couldn't you have picked another way to do it?" Dawn asked. "That dress and those shoes almost look like a costume."

"That's enough." Sienna gave her the evil eye. "If you're going to be on me all night long, you can stay here. It was my idea to go out tonight."

"I know." Dawn walked a little ahead of her. "It's still your idea, and I'm going to let you have it. But don't say nothing when the flies start swarming around."

Sienna folded her arms. *Even some attention from an ordinary scumbag would help me feel better than how I feel right now.*

They took the elevator down to the lobby, then walked to the courtyard that was filled with tables topped by dancing candle flames. Up front, a three-piece band played a whimsical Hawaiian tune. Instead of waiting to be directed to one of the tables, Sienna went straight to the bar.

"I thought you decided you weren't drinking." Dawn followed close at her heels.

"I'm not going to drink any alcohol." Sienna eased into the high chair and crossed her legs.

"Then what are we doing sitting at the bar?" Dawn pulled up a seat beside her. She looked around.

"This is where I want to be. I feel sexy and romantic here."

Dawn sighed. "Look, I know I can't tell you what to do, but this is no way to handle what's happening with Hawk."

Sienna turned on her. "Don't mention him to me. And if you're going to do this all night long—"

"No. No, I'm not." Dawn made a face. "But I want to tell you, you're acting mighty strange."

"You don't know what strange is." Sienna looked down.

"There's no way I don't know what strange is after being your friend all these years," Dawn retorted.

Jason and Steven stepped through the front door of the Kaua'i Coconut Beach Resort.

"Hold it." Steven took hold of Jason's arm. "That's the two ladies from the booth."

"Are you sure?" Jason asked.

"Positive," Steven replied.

"Then our timing couldn't be better." Jason watched the women sit down at the bar. "Seems like somebody's on our side, even though I was beginning to doubt it. I couldn't find out a damn thing about these people."

"Maybe there was nothing to find," Steven replied.

Jason shook his head. "No-o, I don't believe that. Not after what that guy was saying. Somebody knows something, and this is our opportunity to see what we can find out." He squinted. "I want to have a talk with him, and if talking doesn't work I'll resort to whatever means necessary to get him to tell me what I need to know."

"All right," Steven replied. "But we don't know where he is."

"And here's our opportunity to find out," Jason said.

"It could be he's working with some other folks, that these women know nothing about it," Steven replied.

"Or they could be working together," Jason said. "So let's hope they're out alone tonight and interested in a little company."

"Sounds like a good idea to me."

"Which one is the owner?" Jason asked.

"The one with the black dress."

Jason studied the curve of Sienna's thigh, her shapely legs and high, high heels. "She's a good-looking woman," he said. "And from the look of her this won't be too difficult at all. As a matter of fact I'll probably enjoy it." Jason paused. "Go back upstairs and tell Charles and Sammy what's going on. Tell them to stand by, just in case we need them."

"Got ya," Steven replied.

"I'll keep an eye on the women until you return."

"What happens if they leave before I get back?"

"Don't worry," Jason assured him. "They won't. I'll do something to keep them here."

"All right," Steven replied.

"And when you talk to Charles and Sammy make sure everything is firm for that meeting we rescheduled tomorrow. The faster we get rid of our bundle, the better off I'll feel."

"Me too," Steven replied.

"Now go. I'll be right here."

Thirty-three

"*Aloha*, ladies. Can I help you?" A bartender with deep reddish-brown skin smiled beneath a trim mustache.

"Sure," Sienna replied. "I'd like to have cranberry juice with a twist of lime. And give me one of those cute little umbrellas over there." She pointed. "Make me think I'm drinking something even if I'm not."

"Okay." He laughed. "And you, *wicked wahini?* What are you drinking?"

"First you've got to tell me what *wicked wahini* means." Dawn leaned on the counter.

"Oh *wicked wahini* . . ." He licked his lips and looked into the air. "*Wicked wahini* means . . . mm-m-m, a young woman who is full of life. Vibrant in a womanly way."

"Oh really." Dawn's smile broadened as she sat back. "That actually calls for a drink, and I'll have the same thing she's having. And you can give me one of those umbrellas too."

"Your wish is my command." The bartender continued to smile. "I'll be right back."

"I must say I agree with him," a voice from behind them said.

They both turned.

"Hello," Steven said.

"Oh, hi," Dawn replied.

Sienna noticed how her eyes brightened. It appeared Steven had made some headway with Dawn while she was away. "Hello Steven," Sienna greeted him.

"It's beautiful out here, isn't it?" He looked toward the beach.

"It most certainly is," Dawn eagerly agreed.

Sienna simply nodded.

"Aren't you going to introduce me?" the handsome man beside Steven asked.

"Oh certainly. Jason, this is . . . I'm sorry, I never got your name."

"It's Dawn," Dawn spoke up.

"And you're Sienna, right?" Steven attempted to complete the introductions.

Sienna nodded again.

"Hello." Jason extended his hand and smiled beguilingly.

"Do you mind if we join you?" Steven had already pulled out the chair beside Dawn.

"No. We don't mind at all," Dawn said, looking at Sienna.

Sienna gave a nonchalant shrug and motioned toward the chair beside her. "Have a seat." *I said I wanted to be noticed, but now I'm not so sure. Damn you, Hawk.*

Jason climbed onto the seat beside her and by that time the bartender was returning with their juices. "And here you are." He slid both glasses decorated with pineapples, cherries and umbrellas toward Sienna and Dawn.

"Can I get you gentlemen anything?"

"You can get me a *mai tai*," Steven informed him.

"I'll have the same," Jason replied.

"Two *mai tais* coming up," the bartender announced as he walked away.

"So . . . how does Steven know you two lovely ladies?" Jason leaned in a little closer to Sienna.

"We have the booth next to Steven's at the gem show," Sienna replied.

"Oh-h," Jason said.

Sienna could smell his cologne. It had an expensive undertone, and his eyes and skin were gorgeous in a pampered sort of way, but not like Hawk who was naturally beautiful.

"Yeah, that's right," Steven jumped in. "Our booths are right next to each other. Which reminds me"—his brows knitted together—"I saw Dawn throughout the day, but you left right after the incident with the guy. What in the world happened with him?"

Sienna looked down at the counter. "He wasn't feeling very well, but he's being taken care of now." She looked up and tried to keep her gaze steady.

"Boy, he must have given you both quite a scare, huh?" Steven continued.

"What happened?" Jason asked, his eyes wide and innocent.

"I don't know," Steven answered. "It just seemed like he kind of, uh, flipped out. I don't know how else to put it, although I don't want to offend either one of you ladies."

Sienna looked down again.

"Oh no." Dawn jumped in. "We're not offended, but like Sienna said, Hawk's getting some help and uh-h . . . it's just been a very, very stressful few days with getting ready for the show and traveling and all."

"I've never seen anything like it," Steven spoke over their heads to Jason. "The guy was talking, but he looked like he was having an epileptic fit or something. And I could have sworn he said something about diamonds."

"Diamonds?" Sienna focused on Steven for the first time. She searched her memory, but she couldn't come up with a thing.

Steven laughed. "I swear, as bizarre as that sounds." He appeared bewildered. "It was amazing because he was making a little bit of sense."

Sienna's face hardened. "I don't remember Hawk saying anything about diamonds." She looked at the carvings on her silver bracelet.

"What kind of look is that?" Jason tilted his head as he studied Sienna's face. "You would think you hated diamonds, when most women love them."

"Yeah, well. I'm not most women." She tried to control her reaction, but Steven's mention of diamonds brought up all the things she was trying to forget, at least for the night. She closed her eyes and added softly, "For Hawk and I, diamonds are a biggee."

"What is it? You've been trying to get him to buy you a rock and he's refused?" Jason asked in a strange tone.

Sienna glanced at him. "You've only touched on part of it, and believe me, that's just the tip of the iceberg."

"He sounds like quite a character," Jason replied.

"You could say that again." Dawn popped the cherry into her mouth.

"Does he work with you two?" Jason asked.

Sienna glanced at him. "He does but, uh, he's much more than that."

"Oh really?" Jason said.

"Yes. Really."

"So I guess you must be pretty worried, huh?" Jason continued.

"I am, but . . . I know there's nothing I can do about it at this point. Like I said, he's getting help and by tomorrow I'm sure he'll be much better." Sienna tried to smile. "I'll see him then."

"He must be a pretty special guy to have a woman like you on such a tight string," Jason said, his voice low.

Sienna knew Jason was hitting on her, and she felt rather guilty because she liked it. "Yes, Hawk is a very special man." She sighed. "Sometimes a little bit too special for a woman like me."

"That's impossible," Jason replied. "Any man would feel like superman if he had a woman like you by his side."

Sienna took a swallow of cranberry juice. "Believe me, Hawk doesn't need me for any such thing."

The bartender returned with the two *mai tais*.

"I don't believe it," Jason said. "Tell me what makes him so special in your eyes. Maybe a little bit will rub off on me."

Sienna looked down into her juice and shook her head.

"Am I asking too many questions?" Jason asked softly.

"Yes." Sienna replied.

"All right." He threw up both palms. "Then let's turn this thing around. It's your turn to ask questions. I'll be quiet. At least for now." His dark lashes loomed over eyes that were nothing less than hypnotic.

Sienna sipped her juice. She tried to think of something to ask Jason, but she kept seeing Hawk just beyond the edge of the foliage, his eyes wild, his face distorted. "I can't think of anything," she finally said.

Jason placed his hand over his heart. "Am I that boring?"

Sienna chuckled. "No. It's just that your timing is pretty bad."

"But there's no better time than now," he said softly. "And I don't know when I'll get another chance."

Thirty-four

The band struck up a familiar tune, and several couples went to the dance floor. Sienna turned to the side and watched them, while Dawn moved along with the music.

"Seems like you like this song." Steven smiled at Dawn.

"Oh definitely," she replied. "It's one of my favorites."

"Well, I guess I should ask you if you want to dance."

"I thought you never would," Dawn replied.

Steven got off the chair. "Let's see what we can do then," he said as they walked toward the dance floor.

Dawn smiled back.

"Have fun," Sienna called.

"Would you care to dance?" Jason asked.

"No." Sienna shook her head. "Not this time."

Jason made an exaggerated sad face. "Is there nothing I can do to cheer you up?"

Sienna's lips turned a smile, but it was obvious it was no smile at all. "Life has been kind of crazy lately."

"That's no fun," Jason replied. "And you should be having a good time. You're here on the island of Kaua'i. Have you ever seen anything as beautiful as this place? It's magical, isn't it?"

"I'd say," Sienna replied as she recalled how Elikapeka intuitively knew someone had ventured onto the sacred land that surrounded her home.

"I've been on several Hawaiian islands, but none of them can compare to Kaua'i," Jason continued. "It's so untouched. It's so . . . it takes you in, and you get to experience the Hawaiian island of your dreams. You know what I mean?"

"In a way," Sienna replied. "But seeing that this is my first time in Hawaii, and Kaua'i is the only island I have been to, I can't really compare it to anything."

"Believe me." Jason covered her hand with his. "Kaua'i is Hawaii with a capital H."

Sienna smiled for a fleeting moment before she removed her hand. "So how are you connected with all of this . . . Steven and the gem show?"

Jason licked his lips and looked down. "Actually, I'm one of Steven's suppliers. I supply him with some of his higher quality stones."

"Really?" Sienna sat back. "Maybe we can do some business in the future."

"Do you own a shop?"

"Yes, I do. Actually it's my business that has the booth. I have a shop called The Stonekeeper, and we sell a variety of nature-oriented goods. Most of my jewelry has been made of good quality semi-precious stones but it's not very expensive." Sienna felt more at ease talking business. "I'm thinking about acquiring some pieces that are a little more costly, and attracting a clientele that would be interested in that kind of jewelry."

"Well, you're talking to a man who could definitely supply you with what you need."

"Do you have a card?" Sienna asked.

"I sure do." Jason reached inside his pants pocket

and pulled out his wallet. He flipped through the contents. Finally he said, "I don't seem to have any with me right now, but I've got some up in the room."

"Don't worry," Sienna replied. "I'll get it from you tomorrow. Perhaps you can bring it by my booth."

Jason looked at the dance floor. "I'm leaving early in the morning, so I should give it to you tonight."

"I don't want you to go to any extra trouble," Sienna said. "If you give it to Steven, I'm sure he'll pass it on to me tomorrow."

"But I don't want to give it to Steven." Jason looked into her eyes. "I want to give it to you, along with my private number."

Sienna looked at him straight on. "Jason, you're a very attractive man, and I'm sure by now most women would have been more than flattered that you even considered them, but I—"

"Don't say anything else," Jason stopped her. "Because I don't think I could take your rejection. So I tell you what . . ." He put his hands on her shoulders.

"What?" Sienna was somewhat uncomfortable with his touch.

"Let me show you something that will take your mind away from whatever has you in this funky space. I guarantee you, you won't be able to think about your friend, his troubles, or anything else."

Sienna paused. "Don't tell me it's up in your room."

"No." He looked at Sienna as if he were offended. "It's not in my room. All we've got to do is walk down to the edge of this property and look up at the sky. The stars in a Kaua'in sky are unbelievable. And where I want to take you is just dark enough so you can really see them."

Sienna watched his eyebrows rise.

"And I am positive," Jason continued, "once I show you the night sky, I'll gain a few brownie points with you tonight."

She looked into his eyes. They appeared to be sincere. "Okay. You've got a deal."

"Great." Jason got out of the chair and placed some money on the counter. "Let me go to the men's room, and we'll be on our way."

Jason opened the door to the bathroom. He walked over to the urinal and unzipped his pants. *I don't think Sienna knows anything about the diamonds, but there's no doubt that her boyfriend does and she's supposed to get with him tomorrow.* His head turned slightly when another man entered the room. *So I think we're going to have to have a surprise for my man.*

Jason finished his business and washed his hands before he slipped out of the lavatory and onto the elevator. When he arrived on the third floor, he got off and quickly walked down the hall. His knock on room 316 was demanding. It was a matter of seconds before the door opened.

"I don't have but a few minutes, Charles, so listen up. I want you and Sammy to get down to the back of the property, the place where we talked last night. I'm going to bring a woman out there. And uh-h . . ." His eyes brightened. "And she's going to be our guest until tomorrow. I want to take her to the condo because she's going to be our way of finding out what that guy knows."

"I understand," Charles replied.

"Good." Jason nodded. "I'll see you on the beach."

He headed back down the hall, got on the elevator, got off in the lobby and went back over to the bar. "Are they still on the dance floor?" Jason wiped the sheen from his forehead with a manicured hand.

"Ye-es, they are," Sienna said, looking over at Dawn and Steven. "If Steven figures out what's best for him, he might have to drag her from over there. Because once Dawn starts dancing it's hard to turn her off."

"I'm sure he'll let her know when he's had enough," Jason replied. "You ready to go see some stars?"

"Sure, but I want to tell Dawn where I'm going."

"You can." Jason shrugged. "But it's just out back. I'm sure we'll probably be back before they come off the dance floor."

"I know, but I've got to say something or she'll be worried," Sienna replied. "I'll be right back.

He watched her walk across the floor and maneuver between the dancers. Dawn stopped dancing just for a moment while Sienna whispered something in her ear. She nodded, smiled and began to dance again as Sienna returned to the bar.

"All right, I'm ready," Sienna said.

"Wonderful." Jason's eyes gleamed. "You will not be disappointed."

Thirty-five

"I have never seen so many stars in all my life," Sienna exclaimed as she looked at the night sky.

"I told you," Jason said. "Isn't this unbelievable? Kaua'i is right in your face, but it has its mysteries too." He paused and his voice lowered. "I'm the kind of man who likes intrigue."

"I heard something intriguing about Kaua'i." Sienna traced the Big Dipper with her finger.

"And what was that?" Jason moved in closer.

"That if you really want to be welcomed by the island of Kaua'i, the first thing you have to do is go as far as you can go on Highway 56 toward Ha'ena State Park. There's a beach there." She glanced at him then looked away. "And a hiking trail on the cliff above the beach. At the end of that trail there's an altar to Madame Pele."

"Pele meaning the volcano goddess?"

"That's right," Sienna replied still gazing at the sky. "Madame Pele. They say you'll find flowers, *lei*'s, and some special offerings there. I understand it's quite amazing." She smiled. "But that's what you must do if you want to be totally accepted by this island. That way,"—Sienna gave him a coy look—"Kaua'i will embrace you, and not chew you up and spit you out."

Jason laughed. "So did you make your trek to Madame Pele's altar?"

"No, I didn't. I thought about it, but . . . I didn't."

"Perhaps you should have," he said.

Sienna turned and looked at him. There was something about the tone of his voice. "Why did you say it like that?"

Jason shrugged. "We can all use a little protecting . . . sometimes." He gazed at the sky. "The stars look like diamonds, don't they? Millions and millions of diamonds."

Sienna looked at the sparkling specks splattered in the midnight-blue sky. "I hadn't thought of them that way," she replied.

"I did," Jason said. "But a lot of things make me think of diamonds."

Sienna put her hand on her hip. "I guess I never should have told you diamonds aren't my fondest subject. You must be one of those guys that likes to tease and pick at a woman's sore spot."

"Nope, not at all."

"Then why do you keep bringing it up?"

"Because it's important." Then Jason said, slowly, "And because I don't think you've told me everything."

Sienna gave an impatient chuckle. "About what?"

"I'm talking about your friend, and his mentioning diamonds during his act in the booth."

"Act?" Sienna was confused. "Believe me, Hawk wasn't acting. And I told you, I don't remember Hawk even mentioning diamonds. That was something Steven said."

"Yes. That's what Steven told me," Jason agreed. "Actually, he told me several things that your friend,

what did you say his name was? Hawk?" He said the
name sarcastically. "That Hawk said."

Sienna put her hand on her forehead. She didn't
like the way this conversation was going, and she
didn't like the change in Jason. "Look, I didn't come
out her to talk about Hawk or diamonds. I thought
you said coming out here would help me forget what
was bothering me, well so much for that." She
turned to walk back to the building.

Jason grabbed her arm. "Not so fast."

"What are you doing?" Sienna pulled back, but his
grip was tight and hard.

"I intend to find out if you're telling the truth,
that's all."

"Telling the truth about what? Let go of my arm!"
she demanded

"Are you sure you don't know anything about what
your friend is planning?"

Sienna shook her head. "You must be crazy. Dawn
told me not to wear this dress. Talk about flies." She
pulled back again. "Let me go."

Jason obeyed, but when Sienna turned to leave
there was a man standing there. "What's going on?"
She looked back at Jason.

Before Sienna could say another word, a tie was
placed across her open mouth. Her heart lurched
and she tried to remove it, but before she could
her hands were restrained and tied behind her
back.

"Take it easy, Charles. We don't want to hurt her in
any way. Because the truth is,"—Jason rubbed the
back of his hand gently down Sienna's bare arm—"I
like her. She's quite a woman."

Sienna tried to scream at him, but the scream

emerged as a gagging sound. So she kicked instead. Her high heel made contact with Charles's leg.

"Damn it!" Charles spewed. "You better watch it lady."

"All right now, Sienna," Jason said with finality. "If you don't behave I'm going to have Charles tie your legs up too. Then he'll have to carry you like a sack of potatoes." He paused. "And that could be quite entertaining with the dress you have on."

Sienna replaced her kicks with a glare.

"That's good." Jason nodded. "I knew we could count on you to cooperate. And because of that I'm going to let you in on the plan." He moved her hair out of her eyes. "You will be my guest tonight. And I hope during your stay you'll decide to share whatever you might know. If not . . ." He shrugged. "We'll move forward to the main purpose of all this. Tomorrow, you will take us to your boyfriend, Hawk. I'm certain he'll have a lot to say either voluntarily or by whatever means it might take." His voice held a threatening note. "Because, Sienna, my dear . . ." Jason paused again. "I haven't been in this business and struggled to make it where I am today to let someone come in, at this point, and pull the rug from underneath me. And that's what I think your friend Hawk is trying to do." He placed his face close to hers. "But I'm telling you now, it won't happen." Jason stepped back and put his hands in his pockets. "Well, I've done enough stargazing for the night, haven't you?" He smiled charmingly. "So if you promise not to try anything funny, we'll accompany you to our car."

Sienna just stood there, her mind whirling. *What in the world is going on? Jason thinks that Hawk and I know something about his diamonds. And he says he wants me to take him to Hawk tomorrow.* She stared at Jason. Now his handsome features looked cynical under the moonlight. *I have no clue what state of mind Hawk is going to be in tomorrow. None at all. He might not be able to say his name, let alone tell this man what he wants to know. And if Hawk is still not himself, he'd be so vulnerable. . . .* She closed her eyes. *There's no way I will take them to Hawk. I don't know what they might do to him.*

"Where is the car, Charles?" Jason asked.

"Sammy's got it parked right over there." Charles's deep voice reverberated into the night.

"Let's go then. Steven will follow later," Jason instructed.

Sienna's high heels sank deep into the sand as they made their way across the beach. Her heart pounded as she searched for a way out of her dilemma, but Jason chatted as if there was nothing unusual about the abduction that was taking place.

He walked beside her. "And Sienna, you know, if this turns out to be a big mistake, I truly beg your pardon, and I hope that we can still do business in the future."

When they reached the car Sienna heard the car doors unlock. *If I get in that car I am done,* she thought looking around for help.

Jason opened the front passenger side door, while Charles opened the back door for Sienna. Charles stepped aside so she could climb in, and Sienna knew that was her chance. With all she had, Sienna tried to elbow him in the groin, but she hit his lower abdomen instead. Still it was enough to bend Charles over, and Sienna took off as fast as she could. Her high heels slapped against the asphalt as she ran toward the hotel, but the shoes and the tight dress were nothing but a hindrance.

"Get her, Charles," Jason barked.

She heard Jason's command, and Sienna tried to run faster. But before she reached the lit area, Charles grabbed her from behind.

"Come here." He pulled her back against him. "I don't have time for this mess. Jason told you I'd tie your legs up if you don't cooperate. But I'm telling you, I'll bandage you up like a mummy if you do this again."

Sienna struggled against Charles's iron grip, but she could tell it did little good. When they reached the car, he threw her onto the backseat and climbed in after her.

Thirty-six

"You want to go again?" Steven asked as the musicians started another number.

"No way," Dawn replied. "I've never known any man who wanted to outdance me, but I think I've met my match in you, Steven."

He laughed.

Dawn wiped her brow and started for the bar. "I'm surprised Sienna and Jason haven't made it back yet."

"I'm not," Steven said. "If I had you underneath the stars I don't think I'd come back early either."

"I guess it's all in the way you look at it," Dawn said as she climbed back onto her barstool. "I'm sure Sienna might be under the stars with Jason, but believe me, her mind is on Hawk."

They sat through a couple more songs and Steven ordered another *mai tai*. With the bartender's prodding, Dawn ordered a *chi-chi*, a blend of vodka, pineapple juice and coconut syrup, without the vodka. Still she was aware of Sienna's absence.

"What in the world could they be doing out there?" Dawn turned and looked at the entrance.

"I wish you'd keep your mind on me and not on Jason and your friend," Steven complained.

Dawn lifted an eyebrow. "I don't really know you."

She didn't appreciate his remark. "And I'm worried about my girlfriend."

Steven looked as if he were about to reply when his cell phone rang. "Excuse me." He removed his phone from his pocket and pressed a button. "Jason . . . Yeah man." He looked at Dawn. "I'm doing fine. How you doin'?"

Dawn watched him as he listened.

"Oh I see. Un-huh." Steven chuckled in a manner that knitted Dawn's brows.

"What's going on?" she asked.

Steven put up his hand as he continued to listen. "Oh sure, man. All right. I feel you. I'll tell Dawn. Later."

"You'll tell Dawn what?" Dawn questioned before he could hang up.

"It seems that your girl and Jason have really connected."

"Connected?" Dawn's head popped to the side.

"Yep. That was him on the phone telling me, and you,"—Steven gave her the eye—"not to worry about them. In other words, Sienna's going to be coming in a little late tonight if at all. . . . And she just wanted you to know, so you wouldn't worry."

"I just can't believe it." Dawn was shocked.

"Well, believe it. That was Jason on the phone. Seems like she's had a few drinks and has gotten real comfortable."

Dawn's face dropped. "Really?"

"Yep. You know all it takes is a couple of these drinks and you're gone." Steven smiled. "They'll send anyone into orbit."

But Sienna wasn't drinking. And I don't believe she drank anything with Jason because she wouldn't want to hurt the baby. Dawn looked down.

"So maybe I can order you something else and put you in the mood your girl's in." He leaned in close.

Dawn sat back. "Excuse you."

"Ahh-h-h, come on now. I could tell you two weren't alike. She had on that dress that pretty much said it all, and here you are in this flowing thing." He pinched up Dawn's long, airy dress and let it float back down on her leg. "I'm just wondering what's underneath there. That's all."

"Well, you're surely not going to find out tonight." Her eyes dared him to touch her again. "And what do you mean Sienna's dress said it all?"

"Don't get offended." Steven sat back and took a swallow of his drink. "I'm just saying a man looks at that kind of thing. And from the looks of her, your girl looked like she could be down for anything."

"Well that's what you get for judging a book by its cover," Dawn retorted. "Because Sienna isn't down for anything you or your friend may have going." She got down from her chair.

"Hey, wait a minute."

Dawn showed him her palm. She tried to keep calm. "And I want your friend's phone number just in case something happens to her."

"I'm not giving you that man's number. If he wanted you to have it—Uh-uh, if she wanted you to have it, they would have said so when he was on the phone."

Dawn didn't know what to say. "All right." She walked away, then turned and looked back at Steven. "I will see you tomorrow. And before that, if anything has happened to my friend . . ." The words were a threat and a promise. It was all she could do to let him know she didn't trust him.

When Dawn reached her room she didn't know

what to do. But one thing was for certain, Steven hadn't been totally truthful with her. Yet, another part of her argued, maybe Sienna did decide to get with Jason. *He's a good-looking man and emotionally I have never seen Sienna like she was tonight.* Her thoughts raged. *So if I report something to the police at this point and she's with Jason because she wants to be . . . it'll be nothing but a mess.*

Still, deep down inside Dawn felt something wasn't right. She sat on her bed. *I'll give Jason and Sienna a few more hours, but after that, I'm going to take some action of my own.* Dawn thought of Hawk returning, and what might happen if Sienna was still with Jason and it was of her own accord. She kicked off her shoes and laid down, clothes and all. Dawn looked at the clock. "God. This could be the biggest mess."

Hawk heard the huna chant once again in his mind. He didn't know how many times it had played over and over again. The chant had become a part of his psyche and his soul, and now Hawk was immersed in feelings. Feelings . . . the one thing, he now realized, he had tried to avoid all of his life, at least from the time his mother passed away. *It's obvious now, I used logic as a way to escape what I was really feeling. Logic was something I could control.*

Hawk realized he was obsessed with controlling what happened in his life. That's why he chose martial arts, to help him control his body, and education was a means of controlling his mind. Now Hawk saw how he used his academic prowess like a shield. A shield that kept people and life at a distance. His academic surroundings made life predictable and he felt safe until he accidentally deciphered the hiero-glyphed crystals.

After that fateful moment, a different existence opened to Hawk. He discovered a part of himself, a part of human potential that soon dominated his life, a potential that Hawk never believed existed—his intuitive mind. And no matter how hard he fought against it, his visionary abilities seemed to grow with each day, revealing things Hawk did not want to know. People's thoughts. Where they were going. What would happen in their futures. But even after years of possessing this heightened sense of knowing, Hawk never understood it and that was the one thing his logical mind demanded. As a result of this dilemma, this split within himself, Hawk could not accept his intuitive mind. It remained foreign to him, alien, evil, and therefore he could not accept himself.

Now Hawk realized it wasn't really the thoughts and knowing the future that plagued him; it was feeling the feelings of the people who were having them. It was the feelings that overwhelmed Hawk. He had spent his entire adult life trying not to feel his own emotions, so to be bombarded by the feelings of others was pure torture. A punishment for what he had ignored within himself.

Hawk opened his eyes, and the first thing he saw was the candle Elikapeka lit before she went inside her bedroom. Lying beside it was the pendulum the Kahuna used in asking the questions that seemed to go on, and on and on. Questions that made Hawk dig inside himself, and eventually see parts of his life and his being that he did not want to see . . . had never thought about revisiting, and had no clue that they had had such an impact on his life.

Now he realized, when he was a child and his neighborhood friends named him "Hawk, the one who was able to fly," the one with special abilities, it meant worlds to him. It made Hawk believe he could reach for the stars, just as his mother had always told him he could. Being deemed special by his peers made Hawk feel special. Before that, growing up without his father, Hawk had felt handicapped, unequal to all those around him.

Secretly, Hawk sought validation in his imagination. He clung to the super characters in the cartoons and supernatural stories the older men told on the porches at night. He envisioned himself as the hero in the unseen world they whispered about over bottles of booze. Now Hawk realized, that was why, when his homeboys named him "Hawk" it meant so much. Hawk realized the name "Hawk" encapsulated for him the impossible, and because of it he felt a closer kinship to the special beings he conjured up in his mind. It was Hawk's means for self-validation, until his mother died.

When she died, Hawk put away all his dreams. There was no room for dreams anymore. The world was a harsh reality full of sadness, where not even God himself came to put life back into the body of the person he loved the most.

So the motherless Hawk could no longer reach for the stars. He did not see them, nor did he believe in them anymore. The pain of his mother's early death made Hawk close off the part of himself that could love, hate, feel jealousy, envy, joy, pride. It wasn't that he didn't have the emotions, Hawk simply refused to acknowledge them, and as he grew into an adult it became second nature.

Hawk believed pursuing a career as an art appraiser

would be safe, then because of a promise, he married an old girlfriend, but she never threatened the vacuum he created internally. Even her death in a car accident could not bring down the wall. But after Hawk deciphered the crystal, all of that changed. His life became one long search for the Stonekeeper. He could no longer hide from his own feelings. Hawk was tortured by anger and hatred toward those he believed were responsible for his plight.

Then I saw Sienna for the first time. Hawk's eyes misted over. *And from the moment I looked into her eyes I knew my heart was no longer closed. It was as if it had been blown open. It was painful yet exciting. Though in the beginning I tried to deny it.*

Hawk looked into the crystal that formed the end of the pendulum. He closed his eyes. He felt drained, but oddly enough, at the same time renewed. Slowly, scenes of he and Sienna together from the moment they met until the present, presented themselves in his mind's eye. All of the feelings they had experienced together passed through him, and somehow as a result of them Hawk knew he was much more of a human being. "How ironic, all this time the most important thing a human being can do is feel their life, truly feel each moment, exactly what I was trying not to do. If it weren't for Sienna, I would have succeeded. If it weren't for Sienna my heart and my life would still be closed."

In a blur, the visions in his mind tumbled forward in time and Hawk saw himself walk up to a house that he did not recognize, yet he knew it was his house. It was a modest place with a yard full of roses. Just as Hawk reached the door, it opened and Sienna was standing there with a baby in her arms. A fat chubby little boy with round cheeks and bright eyes. Amber eyes that Hawk recognized as his own. Sienna greeted him with a kiss as the baby called him Daddy.

Gradually, the vision faded, but Hawk could still feel the love he felt as he held Sienna and their child in his arms. It was more powerful than anything he had ever known. It dwarfed the consuming drive he had used to become an emotionless intellectual, and it turned the pain, heartache and frustration Hawk felt because of his plight as a scarred visionary into nothingness. But at the same time, this love celebrated the love Hawk felt for his mother. It made peace with his young wife's death, but most of all with his mother's passing. For now Hawk understood, as long as her blood flowed in the veins of her descendants she would always be, and it was okay for Hawk to be as well. It was also okay for Hawk to love and be loved.

"Uh-h-h-h." An anguished cry forced its way out of him and Hawk buried his head in his arms. "How selfish could I be? I sent Sienna away because I felt there was no way she could love me. Deep inside I did not believe it was possible. But now I understand why." His hands turned into fists. "Before now, I could not love myself. And in my self-pity and in my fear, I turned away from the one person who opened life to me again." He shook his head. "Yes. Justice will only be found with the Stonekeeper, but Sienna *is* the Stonekeeper." Hawk looked up. "She is the Stonekeeper. They are one in the same. Sienna the woman and Stonekeeper are one. And it is because of Sienna's love for me that justice was always mine. I just had to be able to accept it. She did not judge me for being a visionary. She did not judge my scarred and blistered face. She loved me no matter what, and it wasn't until this very moment that I could truly accept that."

Suddenly, Hawk felt the urge to close his eyes, and his epiphany was replaced by a vision. He saw Dawn twisting and turning in her hotel bed. She was worried about Sienna. Next, he saw Sienna pacing in a strange room, unable to reach the window that she stared out of with frightened, anxious eyes. Then it was over. When he opened his eyes, the candle flame blurred before it came into focus. "Something has happened to Sienna. I could feel the danger around her." Hawk felt a pain in his chest. "Just as I have come to understand my love for her and her love for me."

So much had happened so fast. Hawk felt the world had opened to him, and now the possibility loomed that it could be taken away. In anguish, Hawk accidentally knocked over his chair as he dropped to his knees. He flinched because he could still feel the danger around Sienna. Danger that had not been planned. Hawk could feel it would be an act of violence that resulted from anger. Anger that was not related to Sienna, but related to him. Sienna had been taken because of Hawk, and the man that had taken her would have no problem harming her if he felt it would lead him to Hawk. This man was trying to protect his diamonds. Smuggled diamonds. Diamonds that Hawk had referred to when he was overwhelmed by the vibration of the herkimer diamond.

Hawk looked up into the rafters of the Kahuna's home. For the first time since his mother died he raised his eyes toward heaven, and not to the powers that be. The force that he had hated since he evoked the power of the crystal. This time Hawk raised his eyes to the God of his childhood. The loving God that he believed in so much before his mother's death. The God that Hawk had denounced afterwards.

"I know I have not come to you in a long time. I know you know I turned my back on you, but I've heard you never turn your back on us, and I hope what I've heard is true." His voice broke. "I have been given a vision of Sienna and me, and our child . . . a happy vision. And I want this vision to come true, God, more than I've ever wanted anything in my life. I believe a vision of such love and hope could only come from you. That you have allowed me to see the beautiful possibility of our future." Hawk swallowed. "So I'm asking you now, God, with everything I have, that you allow me to find Sienna before he hurts her." He pressed his fists against his chest. "And God, if you do, I promise with every part of me, that I will never turn my back on you again. I will be your most faithful servant. I will praise your name, and use whatever gift has been given to me for the highest good." Hawk's chin dropped to his chest. "Please God. Please. Don't let Sienna die because of me. Let me use my visionary ability now to find her, or to do whatever you have deemed for me to do." He covered his face with his hands. "I turn my life and my future over to you."

Hawk remained on his knees. Then it dawned on him his face no longer burned, and the skin beneath his hands felt as smooth as that of a newborn baby. Slowly, he slid his hands downward. The blistering rash was gone. "My face! My face is healed! I know it's a sign!" He rose from his knees. "I know it's a sign! Everything will be all right."

Full of hope Hawk picked up the chair and blew

out the candle. When he turned, Elikapeka was standing at her bedroom door.

"What is it?" she asked, wiping her eyes.

"I'm sorry." Hawk could see he had awakened her. "I didn't mean to wake you. But I've got to go." He stepped toward her. "I appreciate everything you've done for me. You opened the door for me to see my life with new eyes, and I will never be able to thank you enough for that."

"The door was always open," Elikapeka replied. "You just decided to walk through it."

Hawk looked down "Well, I hope it's not too late. Sienna is in trouble." He looked up again. "I had a vision. She's been taken somewhere, and she's very afraid. I've got to go find her," he said almost to himself.

"Yes. You must," Elikapeka replied. "I will give you the keys to my truck. Do with it as you will."

Their eyes locked.

"Now you will be able to fully participate in your destiny," the Kahuna continued. "You will not be a pawn. You will be an active, present, participant. The way is yours. Make of it what you will."

Hawk nodded. "Thank you."

He knew Elikapeka had spoken the truth. There was a strength inside of him now, a kind of rod of power that grounded him in the reality that he and Sienna were much more than they had ever been willing to accept. She was the Stonekeeper, and he was her partner. The combination was key. Together they would make a difference for humankind. Together they would make a difference for themselves.

Elikapeka walked over to a small table and picked up a set of keys. Silently, she held them out for Hawk. He stepped up and took them from her.

"I can't thank you enough," He said.

"What you will do, will be *mahalo,* thank you, enough for all of us," she replied. *"Aloha,* Hawk." Elikapeka drew him into her massive arms. "This time we will say good-bye the Hawaiian way." She bent forward and placed her nose against his. For a second Hawk could feel her breath as he knew she could feel his.

Elikapeka drew back. "We have breathed in the breath of each other. We are one Hawk, and now you and the island of Kaua'i are also one. She will be there for you and your Stonekeeper when the time is right." She smiled into his eyes. "Go now. You will see my vehicle parked behind the house, and the road that I carved out over the years with its tires. That road will lead you to the highway."

"Aloha," Hawk said before he turned and went outside.

Hawk found the truck, jumped in, and turned on the headlights. They lit up the path that Elikapeka had told him would be there. Immediately, he pushed on the gas and the truck nearly catapulted into the foliage. Branches beat the vehicle like an ape beating its chest, as Hawk drove as fast as the forest would allow. All the while his mind replayed Dawn twisting in the bed, and Sienna measuring the distance to the window, as if she yearned to escape.

Thirty-seven

Hawk couldn't wait for the hotel elevator doors to open. When they did he ran down the hall to Dawn's room. He wanted to beat on her door but he held back. Hawk knew it was only seconds before it opened, although it seemed much longer.

"Hawk," Dawn said. "Thank God, it's you." She stepped back so that he could enter. "I was just about to go downstairs." She wrung her hands. "I just don't know what to do. Sienna isn't here, and I'm worried something might have happened to her."

"Tell me what happened," Hawk said.

"We went down to the bar just to have a drink and uh . . ." She looked uncomfortable. "The guy who was in the booth next to ours at the gem show, Steven, introduced another fellow to us, a man named Jason. Steven said he worked with him. The next thing I knew Steven and I were dancing, and Sienna was coming over to me saying she and Jason were going outside to look at the stars."

Hawk's eyes narrowed.

Dawn hurried on. "Now don't jump to any conclusions, because she wasn't interested in that man, Hawk. I know she wasn't." She looked exasperated. "Whatever had gone down between the two of you had her in such a state that I think she was just trying to get away from it. But that was all. Believe me."

Hawk felt something heavy press against his chest. He took a deep breath. "Then what happened?"

Dawn's hands covered her mouth. "That's the last time I saw her. Steven and I danced for a while, then we sat at the bar. I remember asking where they could possibly be, and Steven got this phone call. He said it was Jason." She looked down. "Afterwards he said, uh, not to worry about when Sienna would get back, because as he put it,"—Dawn paused—"she and Jason had hit it off, and she would be coming in really late, if at all." Her last words were barely audible.

Despite all the deep breakthroughs Hawk had experienced with the Kahuna and his love for Sienna, the thought of her being with another man sparked some jealousy. "But you stand here and tell me you didn't believe this Steven, but yet you didn't go to the police?"

Dawn continued to look down. "I didn't believe him, but you two have been going through so much for the last few months I just . . . I wasn't sure." She looked at him with apologetic eyes. "So, I decided to wait and give her a little more time before I did anything."

God, don't let the madness I was going through be the thing that has forced Sienna into another man's arms. Hawk waited before he spoke. "Sienna is in trouble. That's what is important." He forced the thought that Sienna may have gone with Jason of her own accord aside. "Do you know where they went?"

"No. All I know is what I told you. That they went out to the beach behind the hotel to look at the stars."

"That's as good a place as any to start looking for her." Hawk reached for the doorknob.

"I'm going with you," Dawn said as he opened the door.

"I think we might be better off if you stayed here."

"I can't." Dawn followed him into the hall. She kept up with Hawk's rapid steps as he walked toward the elevator. "I was about to go crazy in there waiting for Sienna. For the phone to ring. Anything."

The elevator opened and they stepped in. Hawk pushed the button for the lobby.

"I still think we would be better off if you stayed in your room and waited. I don't want you getting caught up in this. What's happened to Sienna is my fault, and it's my responsibility to get her out."

Steven sat at the bar and took another drink of his fifth *mai tai*. He eyed the woman that had been giving him the eye for the last few minutes. Steven wondered if he should take her up on what he felt was an invitation. To Steven, it was a much more pleasant alternative to what he felt probably lay ahead. *Smuggling diamonds is one thing, and making money off of the diamond trade. No one really gets hurt. At least I've never personally known of anyone to get hurt. But kidnapping a woman is a whole different ball game.*

Steven took another drink as he thought about Jason. He had always been a strange kind of a guy. Eccentric would not be the proper word, although Jason did things that, in Steven's mind, sometimes made little sense at all. But what came to mind now was not Jason's eccentricities, but his nature. Steven knew beneath his cultured exterior lay a man with no tolerance for anything or anybody that got in the way of his making money. *I didn't plan to be a part of any abduction, and I surely don't want to be a part of anything else,* he thought as he stared at the woman who stared back. *I got into this stuff with Jason because it was a way to keep money in my pockets without filling out applications and answering questions that weren't going to do me any good in the end, especially if I told the truth. Hell, how does a man ever recover from having a felony on his record? You want to go down the right road, but once you have a felony on your record there's simply no turning back. Not if you really want to make some money. Especially if you're not the smartest man on the block.* Steven gave the woman what he thought was a sultry look. *If I could have been a doctor or a lawyer or something of that sort, I would have done it, but I wasn't born with the brains for that kind of thing. But I was born with a desire for the kind of money they can bring in, actually . . . a desire for more.* He drained his glass. *But when we were growing up Jason had the brains for it, and the background, but as he told me years ago, those jobs didn't bring the kind of excitement he wanted. Being a doctor or a lawyer was too dull for Jason's blood. And when he discovered the diamond trade, the fringe activities of the diamond trade, Jason knew he had found his niche.* Steven wiped his mouth. He didn't know which was bigger, Jason's ego or his need for excitement. *But eventually he invited me to share in the money. For quite a while now it has been good.* Steven admitted to himself. *But now, this woman and this kidnapping thing, just doesn't feel good.*

Steven wondered if Jason wasn't paddling up the abduction stream just for the excitement of it all. *Well, I'm going to take my time going back to the condo, and I believe the little lady here is going to provide me with the kind of distraction I need to make it worth my while.*

He plopped a twenty-dollar bill on the bar and got up somewhat off balance from the stool. Steven kept eye contact with the woman as he walked over and joined her on the other side of the bar.

She looked at him, smiled, and looked away.

"Hello," Steven said, giving her what he felt was his most inviting smile.

"Hi," she replied.

"Couldn't help but notice you sitting here."

"Really," she said.

"Really." He leaned in a little closer. "I couldn't help but notice how you were looking at me."

She glanced at him. "I think you're the one who was looking at me. Every time I looked up I looked straight into your face."

Steven looked down and shook his head. *You would think after such a strong come-on she wouldn't be playing this kind of game. But what can I say? I'll play it a little while. As long as it gets me what I want.* He raised his head slightly and looked at her. "Well, I guess in the end, what difference does it make who was looking at who? As long as we know we're both interested."

"Interested in what?" a man said from behind him.

Steven looked at the woman who had a strange knowing smile on her face, before he leaned his neck back and looked over his head. "Am I missing something here?"

The man moved around and stood behind the woman. "Yeah, you are. So I think you better get your drunk ass up and away from my wife."

Steven's eyes closed and opened slowly. "Your wife?" he chuckled. "Some wife. Man, you need a leash on this woman, because she was surely giving me the eye."

The next thing Steven knew he was being shoved into the chair behind him, which rattled loudly before it hit the ground.

* * *

The elevator door opened and Hawk and Dawn stepped out into the lobby.

"I don't know, Hawk." Dawn looked around. "I can't stay here and do nothing. Just let me come with you down to the beach."

All of a sudden a clattering sound came from the direction of the bar. They both turned. Dawn grabbed Hawk's arm.

"That's Steven. The guy I was dancing with. I'm going to go over there and ask him where Sienna is." Dawn started forward but Hawk pulled her back.

"Wait," he commanded in a hushed voice.

They watched Steven back away from a man and a woman at the bar, and walk through the lobby with an inebriated lean. Hawk and Dawn hung back as he staggered through the front automatic doors.

"I'm going to follow him," Hawk said. "But I'm asking you, Dawn,"—there was a plea in his voice—"to go back up to your room. Somebody's got to be here in case Sienna returns, or calls."

Dawn looked at Steven as he disappeared down the walkway outside the hotel. "Okay," she said reluctantly. She took hold of Hawk's wrist. "But you be careful, you hear? And bring Sienna back." Her anxious eyes searched his.

"I will," Hawk replied. He watched Dawn get on the elevator and the doors close.

Hawk started to follow Steven outside, but he stopped when Steven turned and headed back toward the hotel. Quickly, Hawk faced the elevator and acted as if he were waiting. Over his shoulder, he watched Steven reenter the lobby and cross over to the hotel counter.

"Hey. There aren't any cabs outside," Steven said, his words slightly slurred.

"No sir, there aren't," the hotel clerk replied. "Would you like for me to call you a cab?"

"I wouldn't be standing here if I didn't," Steven replied.

"One will be here in a moment, sir," the attendant assured him politely.

"Thanks." Steven patted the counter before he walked toward the entrance and back outside.

Hawk waited for the opportune moment to slip out of the hotel and over to Elikapeka's truck. There he sat with the lights off, and waited for the cab to appear. He thought about what Dawn had told him, and her uncertainty about Sienna and the man, Jason. *But as the Kahuna said, I am no longer a pawn in this game,* Hawk fortified himself, *I am going to meet my life and this cycle of the Stonekeeper head on. I own my part in it, and I will not let my jealousy rule over me. Instead, I thank God that this man, Steven, is still here, and for the path He has laid out for me to find Sienna.*

Hawk watched the cab pull in front of the hotel and Steven climb inside. Moments later it pulled off, and Hawk trailed not far behind. The ride was relatively short, before they stopped in front of a complex of upscale condominiums. Hawk watched Steven get out of the cab and slam the door. As the vehicle pulled off Steven shook himself, ran his hands over his hair then walked up the walkway. It took awhile before the door opened and Steven disappeared inside.

Thirty-eight

"You must have been having a mighty good time, Steven," Jason said, lying back in a white leather recliner.

"I would say so." Steven hoped the amount of alcohol he had consumed wasn't too obvious.

"Smells like you brought the entire bar with you," Charles remarked as he walked away from the front door.

"Have you been drinking?" Jason asked.

Steven shrugged. "You know me. I had a few, but I can handle my liquor."

"I hope so," Jason replied. "Because tonight of all nights, we don't need any screw-ups. I need everybody to be on their toes."

"You don't have to worry about me, Jason." Steven walked stiffly toward the nearest chair and sat down. "I can handle myself."

Jason sat and watched him before he spoke again.

"What about Sienna's friend?" Jason lifted a silky eyebrow. "Did she buy the phone call and my saying Sienna and I really connected?"

"Yeah. I believe she did." Steven's head wobbled a bit as he nodded. "She asked a few questions, but after that she just told me that she'd see me tomorrow."

"Well, she should have believed it," Jason replied. "Because it's the truth."

Steven's reddish eyes looked at Jason's closed bedroom door that was normally open. Then he looked back at Jason.

"As a matter of fact, I'm about to finish what I started before you knocked on the door. Sienna was beginning to feel a little more at home here, and I think I was making headway winning her over to our side."

"How has she been doing?" Steven asked as he looked down.

"Just fine. Fine," Jason repeated unnecessarily.

Steven looked up. Mistrust emanated from his bloodshot eyes.

"You don't have to worry about me, Steven. I know you can be a little soft-hearted at times, but I intend to handle her with kid gloves. That is unless something else is called for." Jason rose from the chair smiling.

"Did she agree to take you to her boyfriend tomorrow?" Steven hoped the woman had.

"No," Jason replied. "Not yet. But I'm certain that I will be able to convince her." His voice held a creepy tone.

Steven watched Jason walk over to the bedroom door and unlock it. His stomach griped as Jason entered the room and closed the door behind him.

Sienna stepped back from where she was trying to listen through the bedroom door. *Convince me?* she thought. *There is nothing he can do to me that will make me take him to Hawk. In the state Hawk was in when I last saw him, he would be defenseless against Jason and his thugs.* Sienna looked around the room. *So what am I going to do?*

She had already searched the drawers of the bedroom, and found only a couple of expensive-looking tops inside. Again, Sienna looked for something to throw through the window as a call for help, but they had made sure, with the small chain that was attached to her ankle, nothing heavy was within her reach.

Desperate, Sienna ran to the bathroom and threw open the medicine cabinet. A travel bag was on one of the shelves, along with a couple of boxes of gauze. Quickly, she unzipped the bag and rummaged through it. *If I could only find a razor blade,* she thought as she heard a key being inserted in the lock of the bedroom door.

Sienna zipped up the bag and dashed back into the bedroom. She took a step back as Jason entered and locked the door behind him. His eyes were steady as he looked at her.

"I just thought I'd come in here and check on you. See how you're doing."

Sienna glanced at the locked door. Then she looked at Jason. "I could be better."

"Well, if you cooperate,"—he smiled and his eyes revealed his intent before he raised a key in the air— "I'll unchain you." Jason placed the key on a table that was out of Sienna's reach.

She folded her arms across her body.

"Have you thought about tomorrow?" Jason continued.

Before she realized it, Sienna took another step backwards. "Of course I have. I've thought about that among other things."

Jason advanced leisurely in her direction before he turned and sat on the bed. "I don't want you to worry yourself, Sienna. You see, this is not about worrying. Tonight, I want you to get a good night's sleep so you will be rested tomorrow. That way, I'm sure you'll have a clear head and things will go exactly as they should. You'll be happy, and I'll be happy." He took off his shoes. Then he began to unbutton his shirt.

Sienna stiffened. "What are you doing?"

"Just getting comfortable." He gave her an unhurried glance. "I can't go to bed like this."

Sienna looked at the bed. She looked at Jason, then at the chain connected to her ankle. All of it, topped by his leisurely manner, infuriated her. "I know you don't intend to sleep in here." The words tumbled out before Sienna could stop them.

Jason studied her before he replied. "That's exactly what I intend to do."

Sienna's lips tightened. "Then I refuse to be in here with you." She strode purposefully toward the door. She had overheard the conversation between Jason and Steven, and Sienna thought if she unlocked it, Steven might come to her aid. But before she reached the door Jason grabbed her from behind. His arms locked around her waist, nearly cutting off her breath.

"Wait a minute." His lips grazed her ear as he squeezed her even harder. "You don't run anything around here. I do." Jason pulled her away from the door as he spoke. His warm breath sent chills down Sienna's spine. "And you don't have any choice but to obey me." One of his hands mauled her breast.

"Obey you?" Sienna spat. "I don't want anything to do with you." She brought her spiked heel down on Jason's socked foot.

"Aaargh!"

Sienna ran for the door again. She tried to unlock

it but her hands shook too much. She banged on it instead. "Steven! Let me go! Please!" Her head jerked back as Jason grabbed her hair.

"I'm going to have to teach you a lesson. I can see that right now." His voice sounded raspy. "And you can believe before I'm done with you, you'll be begging to do whatever I tell you to."

Hawk hung within the cover of some flowering trees. His entire being froze when he caught a glimpse of Sienna running past the third-floor window of the building Steven had entered. A million thoughts went through his mind, before he heard a pain-filled cry. *Sienna! My God, he's hurting, Sienna!*

Without thought Hawk scaled the tree as if he was born to it. Moments later he was looking directly through the window, and what he saw filled him with anger. Sienna was struggling to free her hair from the grip of a man who looked as if he derived pleasure from inflicting pain.

In a split second, Hawk grabbed the branch above him with both hands, swung his body backwards and flung himself feet first through the window.

"Hawk!" Sienna cried.

His unanticipated entry was enough to allow her to break free from Jason, but before the sound of Hawk's name stopped ringing in the air, he delivered a powerful blow to Jason's chest. It knocked Jason across the room. Unconscious, Jason slumped against the wall.

Sienna ran into Hawk's arms. "Hawk! You're okay. Thank God, you're okay."

For a moment they drank in each other's eyes.

"What's going on in there?" someone demanded from outside the bedroom door.

"We've got to get out of here," Hawk said as he looked at the chain around Sienna's ankle. "Duck, Sienna." And she knew not to disobey him. Before Sienna could stop Hawk, he spun and used his arm to break the spindle of the bed to which Sienna was chained.

"You're bleeding!" Sienna cried as a large, dark stain on his shirt clung near his shoulder.

He looked down at the wound, but said, "I've got to get that shackle off of your leg."

"There's a key over there," Sienna pointed.

"We've got to get inside!" one man commanded from outside the bedroom door.

"Well, break the door down!" another shouted.

Hawk grabbed the key and freed Sienna. Then he took her hand and pulled her toward the window. It was moist with blood.

"The area below your shoulder is busted wide open." Sienna grimaced at how his shirt melded into the blood-filled wound.

"Come on, Sienna." Hawk urged as the bedroom door rattled. "There's nothing we can do about it right now."

"Wait." She tore away from him. "Just let me get a roll of gauze."

"We don't have time," Hawk warned as she grabbed some gauze from the medicine cabinet and slipped it into the top of her dress.

By then Hawk had opened the broken window. He took hold of a branch with one arm, and circled Sienna's waist with the other. "Here. Grab this," he said, as he swung her toward the tree.

Sienna hung onto the branch, and made her way to the trunk of the tree. She kicked off her shoes and scampered down with Hawk not far behind. When

Sienna looked up at the window, Steven was standing there. Their eyes locked. For a moment he said nothing, but as she jumped from the tree to the ground Sienna heard Steven yell, "They're right outside."

Hawk took her hand. "This way." He made a mad dash for the truck. But before they could reach it, Charles appeared outside the condo with a gun.

"Stop," he demanded. "Stop." Charles raised the weapon and pointed it at them.

As quick as a flash Hawk changed directions. "In here." He ran into the nearest brush, dragging Sienna behind him. "They'll have a harder time finding us!"

Sienna felt as if her breath had been yanked out of her as Hawk pulled her into the plants. Once again, she found herself on her knees.

"Are you all right?" he asked.

"Yes. Yes." She struggled to her feet.

"Where did they go?" Jason yelled, not far away.

"They ran into the bushes," Charles replied.

Sienna held on to Hawk with both hands.

"Well, dammit! Follow them!"

That was the last thing Sienna heard as she and Hawk took off running again. The plants whizzed by her ears, and she could barely see Hawk in front of her it was so dark beneath the canopy of trees. But there was one of Sienna's senses that worked overtime. Her ears seem to pick up every noise Charles made as he pursued them.

They continued to flee, and Sienna flinched when her foot struck something hard, but she did not falter. She didn't know how much longer she could hold out, but Sienna pressed on anyway. "Did you hear that?" The wind carried Hawk's words to her ears.

Sienna looked behind her. She did not see Charles nor could she hear him. "Hear what? Do you hear him coming?"

"No," Hawk replied. "The sound's not coming from behind us. It's in the front of us. It sounds like music."

Sienna strained to hear what Hawk was hearing, but the sound of them crashing through the brush seemed to drown out everything else. But it was only a matter of seconds before Sienna heard the music too. At first it was subtle, but then it grew louder. The melody was uplifting and beautiful, a hypnotic East Indian tune. It was surreal compared to the feeling of Charles with a gun on their tail. "I wonder what's going on." Sienna asked.

Finally, Hawk slowed his run to a rapid walk, and no sooner had Sienna slowed down too, then they emerged out of the bush. A group of people were congregated nearby. Sienna looked about her as she removed the box of gauze from her dress and held it in her hand. People were sitting on the ground and on rocks. Only a few of them sat in chairs. Most focused on a belly dancer who was performing on stage to the music Sienna and Hawk had heard.

Sienna walked close to Hawk, covering the blood that stained his shirt with her body. But she also hung close just to feel him, as they passed by a small, tented market where vendors were selling jewelry, books and food. Sienna could feel Hawk internally slowing down as they endeavored to get lost in the crowd and that wasn't difficult to do. A large ring of candles provided the majority of the light at the gathering, along with a couple of spotlights that pointed toward the stage and to the market.

As they made their way around, Sienna looked behind her. She saw Charles emerge from the brush. "Charles is here." She clung to Hawk's arm.

Thirty-nine

Hawk nodded his awareness of Charles's presence, and he maneuvered over to a hill of jagged stones where several children played high on top. Hawk and Sienna went behind the mountainous structure, and quietly out of the crowd's sight. Just as Sienna felt she could go no further, they came to a nearly hidden opening inside the rocks. She and Hawk slipped in and went deep inside.

Once they stopped Sienna slumped to her knees. She was grateful for the soft plants beneath her. Hawk sat down as well. He leaned against the wall before he pulled her into his arms. They didn't say a word as they sat and caught their breaths. Eventually, Sienna closed her eyes and listened to the music. She was thankful that Hawk had come. Thankful that he was well. Thankful that they were together.

Hawk and Sienna stayed wrapped in each other's arms until the music stopped. Sienna didn't know, between the two of them, who held the other the tightest, but when she opened her eyes and moved just a little, she felt something sticky against her face. Sienna realized she had been lying against Hawk's wound and he hadn't said a word. "I'm hurting you." She pulled back, quickly.

"No." Hawk shook his head. "Now you're hurting

me." Hawk looked into her face. "Now that you are out of my arms, you are hurting me."

Although it was dark inside the opening, enough moonlight filtered through the staggered slabs for Sienna to make out Hawk's features. Especially his eyes, which seemed alight with something special from within.

Hawk pulled her into his arms again. "This is where you belong, Sienna. You belong with me, every part of you. Sienna the woman. Sienna the Stonekeeper. It does not matter because I love you and I always will."

She threw her arms around his neck and covered his face with kisses. "I love you too, Hawk. I've always loved you, and I always will. There is nothing that will ever change that."

When her lips found his, they clung together, savoring each and every moment. Savoring the sacredness of their union. Through the kiss Sienna and Hawk acknowledged the miracle of their lives, and the miracle of their love. Sienna only moved away when she felt Hawk wince as he tried to pull her closer.

"Wait," she said, then she kissed his eyelids. "I *am* hurting you. You must let me bandage that."

Hawk was reluctant to let her go, but Sienna gently extracted herself and opened the box of gauze. Hawk began to unbutton his shirt, but Sienna gently stopped him. Tenderly, her fingers unfastened the buttons and pulled the shirt from his shoulder. Afterwards, she kissed the area above his wound.

Sienna removed the gauze from the box and began to unwrap it. Suddenly, she felt two cool, hard objects fall into her hand. When she looked down, despite the thin moonlight, two large diamonds sparkled with an alluring light.

"Hawk! Look!" She held her hand out for him to see.

"So these are the diamonds. These are what this is all about." He took his finger and moved them around in her hand. "Those men are diamond smugglers, Sienna, and they think we are trying to cut into their stash."

"And we have." Her eyes filled with apprehension.

Hawk nodded, slowly. "Yes, we have. But obviously it's a part of a bigger plan." He touched her face. "And Sienna, there's one thing I've finally learned, and that is not to fight the wind that is our lives. To fight who we are is useless." Hawk kissed her, lightly. "You now hold these diamonds in your hand because it is a part of God's plan."

Sienna's eyes opened wide before they filled with tears.

Jason ran past Steven and into his bedroom. He nearly tripped as he entered the bathroom, threw open the medicine cabinet door and looked at the contents. As he had feared, a box of gauze was missing. "Which one of you bastards are playing the candle from both ends?" he roared.

"Wha-at?" Steven slurred.

"You heard me. Somebody is working all ends of this deal, and they're going to wish that they weren't when I get through with them."

Steven entered the bedroom. Jason's eyes were beaming anger.

"Man, calm down. What are you talking about?"

"I'm talking about the damn diamonds that are missing. My diamonds that that woman took." He could barely speak he was so angry. "And I know one of you set me up."

"Do you know how crazy that sounds?" Steven asked, the alcohol loosening his tongue. "One of us helped you? One of us helped *her?*" he corrected himself. "We didn't even know the woman was going to be in here. So how can you say we're playing the candle at both ends?"

"Well, how did she know some of the diamonds were in the gauze? Tell me that?" The veins bulged in Jason's neck. "How did she know?"

"Diamonds in the gauze?" Steven reared back. "I know you're not telling me you hid the diamonds in some gauze?"

"What's going on?" Sammy asked from behind Steven.

Steven turned, almost laughing. "Our fearless leader, Jason here, hid the damn diamonds in some gauze in his bathroom."

"Say what?" Sammy seemed confused as he looked from Steven to Jason.

"I'm telling you, man, the diamonds," Steven laughed, "he hid them in—"

"Ah-hhh!" Jason roared before he latched on to Steven's throat. "I'm going to kill you. Nobody messes with me like that. Do you hear me? Nobody."

Steven's eyes bulged as he tried to move Jason's hands, but the madness in Jason's eyes revealed itself in his strength.

"Stop, Jason! Stop!" Sammy warned, but he kept his distance. "If you kill Steven it won't do us any good. You certainly won't get the diamonds back this way." He tried to reason with him. "And eventually we'll have the cops all over the place."

Jason stopped just as abruptly as he started, but his

hands remained around Steven's neck. Finally, he backed away.

Steven's face contorted. His mouth moved as if he was trying to speak but only a strangulated cough emerged.

"Somebody told that woman where those diamonds were." Jason's eyes narrowed as he looked at Steven and Sammy.

Sammy threw up his hands. Steven tried to reply but couldn't.

"Well, you can believe I'm going to get to the bottom of this," Jason warned. "But first I'm going to get my diamonds back. And I don't care who gets hurt in the process."

Forty

Sienna looked down at the sparkling diamonds. "But how? How did I—"

"You know how, Sienna. You know how," Hawk said firmly. "You are a Stonekeeper. The Last of the Stonekeepers. It doesn't matter that that sounds so grand. So out of your reach. It is who you are! But at the same time you are just a woman. You are just Sienna Russell, a shopkeeper, and the woman I love. You can be all of those things, Sienna. That's what I've realized with the Kahuna's help." He bore deep into her eyes. "That's what I have accepted about you, about myself. I am Hennessy 'Hawk' Jackson. I am a visionary, but I am an ordinary man. We are all much more than we believe we are. The key is to accept our grandness, and to be it to the best of our ability, and to understand that it is our right."

Sienna looked down at the diamonds and she shook her head as she looked back at Hawk. "But why us, Hawk? Why?"

"Why not us?" he replied. "We are a part of God, Sienna, just like all things are. All things. Be they ugly or beautiful. Be they our heart's content or our greatest fear." He took her shoulders in his hands. "And it is through those things that frighten us the most that God is reaching out to us in a way that says wake up. Wake up, Sienna, the Last of the Stone-keepers. Wake up, Hennessy 'Hawk' Jackson, visionary, intellectual. Wake up! You can be any and all things, because I am any and all things, and you are my creation."

Overwhelmed by what Hawk said and his vehemence, Sienna looked down. Silently, she picked up the empty box of gauze and dropped the diamonds inside of it. With hands that trembled, she began to tend Hawk's wound again.

"Do you hear me, baby?" Hawk asked softly. "Do you? All this time we've been battling, you and I, struggling with our reason for being together. Yes. I admit it now. I *was* struggling. I knew I loved you, but I was afraid that I needed you more as the Stone-keeper to help me out of my own personal hell. I was afraid that my need for you, my fear, was greater than my love, and that's what you felt. You felt that from me, Sienna. That's why you always threw it in my face. But you don't have to throw it in my face anymore." Gently, he turned her chin toward him, and made her look into his eyes. "No more, baby. There is nothing, nothing greater than my love for you, and if I do love the Stonekeeper, I know now, it is simply an extension of my love for Sienna, the woman."

Sienna stared down at the strip of gauze before she bent over and tore it with her teeth. Finally, she tucked the end against Hawk's body and then the tears were streaming down her face. Tears of gratitude. Tears from exhaustion. Tears of hope, a real hope, for their future. Sienna didn't know why she couldn't lift her head up and allow Hawk to see how she really felt. It was so overwhelming. Maybe it was the weight of all of it.

"Come here." Hawk wrapped his arms gently

around her and pulled her to him. "My woman. My Stonekeeper," he whispered against her hair. "My Sienna. My love."

Her body trembled as Sienna placed her arms around him. Hawk trembled too. Sienna felt as if for the first time they were truly one and the love she felt was so profound that there was no barrier it could not cross.

Gently, she pulled back and looked into Hawk's eyes. Her hands went to his face, and she stroked it over and over again. The face she had loved for so many years, the face of the man that would be the father of her child, the face of the man that she knew loved her as much as he loved himself.

Their lips were drawn into another kiss that was the essence of love, the essence of sweetness. Afterwards Sienna decided of all the poets, through all the ages, there had never been a poet who had expressed the substance of the kiss she had shared with Hawk. Not Rumi. Not Elizabeth Barrett Browning. No one had relayed this kind of bliss.

Sienna's tears flowed like nectar from her eyes, and that's when she realized Hawk had tears too. "Oh-h Hawk," she said softly. She kissed the salty drops, kissed them, hoping it would help heal the wounds that they had inflicted on each other through the years. The wounds that they had unconsciously made in the name of love, but in truth, it had been in the name of fear. "Hawk. Hawk." Her lips touched his face in feathery motions. "Hawk, my love, my man, the father of my child. I love you."

She felt his body still. "What did you say?" he asked as her lips continued to caress his face.

She repeated the words softly. "I said, 'Hawk, my love, my man, the father of my child.'"

This time it was Hawk who gently pulled back. "You are pregnant."

"Yes," she answered.

"Oh God." He threw his head back. "Oh God." When he pulled her into his arms again, he buried his face in her shoulder, and Sienna held him as if he were a babe in her arms. "I have experienced a rebirth today, Sienna, and I pray that I will be allowed to experience the birth and life of my child."

Again his lips came down on hers. Sienna felt submerged in the whitewaters of an unadulterated love. Hawk turned Sienna over onto her back, and gently laid her against the moist ground. "This body is the body of my love, the body of the mother of my child. It is a temple," he said as his fingers lightly traced her arm, then proceeded to her ear. "The temple of love where I have worshipped for eight years. I am so honored, Sienna, that God has blessed me with your love. Not every man has been able to feel this. I know that now." He spoke into her eyes. "I know that we are special, we are blessed, not only because of who we are as the Stonekeeper and the visionary, but for the love that we have shared. How many people spend their entire lifetime longing for what we have known? But I know one thing . . ." Hawk closed his eyes. "I will never take it for granted again. Never."

"Nor will I," Sienna said, touching his lips.

In silent agreement they removed their clothes and Hawk's head lay gently between her breasts. Appreciatively, he rubbed his face against her body, where the mark of the crystal lie. When Hawk kissed the mounds that framed it, there was no hurry in his touch. But there was a knowing of the priceless gift that he had been given, the gift of love for a woman who loved him just as much as he loved her.

Hawk worshipped Sienna with his lips, and caressed her with his hands, and the love that emanated from this made Sienna forget that they were lying on the ground between craggy rocks. Made her forget Jason and Charles, the people outside and the children playing high above them. For all the feeling that welled up inside of her, she could have been lying on a bed of roses. Roses handpicked by Hawk.

Sienna focused on the warm, downward trail of kisses that Hawk made, but something inside of her wanted him to stop. She wanted to be able to look into Hawk's eyes and to tell him how much she cared. "No, my darling." She helped to pull him up. "Come here, to me. I want to see you. I want to see your face. I want to see your eyes, Hawk. Your eyes. The eyes that have haunted me and loved me for so long."

Slowly, he did her bidding, and when his rock-hard chest pressed against her breasts, they hugged again.

"I've never been so present for you before," Hawk said as he held her close. "I've never known how. I had to hold part of me back. It was the part that was afraid to give completely. It was a part that was afraid I wouldn't be enough for you."

"But you always were enough," Sienna assured him. "Even from the very beginning. And you've always been the light of my heart."

They caressed and rubbed against each other, and as the moments passed, every inch of skin became a sensuous instrument, an instrument of love. Sienna slid her leg between Hawk's and she pressed her feet against his. It seemed every nuance was an incendiary message, and the fire within their bodies grew. But there was no need for acrobatics, no need to prove themselves, because for the first time Hawk and Sienna truly knew and accepted their love.

His mouth covered hers in another kiss and as Sienna moaned, Hawk chose that moment to enter her. Sienna's moistness had barely settled around him before Hawk could feel her pending orgasm as it pressed her insides, until it bubbled into fullness. An orgasm sparked by their love.

A passionate sigh eased from her trembling lips and Hawk stilled his body as their tongues met again. Patiently, Hawk waited for Sienna to come back to him from her place of ecstasy and when she did, he knew his time had come.

Hawk took advantage of her parted lips, savored her mouth, and he entered her repeatedly for the sake of closeness, for the sake of love. As Hawk's body mounted in speed he pulled Sienna's legs up and placed them around his body. It was there that he found it, a place within her that tingled like ecstasy itself, and it sent shockwaves through them as Hawk strummed it over and over again.

Finally, after a time of unsurpassed pleasure, Hawk reached his own release, and Sienna found rapture again as their lips melded in a kiss.

Forty-one

"Have you two seen Keith?" a concerned female voice demanded from someone outside.

Startled, Sienna pulled Hawk to her in an effort to cover her nakedness.

"Yes, we saw him," a child replied. "He was playing over there on the rocks."

"When was that?" the woman demanded.

"A couple of minutes ago."

"Keith. Keith," she called, her voice fading as she passed the opening.

"See, she's not coming in here," Hawk whispered in Sienna's ear.

But still Sienna and Hawk swiftly put on their clothes and slipped out of the enclosure, just as the woman returned. She eyed them suspiciously.

"I'm looking for my son. You haven't seen a little boy, have you?"

"No," Sienna replied as Hawk put his arm around her.

"Mama," a voice called from above them.

"Is that you, Keith?" She looked up and irritation replaced the relief in her voice. "You come on down here. Didn't I tell you not to climb up that far?"

The boy jumped down from the rocks and Sienna

watched the mother put her arms firmly but gently around his shoulders.

"You've got to learn to obey me. You see how dark it is out here? What would have happened if you had had an accident?"

The boy looked down. "I'm sorry. But I didn't have an accident."

The woman took him by the hand and began to walk away. "But that's not the point, Keith." Her next words faded as they disappeared around the rocks.

"Oh." Sienna frowned and touched her abdomen.

"What is it?" Hawk's eyes filled with concern.

"I feel sick to my stomach." She tried to breathe through the nausea. "There was so much on my mind I guess I forgot to eat." Sienna looked at Hawk.

"It's the baby," Hawk said, gently touching her middle.

Their eyes met.

"You need something to eat," Hawk concluded.

He led her to the edge of the rocks. The crowd had thinned to a few stragglers and the market vendors were shutting down their booths.

"Do you see any of them?" Hawk asked.

"No." Sienna touched his arm.

"All right. Well, maybe I can get that vendor over there to sell us a little something before she puts everything away." Hawk stepped from behind the rock.

"Careful," she whispered as he moved away.

Sienna watched Hawk walk over to the vendor, who was bagging up the last of some freshly fried taro chips. Sienna saw the woman nod her head. She gave Hawk a bag of chips and he put something in her hand. Hawk turned to come back to her but Sienna's heart lurched when she saw Steven, Sammy, and Jason step out of the foliage.

"Isn't that him?" Steven shouted.

Hawk turned at the sound of Steven's voice, then quickly yelled to Sienna. "Run, Sienna." As he ran toward her.

Sienna ran back behind the rocks and she could hear Hawk close behind as she reentered the foliage.

"Whatever you do, don't look back," Hawk warned. "It will only slow you down."

A deep rushing sound permeated the air as Sienna tried to zigzag through the forest, but it was obvious her tactic was doing little good. "I'm getting tired, Hawk," she gasped over her shoulder.

"I know, but try to keep going." He tried to take her hand and move in front of her.

"I don't think I can." Sienna filled with fear. "And oh my God! Look what's ahead of us! A waterfall! There's no way to get around it." Shocked, she stopped running.

Hawk took her face in his hands. "Then you've got to do what I tell you. Go!" He shoved her gently. "Hide over there!"

"No!" Sienna refused.

"I'm going to take care of them," Hawk assured her. "But I want you to go."

"No!" Sienna insisted. "They've got a gun!"

"Sienna." He grabbed her shoulders. "I love you." Hawk looked deep into her eyes. "And no matter what happens to me, if you and my baby live, I live. Don't you understand that?"

"No, Hawk!" Sienna put her arms around his neck.

He pulled away. "Sienna, if you love me, you will go! Now!"

They could hear the men yelling.

Torn, Sienna ran into the brush as Jason and his gang emerged.

"There he is!" Jason screamed. "But don't let that crazy-eyed bastard get near you. You better shoot him. Shoot him now," Jason commanded.

Charles looked at Hawk who stood still as death. "I'm not just going to shoot the man. He's not doing nothing. He's simply standing there. Hell, it's four of us and one of him."

As Charles turned his head to look at Jason, Hawk ran forward and exploded in a flying jump kick, knocking the gun out of Charles's hand.

"See there? I told you." Jason scrambled for the weapon. When he reached the gun, he picked it up and pointed it toward Hawk. "I got to do every damn thing myself. Where are the diamonds?" he demanded.

Hawk silently stared Jason down.

"Where are they?" Jason shouted, shaking the gun.

"Right here," Sienna said as she stepped out of the foliage. She removed the diamonds from the box and held them in her outstretched palm. Her heart was beating extremely fast, but she could not let Hawk face Jason and the smugglers alone. Sienna could not let Hawk die.

"Sienna! No!" Hawk cried.

Sienna glanced at Hawk. "I love you, Hawk, and I love our baby, but I can't let you die." Her voice trembled with the fear that he might be killed, and her determination to keep him alive. Suddenly, as if her love for Hawk was the opening, every feeling of every person present became known to Sienna. Hawk's love for her, and his willingness to die so she and their child might live. Jason's anger, and his obsession over the diamonds and the lifestyle they provided. Charles and Sammy's desire to be more than tools for Jason, and Steven's fear of his lifelong friend, Jason, and how he wished he had never gotten involved in smuggling.

Their emotions gelled and through them Sienna could feel the essence of the violence that engulfed the world, violence as a plague, a means to an end that brought only sadness and pain.

Sienna felt strengthened by her awareness, and a sense of purpose began to shine through. She looked at Jason and lifted her chin. "If you want these diamonds you better come get them." She began to walk backwards toward the waterfall.

"That won't be necessary," he replied, smiling. "I'll just shoot you and take them."

Jason's hate and insecurity washed over her, but there was a strange hint of excitement underneath. "Not before I can throw them into this waterfall." She threatened as she took several steps back toward the roaring waters.

"Don't play with me woman, because you're no match for me. You think you're tough?" Jason taunted. "I'm going to see how tough you are." He pointed the gun at Hawk. "I'm going to shoot one of these sons of a bitches because they helped you." He pointed the gun from Sammy to Steven. "You won't know who's going to get the bullet first. Will it be your precious Hawk? That's how tough I can be."

Sammy's eyes grew big and Steven wiped his mouth with a shaky hand.

"But you can be sure I have enough bullets in this gun for your man here." He aimed the barrel at Hawk again. "I want to shoot him just for knocking me across the room."

"None of them helped me." Sienna said boldly. "I didn't need it because I am the Last of the Stonekeepers, and you and your friends, Jason, are just a part of a bigger play."

"What the fu—" Jason replied. "You've gone crazy. You're what?"

"The Last of the Stonekeepers." Sienna seemed to grow in stature as she looked at Hawk. "Women who are born to capture the emotional history of humankind inside gems, just like these." She lifted the hand that held the diamonds higher. "So humanity will not have to relive its mistakes. Mistakes that you have made, Jason, because of the allure of danger and the fast life. You felt you needed it to make you feel alive, when in truth, what you needed was always inside of you. Available because of your oneness with the highest power there is." Sienna's voice held a commanding tone. "The allure of diamond smuggling was only an illusion, Jason, a cover for your desire for God."

Jason's face trembled. "You are out of your freaking mind." He stared her down. "But you had one thing right." He pointed the gun toward her again. "You are the last. Of what?" His face held a hideous grin. "I don't care."

"Si-ee-nna!" Hawk screamed as he ran toward Jason.

And as Hawk screamed her name, in a flash, memories of the Passion Ruby and the Pirate's Emerald whipped through Sienna's mind with all the people and all the events that surrounded them. But most of all, Sienna recalled how Mother Earth herself came to her aid at the moment she needed it most.

Sienna turned to the waterfall. Hawk's profound words before they made love between the rocks welled up inside her. Sienna knew, without a doubt, that she and Hawk were more than just their physical bodies. That they had come into this life with a purpose that was a part of a bigger plan, and her standing at the edge of that waterfall was part of it. "I am the Last of the Stonekeepers and if this act will have purpose beyond me and my child's life, I perform it willingly. I claim this part of myself as an act of faith in a higher plan. It is this peace that I feel now that is my gift to humanity. It is the peace that God has always desired. Perhaps my death, at the moment that I deliver this diamond back to the Earth, will be the vehicle for humankind's peace." Sienna surrendered herself to her destiny.

She could hear Jason scream "No!" and the gun go off as she threw the diamond into the waterfall. Sienna closed her eyes and waited for the bullet to hit her, but instead she was greeted with the overwhelming sound of rushing water. When she opened her eyes Sienna was shocked to see the massive waters of the waterfall rising far, far above their heads. She turned and looked at Hawk. He was looking up. Sienna looked at the frightened faces of Jason and his gang just as she heard her own voice cry Hawk's name as the water from the waterfall tumbled down on them.

Sienna closed her eyes and waited to be struck down by the powerful force of nature. To feel water rush into her nose and into her lungs, but the moment never came. When Sienna opened her eyes again, she saw the water lift from the ground before it returned to its natural state as Olekapeka Falls.

Stunned, Sienna looked down, and she realized she had not been touched. The ground under her feet and her clothes were as dry as a bone. Quickly, she looked for Hawk. He too was standing there dry, as if the water had never washed over them.

Their eyes locked as Hawk walked across the sodden ground toward her. When he reached her Hawk drew Sienna into his arms. "It's over now, Sienna. It's all over. And you proved to yourself, to all of us, that you are the Last Stonekeeper."

Sienna looked at Jason and the others who had been lying still as death. Then, one by one they began to emit choking sounds as they tried to clear their bodies of water. "But is it over, Hawk, is it really over?" She held him tightly, still stunned by the miraculous act of nature and her own courage.

Hawk's body stiffened as a quiet but clear voice spoke within him. *It is over. The job of the Stonekeeper is done. Her acts, especially the peace that came upon her, will affect humanity like the ripples of a pebble tossed into a pond. The results will not be seen immediately, but they will come.*

"What is it?" Sienna pulled back to look into his face.

"I was told your job is done and the results will come in the future," Hawk replied. "But the voice was so gentle within me, Sienna." His amber eyes filled with gratitude. "I didn't feel like I was being forced to listen. It coerced me, so gently, I wanted to know."

"Then it is really over," Sienna said.

"Yes," Hawk replied. "We can begin a new life with no fear of the Stonekeeper's cycles and what they might bring."

Again, Sienna looked at Jason and his friends. Then she looked at the sky. "The waterfall actually rose up above us, Hawk," she said bewilderedly. "I truly am the Last of the Stonekeepers." She looked back into Hawk's eyes as if she believed it for the first time.

"And you always will be," Hawk assured her. "Now there's something else you need to become."

"What?" She asked softly.

"My wife," he replied.

Sienna searched his eyes. They were soft and tender. "You're asking me to marry you?"

"Yes."

There was a moment of utter silence. For Sienna, it was almost impossible to believe that Hawk was asking her to be his wife. Almost as impossible as everything that had happened in her life over the last eight years.

"Will you marry me, Sienna?" Hawk asked again.

"Yes. Yes, I will marry you." Her eyes filled with tears, before he drew her into his arms, and they walked back, slowly, into the brush together, leaving Jason and the others to fend for themselves.

Forty-two

"I did not bring the right clothes for this, Sienna," Dawn complained in the front room of the tiny beach house.

"You look fine," Sienna assured her as she fingered the Stonekeeper's pendant that hung around her neck.

"That's easy for you to say. Look at you." Dawn stepped back. "You've got your flower lei encircling your head, your pretty little off-the-shoulder white dress to wear."

"But I'm the one who's getting married," Sienna reminded her.

Dawn finished tying the pareo around her waist. "That's no excuse," she replied mischievously.

They looked at each other.

"Are you ready?" Dawn asked.

"You know I've been ready for a long, long time," Sienna replied.

The two friends hugged.

"Well, let's go get him." Dawn opened the door.

Sienna smiled as she and Dawn walked out and onto the beach. Next to the beach house, a lone musician wearing matching Hawaiian-print pants and shirt played a pan flute and bowed over and over again.

"What's with the pan flute, Dawn?" Sienna said as she smiled at him.

"What do you mean?"

Sienna gave her the eye. "A pan flute . . ."

"Huh," Dawn sounded. "You better be happy I found him." She straightened the ring of flowers around Sienna's head, "I couldn't find anybody else at this short notice."

Sienna smiled and shook her head. When she reached the back of the beach house, she saw Hawk standing shirtless in a pair of white pants. His light brown locks were down, and the wind blew them, gently, around his face. Elikapeka stood behind him.

Hawk met Sienna halfway. He reached out his hand and Sienna took it.

"Are you ready to become my wife?" Hawk looked deep into Sienna's eyes.

"I've been ready for a long time," she replied. "But I want to show you something."

"What? Now?" Hawk looked at the Kahuna then back at Sienna.

"There's no better time." Sienna cupped her hand and Hawk leaned over to see. "This will make a wonderful ring," she said as the sunlight turned the facets of the diamond in her hand into countless colorful rainbows.

"Sienna." Hawk was clearly shocked.

She smiled. "I figured it only took one." Aunt Jessi's bracelet caught the sun as Sienna threaded her arm through his and they turned toward Elikapeka to take their vows.

Dear Readers,

I have something to confess. While I have discovered I have a talent for writing, I've also discovered I am not the best at using the Internet as an interactive tool to stay connected with you. Please don't hold it against me. It doesn't mean I don't honor you and appreciate all of your support. I want to thank each and every one of you for reading my novels, which have not been the "norm." I hope you continue to hang in there with me. I promise to work harder with the Internet because it can forge a stronger bond between us. And as a gesture of good will, I am hosting **"A Diamond's Allure Contest,"** and one of you will be the lucky winner of the **Grand Prize . . . a beautiful pair of diamond stud earrings and a romantic dinner for two!**

What do you have to do? Send in your name, address, phone number and E-mail address (if you have one) along with the correct answer to the question . . . Who was the Stonekeeper before Sienna? There are two ways to enter this contest. 1. Mail a 3 x 5 postcard or index card addressed to: A Diamond's Allure Contest, P.O. Box 71932, Salt Lake City, UT 84171-0932. 2. Go to my website www.ebonisnoe.com and click on contest.

The entry deadline is June 30, 2003, and the drawing date will be announced in the future.

Good luck!!! And remember . . . if you keep reading, I'll keep writing.

Eboni Snoe

ABOUT THE AUTHOR

Eboni Snoe, also known as Gwyn F. McGee, has ten novels to her credit, novels that she hopes open the heart, mind and spirit. Her permanent residence is St. Petersburg, Florida, although she has spent the majority of the last year and a half in Salt Lake City, Utah.

More Arabesque Romances by
Monica Jackson

DO YOU KNOW AN ARABESQUE MAN?

1st Arabesque Man HAROLD JACKSON
Featured on the cover of "Endless Love"
by Carmen Green / Published Sept 2000

2nd Arabesque Man EDMAN REID
Featured on the cover of "Love Lessons"
by Leslie Esdaile / Published Sept 2001

3rd Arabesque Man PAUL HANEY
Featured on the cover of "Holding Out For A Hero"
by Deirdre Savoy / Published Sept 2002

WILL YOUR "ARABESQUE" MAN BE NEXT?

One Grand Prize Winner Will Win:
- 2 Day Trip to New York City
- Professional NYC Photo Shoot
- Picture on the Cover of an Arabesque Romance Novel
- Prize Pack & Profile on Arabesque Website and Newsletter
- $250.00

You Win Too!
- The Nominator of the Grand Prize Winner receives a Prize Pack & profile on Arabesque Website
- $250.00

To Enter: Simply complete the following items to enter your "Arabesque Man": (1) Compose an Original essay that describes in 75 words or less why you think your nominee should win. (2) Include two recent photographs of him (head shot and one full length shot). Write the following information for both you and your nominee on the back of each photo: name, address, telephone number and the nominee's age, height, weight, and clothing sizes. (3) Include signature and date of nominee granting permission to nominator to enter photographs in contest. (4) Include a proof of purchase from an Arabesque romance novel—write the book title, author, ISBN number, and purchase location and price on a 3-1/2 x 5" card. (5) Entrants should keep a copy of all submissions. Submissions will not be returned and will be destroyed after the judging.

ARABESQUE regrets that no return or acknowledgement of receipt can be made because of the anticipated volume of responses. Arabesque is not responsible for late, lost, incomplete, inaccurate or misdirected entries. The Grand Prize Trip includes round trip air transportation from a major airport nearest the winner's home, 2-day (1 night) hotel accommodations and ground transportation between the airport, hotel and Arabesque offices in New York. The Grand Prize Winner will be required to sign and return an affidavit of eligibility and publicity and liability release in order to receive the prize. The Grand Prize Winner will receive no additional compensation for the use of his image on an Arabesque novel, website, or for any other promotional purpose. The entries will be judged by a panel of BET Arabesque personnel whose decisions regarding the winner and all other matters pertaining to the Contest are final and binding. By entering this Contest, entrants agree to comply with all rules and regulations.

SEND ENTRIES TO: The Arabesque Man Cover Model Contest, BET Books, One BET Plaza, 1235 W Street, NE, Washington, DC 20018. Open to legal residents of the U.S., 21 years of age or older. Illegible entries will be disqualified. Limit one entry per envelope. Odds of winning depend, in part, on the number of entries received. Void in Puerto Rico and where prohibited by law.

ARABESQUE
A PRODUCT OF BET BOOKS